THE GILDED

by

A CANDID, THOUGHT-PROVOKING, partly humorous look at escapism and the quest for acceptance through the eyes of college students on the verge of adulthood. . . . If you're a fan of the teen movie *Mean Girls* or you love fiction about college years, complex friendships, self-worth, and the pressures to fit in, this novel is a must-read.
  READERS' FAVORITE

MUCH LIKE A frat party . . . but with manic, fizzy energy.
  KIRKUS REVIEWS

FILLED WITH ENLIGHTENING moments of self-discovery and insights into male and female relationship-building, *The Gilded Butterfly Effect*'s powerful study in contrasts is hard to put down.
  D. DONOVAN, Sr. Reviewer, *Midwest Book Review*

A SHARPLY OBSERVED novel that deploys innovative language to get deep into the psyche of women at one of the most pivotal times in their lives. An engaging and thought-provoking read.
  AMANDA EISENBERG, author, *People Are Talking*

THINK *MEAN GIRLS* on uppers. By turns savage and sympathetic, Heather Colley's *The Gilded Butterfly Effect* skewers the absurd theatre of college life with ferocious wit and style. Told in alternating first-person narratives, it lays bare the dark, narcotic heart of sorority culture.
  DAMIAN FOWLER, author, *Falling Through Clouds*

SPREADS LIKE A stain, dark and irrevocable, as the characters chase the edges of their own destruction. At once jarring and hypnotic, bitter and full of desperate hope, the voices of its two narrators entwine and pull each other to pieces. Heather Colley has invented a new rhythm of language, or perhaps pulled one out of the depths of consciousness. A singular and unforgettable debut.
  DEVON HALLIDAY, author, *To Stay, To Stay, To Stay*

WITH AN ACADEMIC laxness that's almost charming, and armed with pharmaceuticals taken not for recreation but to restore the humanity the Greek system has taken away, Colley's characters collide with a system where betrayal is as transactional and expected as a course assignment. *The Gilded Butterfly Effect* is a rowdy, utterly compelling journey through the debauchery and moral reckonings of contemporary university Greek life.
  LAURA HULTHEN THOMAS, author, *The Meaning of Fear*

THE GILDED BUTTERFLY EFFECT

THE GILDED BUTTERFLY EFFECT

A NOVEL

HEATHER COLLEY

THREE ROOMS PRESS
New York, NY

The Gilded Butterfly Effect
A Novel by Heather Colley

© 2025 by Heather Colley

All rights reserved. No part of this book may be reproduced in any form or by any electronic or mechanical means, including information storage and retrieval systems, without permission in writing from the publisher, except by a reviewer, who may quote brief passages in a review. For permissions, please write to address below or email editor@threeroomspress.com. Any members of educational institutions wishing to photocopy or electronically reproduce part or all of the work for classroom use, or publishers who would like to obtain permission to include the work in an anthology, should send their inquiries to Three Rooms Press, 243 Bleecker Street, #3, New York, NY 10014.

This is a work of fiction. Names, characters, businesses, places, events, and incidents are either the products of the author's imaginations or used in a fictitious manner. Any resemblance to actual persons, living or dead, or actual events is purely coincidental.

ISBN 978-1-953103-62-8 (trade paperback)
E-ISBN 978-1-953103-63-5 (Epub)
Library of Congress Control Number: 2025937118

TRP-120

First Edition

Pub Date: October 21, 2025

BISAC category codes:
FIC076000 FICTION / Feminist
FIC044000 FICTION / Women
FIC071000 FICTION / Friendship

COVER AND INTERIOR DESIGN:
KG Design International: www.katgeorges.com

DISTRIBUTED IN THE U.S. AND INTERNATIONALLY BY:
Ingram/Publishers Group West: www.pgw.com

Three Rooms Press
New York, NY
www.threeroomspress.com
info@threeroomspress.com

For Dad
My forever first reader

THE GILDED BUTTERFLY EFFECT

STELLA

I don't really get weak at the knees. I'm not much of a romantic. Quite honestly, I haven't got the time. Romantic types make me feel strange, as if I'm playing the part in a movie for which I've been entirely miscast. Romantics are all well and good until they use up my time for fun, and glory. There is only so much weekend, and after I got to Michigan, I stopped wasting it on romantics. I wasted a great deal of time on boys. But there was nothing romantic about it.

So that's how it was on that night, and how it had been for many nights before. It was Sterling's birthday party. He was a sophomore like us, but he was twenty-three or twenty-four, so we perceived him as archaic, washed-up, a bit creepy. Someone perched at the perimeters, hunting and drooling. And always, of course, watching. We had to be so beautiful because they—the boys—were always watching. Unzipping our skin, and looting whatever they found underneath.

It was an outdoor party, stacks of beer cans, taller than the tallest brother, and a bar with no bartender, you served yourself, and there was only one type of liquor. Clear, burning liquor that only rolls in Middle America, the type of thing that hurts on its way down, and makes me cry late at night. Music played. It was the kind of music that you knew, even if you didn't. The air was warm with the receding summer, and

Michigan seemed like a dream to us then—it always did, at the beginning of the academic year, when everybody was so pretty, and plumped up from long summers spent being overfed, and over-tanned by yoga moms and finance dads. At the edge of the yard, fraternity pledges stopped God Damn Independents from breaking in, laughed in their faces. They said, you'll have to rush, then. And when girls were turned away, they looked up to us. Hated us deeply; and we loved that, how that felt.

It was easy to express that love through our fake, crackling laughter.

Kappa Alpha—us—and Sigma Rho—them.

There were wooden risers, the pledges built them every August and destroyed them every May. They lined the backyard, and blocked off the nearby shrubbery, where we went to undress, and admire one another naked, or to empty our bodies of excess toxic waste, because there was a certain unbeauty about alcohol poisoning that called for the quiet, and rapid disposal of it by manual force. These risers were the hierarchy in architecture. Right then, we must've been eight or nine feet up. From up there you saw the tops of other girls' heads, the Betas, and the Gamma Phis, and even some God Damn Independents who'd snuck in. We saw these girls below, and knew that if we wanted to, we could toss a drink onto their dull hair, and watch it run cold under their tank tops, and into the fibers of their jeans, and nobody would say a word, apart from us, and our words would only be in laughter. Hysterical, tons of it, and I was always the one that spoke English first, and I'd say something like, "Isn't this amazing?"

We didn't throw any booze that night. It was too soon in the new semester to wreck the house's image. That year was meant to be our attempt at re-affirming our prestige and decorum, an effort trailblazed by Kathy Van Tassel since she'd been elected Chapter President at the end of the last academic year.

Van Tassel was composed at this party, I saw no drugs. She was the cocaine type, and from my elevated vantage I saw that she was wired like a caged songbird, beautiful but sweaty. She never used in company.

And we all know it's a problem when you start using alone like that. Back in August I was only a coke user socially. It was still a group effort back then. Things changed, of course; things always change in the fall.

Never mind President Van Tassel. Sigma Rho was a top fraternity, and rising every year, so this was the coupling that both chapters needed. There were constant male grips, Sigma Rho hands, pulling me back to the very top of the risers, where we pretended to have panoramic views, and loitered in heaven.

Always a boy's hand lingering for too long, a hand perched where he assumed my butt crack started underneath my jeans, an accidental—yeah, *okay*—brush against my tit as I teetered up on the risers.

After a while of dancing, it got to be only pretending, for the sake of something to do. And that's when it's time to move on.

Millie, who was my drug-dealer firstly and my friend recreationally, had also picked up on the evident death of the party.

Yet still she said, "One more song, and one second," and I nodded all right, the bars wouldn't be open for a while anyway. Millie hopped down to sea level and left me amongst a dwindling group of Kappa Alphas who all looked variants of Millie, who looked a variant of me.

On the ground, Millie embarked toward a pong table with that particular focus that can come only from strong speed.

She snorted something off the table, and turned around to a good-looking Sigma Rho, thanked him, and laughed. It couldn't have been coke, not yet, since it just wasn't an August drug. We reserved it for depressed Michigan winters, when sunlight was no longer even minimally on call. It might've been caffeine concentrate, I thought, which was a silly trend then, or, given the character of its user, it might've been something that one of her many psychiatrists had prescribed, pills which she'd crushed and broken down for easy snorting.

Who could've known? Who could've asked?

Millie hopped back up the riser staircase to join me again, and she did so with angular spins, and focused footsteps, which made me sure that it was Adderall. She shoved aside some God Damn Independents, who stood nearby, unmoving, pretending to sip their mixed drinks while they waited, and sweated, and tapped their feet to songs inside their heads.

So now here was the funeral parlor to the night. The first night back at school, and yet it felt like an early ending, the music fading, and tuneless singing for somebody's meaningless birthday. I committed myself to belligerency; downed vodka from the cup that I'd been attempting to sip slowly. My head was grateful, but my stomach was shocked, and it called out a warning.

Here's a laugh, (and you have to laugh, otherwise somebody else will first): to the sounds of pop music, I attempted to dance, and then my body notified me that I was falling. I toppled all the way down—down three riser levels, the middle of which stunted the fall, and delivered me to the pillowy earth, where I ended up on my knees in the gravel.

I opened my eyes to a new horizon of stamping sneakers and the purview of an insect, but I was not unhappy with my tumble. It is better to be sobered up on the gravel of the people than lost in my head up above them. And anyway, right then I felt no pain.

I straightened, and saw that tiny stones were crunched into my right knee, at which point I stood up to analyze my whole leg, and I discerned that it was bloody, and coated with dust and pebbles. From above I heard their laughter, the Kappa Alphas, the sound of a defunct Disney ride with dolls who sing showtunes in all vowels, not totally sane. And as if my lever had been pulled or triggered by theirs, I laughed too, and was still laughing when Millie hopped down and hauled me to my feet.

Suddenly, the darkness lifted—like Friday nights have a way of doing—and the mood? It came back. How lovely and perfect it was, we thought, that the gravel acted as a Band-Aid, stifled the blood. Millie poured liquor on it, "We have to sterilize."

I thanked the night for not quitting yet. Millie draped over the pong table from which she'd only just snorted, wheezing with laughter, and others joined, identical faces and names—Leah, Emma, Sarah—they let out low laughs, and one tried to puff on some cig or spliff, which made her suffocate, which made us laugh more, and also reminded us that we had our own cigs to light, so we did, and I cracked a new beer, and poured some over my knee, to observe the effect of its mixing with blood, then drank the rest, and splashed some on Millie.

Above our nonsense rang the steady song of a hammer wielded by some nameless fraternity pledge—they're always nameless till they're brothers—as he fixed a wooden riser, and the sound knocked around amidst our cackling, which, as it happened, was starting to become a kind of reflexive reaction; nobody remembered what we laughed at anymore, but we labored on, just for something to do, and somebody to do it with. The pledge hammer stopped, and Millie cackled still, but I couldn't force anything more from my own tired lungs, and then silence hung again. The party had died, and we'd mourned it, but here might be its afterlife, and everything—parties included, parties especially—deserves a second go.

There was a group of three, over by an otherwise empty bar. I saw Nico, who was a Sigma Rho in my year, and he saw me seeing him. He elbowed another guy that I hadn't seen yet that night, who spoke to some blond girl, a Beta. The Betas were creeping into the top tier, and we were well aware of this ascendency, their increasingly good looks, and their honest recruiting style. They advertised a "Values-Oriented Sisterhood," a premise that attracted a growing percentage of the incoming girls of good quality, the ones we might've wanted for ourselves, and this blond Beta—she looked like a Beta, they always do match up to their letters—she doted on the boys, looked exactly like somebody of a self-described sisterhood of ethics and morality.

I fixated on the Beta. She saw Nico see me. The Beta had this terrible high laugh which she forced out and upward, trying to keep their group together, but the noise was jilted when Nico ripped the other guy away, and came toward us. That other guy was Jack.

He was already smiling when he reached us. That was my first look at Jack's smile, all self-composure. He was good-looking in a Midwestern sort of way. But they all were. Jack struck me especially, because he looked like the sort of guy who believed in God, in a totally unforced and unhurried sense of the thing, not bullied by parents or creeps in capes, but just earnestly believed in Him as a source of, like, hope.

Nico introduced all around, the Beta girl forgotten, didn't even bother telling us her name.

THE GILDED BUTTERFLY EFFECT

Jack was in the trail of my cig smoke. Nico entertained Millie and the others, they were off in jokes again about something new, so I offered Jack one as a courtesy, because I felt him watching the cig or the smoke or me. He took one. He had no light. I offered him mine.

"Did you take a fall?" he asked, and looked down at my leg, which was an ornament of dried blood and beer.

"No," I said. "It was completely deliber—"

And then Nico shifted toward me, while the others laughed on, to touch my hand, and instruct: "Listen. Talk him up."

Right. Jack was a prospective pledge. And prospective pledges make their final decisions on which fraternity to join in the fall based not on the boys, but the girls, the girls that the boys fraternize with. And that was the whole reason behind this guise of family reunion: Sigma Rho had to prove it to the new ones that their girls were worthwhile. They wanted us to be their girls—and we were split, of course, between them and The Church. Which meant that old house rivalry would carry on.

"I need a drink," I told Jack, which I did not, but he led me over to the bar—as if I really needed somebody to show me the way. On the short walk he said things like, "How do you find life at Michigan?" to which I said, "Yeah, sure. All good and great, right," and he looked at me strange, as if I hadn't really understood the question.

At the bar he took a beer, and I took a new cupful of the vodka, drank it as quickly as I'd poured it.

If he was at all alarmed by the speed at which I put away the toxic waste he remained outwardly neutral, grabbed a new cup from the stack, poured some more in—not as much as I had done—handed it to me, said, "So where are you from?"

Silence ached as I sipped again. I had an awareness, tucked away somewhere primitive, that this was abnormal behavior. And I understood why: this was not a question that boys asked girls. This was a girl-to-girl question.

"Well," I said.

Now he looked at me with a tired unease. Of course he did, he'd assumed that I was an upstanding and representative Kappa Alpha, skilled in conversation, and subtleties, and whatever other feminine wiles, and he did not know yet about my other bits, the bits of me that were trashed and deficient.

"Forget it," I said. "I'm going out."

"Ah—where's that?"

"South U."

I spoke as if to a listening crowd, slowly, and with attention to inflection and syllable, which I thought might promote an illusion of sobriety.

"Are you all ri—do you need me to walk you there?" he said.

He'd never been downtown on a night in August, when the weather was fine, and the kids were antsy. So he did not know, yet, how one small step onto the Ann Arbor sidewalk would sweep me unilaterally toward town, how the night itself would lead me to the bars, a cardinal magnetism. He also did not grasp how very profoundly I did not need him; how profoundly I had promised myself to stay uninvolved this semester, because the prior Spring had proven that involvement with fraternal men is shady at best, misery at worst, and it's all business to them, all exchange, and buy, and sell.

"I'll find my way," I said. "Maybe I'll see you there."

So, we went to rejoin our respective coalitions. Jack didn't hang around long, spoke briefly to Nico before turning back to the denser badlands of the party, the vomit-soggy brush, and mud, and the splintered risers, and the discarded solo cups all chewed up and teethed, out of nerves or speed, and I watched as he was subsumed into it.

Millie and I left Sterling's, didn't look back to say goodbye to Nico. He called *see you later?* after us, and then the sidewalk was a coddling migration, my whole pledge class was suddenly around me. Everybody walking downtown toward the bars, which were lit up and ready for the school year after the long and empty summer. And everybody yammered their own fictions of what had happened to them in June and July, who had fucked who, and acquired what experiences, and then, *did you do the coke or what?*, and it was Millie who had said that.

"What coke?" I asked.

Silly of me. She'd already done some, she'd done it at the party, and now wanted more: "I need a come up," she said.

"Another?"

She nodded. Upon the suggestion, coke sounded all right. We drew up to the beginning of South U, and the lights on the sidewalks filled everything, they tangled around barstools, and unhappy waiters, and singing undergraduates. I should've known—I should've known then that the natural order was awry, cocaine in August? It just didn't fit, it wasn't life as usual, but I tilted into an unlit backstreet where the 7/11 delivery trucks park to unload in the daytime, and I did a bump from the head of my housekey. You could feel it, the night unraveling, manic summer ending, and it drives everybody mad, the few days between the seasons, and we went like heroes toward our merry catastrophe.

PENNY

My parents used to call me a *problem* before I was psychiatrically diagnosed. Now I am just a bit of an issue.

In high school, they gave me advice. My mom said, "Have you tried making some friends? Girls are always looking for new friends."

This turned out to be overwhelmingly false. My looks did not help. I won't get into any specifics about that. People want to hear all about the beauties. It's intriguing, almost scientific, the communal fascination with beauty; there is no need to detail, really, the specific elements of the opposite. We all know exactly what beauty is. And we know what it is not.

And anyway, about topics like this, I've explained, and I've explained, and I've explained—to therapists, to myself. The more I try to explain, the more hopeless my case becomes.

I did have one friend back in high school, Leah, who liked me because she talked a lot, and I never did, and her popularity and good looks allowed me a degree of group interaction, or rather, her group interacted around me, as I looked for ways to insert myself. Once, our high school rented a stand at the New York State Fair, and Leah volunteered us to help sell the PTA baked goods and undesirable raffle prizes. Leah was a true natural under that striped awning, chatting up attractive fathers with small kids knocked out in sugared hazes, complimenting the women on their boots, and denim, and athleisure. She did not notice that I escaped an hour into our shift, spent the day hopping between stalls in the food field, slowly intoxicating myself with trans-fat, lumbering with increasing difficulty as the day dragged, and the sun hurt. When I returned to the school stall, Leah was gone, and the next students had taken their posts; no messages from my friend, but mom had been around, wondering where I'd got to.

I know in my ribs that Leah liked me because of the State Fair dynamic. I was an ornament beside whom she glowed and glimmered. Once, in middle school, I'd got this weird urge to grab her and kiss her on the neck. It was immediately followed by a new feeling, which was the desire to unzip her, and crawl inside, and become her, exist in her beauty and luck. It passed, and I said nothing.

Now, it's been over a year since I've seen my high school friend. I'm stuck at this dark, small campus, while Leah lives a new life out in Michigan, where football is King. She used to call me every so often, in our first year away, but we're sophomores now, and she calls less. I get the sense that she has moved on, and I understand why. My college is within the same geographical remit as our old high school and my parents' house. It does not feel like I've gone anywhere, done anything. In fact, when I walk by the school kids in the McDonald's parking lot during lunchtime or see them parked in shadowed lanes doing things in back seats, I feel I've actually moved backwards, somehow. A scratched vinyl that keeps spinning despite itself.

And now, I'm sat across from Professor Peterson, who asked me to stay after class to discuss the first assignment. I already know I haven't done well on it—one thousand words on *The*

Beautiful and Damned—so only one week into this year, the terrible nothingness is back again.

Peterson says, "You have promise, Penny. Your summer assignment started off a wonderful reflection of the degrading reality of an enclosed system. But really, Penny. It goes off on tangents. What is your actual argument?"

"Uh – I'm sorry," I say. "I think I was just looking for something new to say. Some interpretation. It didn't come out right." Surprise, surprise. "I was looking for something that hadn't been written."

"Well, perhaps for your next semester, consider the postmodern seminar," she sighs. "Somewhere, you allowed the trials and tribulations of the collegiate experience to distract you from the *academics* of this essay, and you've diluted yourself."

I think it's strange that I'm becoming diluted, but she might be right. Everyday bits of myself are becoming weaker, like I'm disintegrating into a person who's not-fully-there, not wholly involved in my own reality.

She snaps at me, "Penny? Are you present?"

"Yes," I say. "Thank you."

It is cold for the end of August, and I walk by fraternity row on my way back to the dorm. Sometimes the front yards rage. On this Monday night, it is only remnants: damp beer pong tables, and dark bedrooms, and brothers sitting on porches, talking low, smoking, and the smoke looks like it's following their orders.

I see some familiar faces on my walk.

Hi, Sheila. Remember when you dragged me to a party on the second night of our freshman year, last August, the first party I'd ever been to? I never have much of a good time, but

I figured I was having something like it that night. Remember when you got drunk, so drunk that you thought you could talk to me about other things, and then we realized that both of our aunts have breast cancer, or rather, that mine has, and yours did, before she died? Remember when you rushed a sorority, and now you wear your letters on your baseball cap every day, and you don't talk to me anymore, not even drunk? I remember, too.

Sam. Remember when you slept with the girl across the hall named Maeve, and she sort of fell in love with you, and then you told her you really only wanted to be friends, and now she's still in love with you months later, because you took her virginity, and you didn't know it? And how do I know all of this private information? Well, it's the same syndrome, the one that is virulent around here: the drinking, and then the revealing. One night I went out to pee, and Maeve was gagging in another stall. I tried to be quick, but my bodily functions stalled from the sudden human closeness, and the pee wouldn't come, so I just sat there. She called out, who's there? And then she shrieked, talk to me! So I did, or rather she talked, and she told me that she loved you, and that she'd fucked you so you'd do it back, the loving, but you hadn't done that bit.

I realize that I miss Leah, immensely and suddenly.

She's told me that Michigan is a complete party. It's huge, it's alive, she says, and the people are so indescribable. She has never even tried to describe them.

Which might explain exactly why it is that I'm seated on a cross-country bus to Michigan. And Professor Peterson's voice comes back to me in bits. But at least she cannot accuse me now of absolute deadness, of diluting myself completely. The bus breaks through to Pennsylvania as the lonelinesses come back again.

* * *

When I awake, it is to the sunrise over the American Midwest. In a panic that is only mildly interested in itself, I recollect the previous night, in which my mind had succumbed to blank determination, and I'd packed a bag like a mechanic: only the basic necessities, some clothes, cash, my remaining meds, only one weeks' worth left.

I'm on three different ones, since the second one addresses the increased anxiety that comes along with the first one, and the third one addresses the chronic lethargy that comes with the second one, and the first one is meant to get to the root of it all, which is the deep dark dreariness. I am almost depleted, since Shelly is meticulous about prescribing exactly a month's worth—last February, she'd mistakenly forgotten about the leap year, and I'd gone a few days without anything at all. Those were damp and dreadful days, in which all of my terrors had come in double.

On the bus, I start thinking, which is an extremely dangerous thing for me to do. In order to counteract this danger, I employ one of Shelly's cognitive techniques, which I do not wholly subscribe to, but which I use as a last resort. I take three deep breaths (which should've been five), and I focus my eyes outside of myself, out the window. And I observe.

I've never before considered that upper Ohio is anything spectacular. There is a sunrise now, and hanging clouds. The sort of scene that people might try to paint, and they would only get the effect about halfway, since it is something unspoken, the general feeling about Middle America, where it seems like no one lives, and no one dies—and no one does anything in between.

The bus halts at a rest top, one of those uniquely American combinations of bathroom, fast food emporium, and truck services. Weird souvenir shops, which sell nothing much. I take my phone from my backpack, and call Leah. I haven't spoken to her yet this year. I've had such little interest in old friends and conversations. Still, I hope that she might bring me into a collegiate world from dreamy films and dark novels, with beautiful characters who make fixable mistakes.

It rings for so long that I almost hang up. And then:

"Hi?"

"Leah. It's me—it's Penny."

"Jesus. Hey. How's school?"

"I'm good, actually, but I'm not there anymore, I've left—"

There was some unidentifiable commotion on her end.

"Hang on one sec, Pen—WOULD YOU SHUT THE FUCK UP I'M ON THE PHO—sorry about that, hard to have a private conversation, but listen, I have so much to tell you, but not right now, okay?"

"Leah, I need to ask if you could please go to the Ann Arbor station—"

"What do you mean, Ann Arbor? SHUT UP FOR ONE SECOND—did you say something about Ann Arbor?"

"Yeah, could you be there around—what time is it—could you be there around six o' clock tonight?"

"Are you all right, Penny? What are you talking about—JESUS CHRIST—did you say you're not at school?"

"My phone is almost dead. And I didn't bring a charger with me. But honestly, I might get rid of it anyway. I just feel like I should. Okay?"

"Wait, are you out of your mind?"

And my phone dies, which I take as some divine signal to, at last, finish off what I've been contemplating. I go to a stall in the public bathroom, and toss the phone into one of those garbage bins specifically designed for women's hygiene, and there it muddles with half-hidden tampons stained slightly in blood.

I wait at the bus for the driver to signal his departure, and I climb back aboard for the last time.

I try to put all of the nagging riddles out of me. Still half my thoughts are occupied by terror. Yes, it's a mess in there, my brain. It buzzes on, somehow, and that's how it goes. Buzzing. It buzzes for the next few hours toward Ann Arbor. The afternoon passes like twenty minutes, or like half an eternity—I wouldn't know, I wouldn't know.

* * *

LEAH'S HAIR IS SHORTER BUT JUST as curly as I remember. She'd once looked like the small and friendly type, the type that took gymnastics lessons, and made good impressions on adults, but now she is a sleek and sophisticated-looking girl, a *woman*, with curls that sculpt at an angle, and cut her jaw line in a way that I understand to be fashionable.

When we meet in the station, she doesn't touch me. She looks confused, as if she doesn't realize that I can exist outside of the old world of high school.

"What are you doing here?" she says.

"I couldn't think of anywhere else to go."

"So, your first idea was to trek to the *Mid fucking West?*"

Hearing it spoken aloud like that, I feel ludicrous, wonder if I've been overcome by temporary insanity.

"Well. Yeah, is that okay?" I say.

"I mean, it's psychotic. But that's okay. Wait till the people from high school hear."

I'd forgotten that she still had ties back home.

"No one knows," I tell her.

She looks at me as if I've suddenly become an entirely new person.

"I never thought you had it in you to just up and leave," she says, and that makes me feel very tired.

"Can I put my bag down and get some food?" I ask.

"At my place?"

"Yes. Yeah. Please."

Two moments pass. It is the second moment, the one that attracts an unnatural bit of attention to itself, that makes me think she might reject me, leave me here, tell me to convince a motel concierge to give me a room on credit; it was silly of me, I think, silly and childish, to come here.

Leah just walks out of the station, toward Ann Arbor Central Campus—according to the street signs emblazoned in blue and yellow—and says, "Let's walk."

I follow with unfamiliar anticipation. Activity picks up around us. Bar and restaurant patrons—many of them no older than me, I notice—tumble onto sidewalks. *Welcome to the University of Michigan,* a massive sign reads. The sort of sign meant to be photographed in bright colors for promotional material.

Soon there are people everywhere—I mean really everywhere—and they are all young. Everyone seems to have something interesting going on, lots of laughter. A herd of girls walk by, talking so urgently that their voices overlap. I've always had such trouble seeing myself in others. Never thought

I could do it right, like they do—the friendship thing, the hobbies and goals thing—but as the girls pass, I can see myself in them. Or bits of them in me.

We turn right down a street called South University, and pass a bar called Canteen, which has a red staircase leading up to it. There are three pizza shops in succession, and a 24-hour bakery shop ("We delivery warm cookies until 3AM!") within which a bunch of kids gather and gesture histrionically over the menu. Their laughter is not explicitly audible, but I know that it is there.

There are calls in our direction from across the street.

"LEAH!" a chorus of light voices ring out from a moving conglomerate, and the group cuts diagonally toward us. Leah looks at me for two moments again, and smiles by pushing the vertical ends of her lips together, as if in pre-emptive apology. Then she turns away and greets each person individually with a hug.

I try to be unobtrusive as I scan them. There are eyebrows that cut across the girls' clear foreheads in Pythagorean angles. An unbothered way about the boys, like they could be here or not, and they'd feel the same way regardless. Aggressive plastering of Greek letters across their clothing, and shoes, and backpacks, and *jewelry*. There is a Kappa, and an Alpha, and a Delta. Even as I stare, not a single eye looks back at me.

They pass then, their voices rising into a two-toned chorus.

I have spent a lot of time cultivating my anxious and depressive tendencies. They follow me like friends, sometimes hug me like parents, often ask me, again and again, why I'd ever try to expel them forever. And right now, it feels like they've come back once more, to remind me that they are not going anywhere. Because there is something about those bright letters, some in sequins, some in gold, and all of them in money—there is something about those letters, and everybody wearing them, that cuts the music, and flicks the lights back on. Everyone in a conversation together except you.

"Who were they?" I ask Leah.

"My friends," she says, and then she points to a different bar, and adopts a reverent way of speaking, with inflections of worship. "Right," she says. "So, over there is South U Pizza. They have the best slice in town, and they're open until four AM, so we go there for drunk pizza. We go after a night at Scholarly Lounge, which is a bar. They don't shut off the music until sometimes a little after four if the crowd is big enough, and having a good enough time. Which we usually are."

Leah goes on, pointing and explaining. Another bar pops up, and another joint ahead of it, or another person excited to see her. Leah does not stop again, only shouts hellos to people who shout them first.

Then South University changes: it becomes residential and grassy, and in place of the bars and restaurants there is now sprawling land, bright green yards which meet sidewalks in straight lines. Each front yard is meticulous, and an almost sickening shade of lime. And well away from the sidewalks are massive homes, planted angrily in their bright yards. Mansions, in the true sense of the word, with east and west wings, and columns, and wrap around porches.

I realize that Leah is pointing to one of them now.

"Sorry?" I ask.

"*There,* Penny. That's where we go sometimes. For parties and mixers. That's Sigma Rho."

This house has a deep black roof and white columns that never end.

"Sigma—what?"

"Rho."

She looks at me sideways again. I tell myself to enjoy the present, which is light, and bright, and mine.

"That's who we hang out with. The Sigma Rho boys. And some of us hang out at The Church."

"Who is *we?*" I ask.

Leah gives a sort of empty sigh, as if to scatter away some pretension. And then she looks at me finally straight on, and she has that apology smile on her lips again. We stop at the end of South University Street. Ahead is wilderness, and behind is town. And it feels, to me, like there is simply nowhere in the middle.

Leah lifts a hand to my face, as if to sooth me like a child, but she hasn't told me, yet, what there is to worry about.

"Penny, I live there. See? That one is my house."

She flicks a hand across the lawn that met the edges of our feet. To call it a *house* is a grotesque misappropriation. It is different than a mansion. Rather it is a community of mansions, with additions, and balconies, and side porches, and front porches, and—is that a stained-glass *window?* It is long, but it is also tall, the columns something ancient, you could wrap three girls' wingspans around each, and only just make it around. Two figures stand on the balcony with their arms draped over the handrail and their toes scrunched into the spaces in the barrier that separate them from open air. They stand still and unbothered. Their faces are pointy, the kind of genetic precision that is visible even from a distance. I feel them look down at us, feel them see and register; and then I watch them look away and out again, into still skies.

And I've never in my life felt so prominently like an Earthling, as if everybody else has the beautiful, self-assured, extraterrestrial gene somehow, and that they are exposed to boundless knowledge, and imposing architecture, and good hair, and that I, alone, don't understand it all.

An empty porch swing creaks back and forth, as if only just vacated. And just behind the swing, above the great door, written out in both English and in what I understand, now, to be the corresponding Greek, is the house's title.

Leah watches me closely as I say, "You live in a house called Kappa Alpha?"

"Well," she says, as she starts up the steep stairway to the great front door, "You have to, your sophomore year. All second-year members live in."

I feel an abandonment coming, so I hurry after her. Those eyes still watch keenly from the balcony. I look up and see their fingers twirl.

"Leah," I whisper. "I don't think I can go in there."

Because I know what they are like in there. They are the type of people I will never be—beautiful, and happy, and joyful. And excited about things.

"I knew it," she says. "I knew you'd panic."

We reach the front door, which looks so heavy that I wonder whether people actually use it, or if there is a more functional secret entrance somewhere else. "Penny, it's not that you can't stay here for a little bit," Leah continues. "It's just that if you do, you can't be all anxious the whole time. This is where I *live*. And they're good people, once you get to know them. They're no different than you or me."

I am silent, but the fact remains: I need a place to sleep.

"But—I mean—will they *like* me?"

Leah smiles and heaves open the door, giving me a little shove inside.

"I don't even think they'll notice you," she says.

Which, to me, is a dream.

"And Penny," she says. "I'm glad you're here." She shakes her head a little. "You psycho, all the way in *Michigan*."

"I'm glad, too."

I take my first Midwest Prozac in Kappa Alpha, and it calms my thoughts, which have crumbled into simultaneous euphoria and doom. The pill silences them; thank God, I think, for the pharmaceutical industry. I don't hear anything anymore, not even the omnipresent worries, and I wait in a dark living room for Leah to return with a pillow.

STELLA

EVERYONE WAS OUT. OF COURSE THEY were, it was still that first week back at school, only a few days after the first night at Sterling's, which had crumbled into a blackout. Nevermind—we needed a drink, and we needed some drama.

We went for the center of town. And further down, past the bars, is The Church. There was a Church party that night. Even over the pop music from the South U bars, you could hear The Church's bassline. All of The Church brothers, they would be coming out too, eventually. This was where everybody always wound up. And it was beneficial, that you could rely on other people, other people and a certain familiarity amongst them. Because I knew that I'd lose Millie and the rest of the rat pack early—their prerogative is always other people, and those other people are always male.

Millie slipped into Charley's, so I did too, but she was distracted by men—Jimmy Crawford, in particular, one of Trip Swindle's froggy bodyguards. I sat in the toilet stall, and thought of how to leave without notice from The Church boys, but then Millie rushed into the bathroom herself. She shoved her foot through the gap in my stall door, and she called for me to join her at the bar.

I opened the door as she moaned something about Jimmy, then something about the way her underarm looked in the mirror. Somewhere in there I took a bump from her plastic bag. Even at that shallow point in the semester it was clear that she'd become a coke girl over the summer. And since my own summer had been cokeless—dry out, calm down, sober up, whatever my mother had suggested to recover from what she called my *little hiccup* —I welcomed it back like a friend.

And then I left Charley's alone. The Church boys had vanished, and I felt summoned by something outside. You could tell who was a Tri Delt or who was a Kappa or who was a Sig Mu based exactly on how they walked and talked, which was based on how they looked. There were Greeks all around me, calling out to one another, and I tried to see faces, to remember my connections, except I couldn't get myself to know anybody.

Crowds leapt into Scholarly Lounge and lined up at Canteen, or individuals sat on stoops with pizza, or cried and carried shoes in hands—I knew it all like home, and yet not a single friend, not one sister. Then, just like that: Jack Ellis, the pledge, came loping around the corner of South U and South Forest. He could've been stargazing, I don't know, he was odd like that, in an unbothered way.

"Hey, Stella. What happened to you the other night? After Sterling's?"

I thought his sneakers looked misplaced, sitting there like duck feet at the end of his blue jeans.

"You looked?" I said.

"Sure. What are you doing?"

Coke. That's the zeitgeist, Jack. That's the zeitgeist of the hour, of the year.

He was stopped in front of me now, and then he shuffled me out of the pack's way, below a dark awning. So we stood close but unclose. Something feral instructed me not to tell him about the coke.

"I'm going to Canteen," I told him, which I hadn't been. He looked up the bar's red stairs, then back at me. I thought sporadically that even if he was smart, I was smarter—and that either way, it was my move.

"I mean, I'm going to Canteen with you," I said. "I thought you knew that."

I didn't yet have any particular interest in Jack apart from the fact he was there. There was nothing romantic about it, not with echoes from last Spring still reverberating in my head.

And—I'll say this now, I'll admit it—I'd been going to The Church. A dark place. I thought I'd do some talking there, some screaming. The coke had stimulated that anger in me, the jilted slut, the forgotten bitch, and it had made me want an answer. I wanted to be myself again.

His laugh rang into the air and vibrated there, amongst the streetlights.

"I did know that, actually," he said. "Let's go."

He couldn't have known, but we were both out of it, just looking for something to do, and somebody to do it with.

It was strange that he grabbed my hand in order to lead me up the stairs to the bar. Strange in that he shouldn't have, and strange in that it was still sort of all right.

We flashed IDs to the bouncer at the entrance. When we were in, I nodded toward his license.

"Fake?"

And he shook his head,

"Gap year," he said. "And an early birthday," and a screw jammed through the cocaine brightness. This was something that I might've been able to gather last year, back when I was more perceptive, and more insightful: no nineteen-year-old takes your hand on the sidewalk like that, not in the first week of college—handholding is marriage and suicide. And anyway, he didn't *look* like a freshman—I stared at him while he stared back.

So I said, "I need a drink," which I did. And then I made a movement to get cash from my right pocket, which was empty of cash.

"Wait, let me get it," he said, and reached again for his wallet.

"No, no."

"Don't worry," and he was already ahead of me, with one arm leaning on the bar and the other waving down the bartender.

I went up beside him, and placed an elbow on the bar, and my chin on the hand connected to it.

"What do you drink?" he asked, as if it were really so simple.

"Rum and diet, please."

Effective, unpretentious, goes down like water.

"One rum and coke," he said, "And a Stella," he told the bartender, who took his cash.

Jesus Christ.

"Diet coke, that's a diet!" I called.

But it was already poured and served, a rum and regular. I could taste the pure sugar immediately, so vile on my teeth.

I also pretended not to notice his choice of beer.

"Thanks for this," I said, took a sip, and he brought the beer to his mouth.

"I was glad to find you," he said, placed the bottle down. "It feels like I meet a hundred new people every day, but barely know anybody really."

Cruelty flashed. I wanted to tell him that he'd chosen this

when he penned his name to the Sigma Rho recruitment scheme, but I only said, "There's nothing that bad about it."

"I didn't think there was," he said, and he looked at me strangely again.

"Where are you from?" he said, tipped his beer, took a gulp, puffed his cheeks out full of fizz, and then swallowed. Like most men he was graced with the easiness of not really considering how he looked, moment-to-moment.

And here I will say that Jack Ellis wasn't bad looking at all. Jack Ellis was bulky, like an ex-football player, with coarse, dark hair that was longer than his brothers' (or soon-to-be brothers), and one eye was slightly bigger than the other. This was especially pronounced when he smiled, because his smile was crooked, and so one eye squinted up while the other did not. At the smiling phase he looked briefly maniacal. Those imperfections could not be masked by artful facial hair or intense skin regimen; they were built into the architecture, and they prevented him from being beautiful, which made him the kind of handsome that waits awhile to be invited in, and is always the first one to leave.

And now he looked at me, with one eye scrunched. I considered mentioning the cocaine, in order to explain the tunnel vision that I was sure had warped my face into a farce of itself.

"Sorry—what was that?"

"Is everything all right? I'm sorry if I was too forward—I'd wanted to talk more at Sterling's, and thought—"

"Jesus, you ask a lot of questions."

"You never *answer* any of them."

"New York," I said. "I'm from New York. And sure, everything is all right. What else was there?"

He shook his head microscopically. A voice—my mother's, I think—asked why I was so bent on being difficult, why I couldn't just sit and flirt like I was sure he wanted, why I could not flutter so prettily, like a bred creature. Jack looked at the ice in my glass, nodded at the bartender, held up two fingers, and more cash—

"Uh—Jack. I see my pledge class over there. I have to say . . . I have to tell them I'm here. I'll be back."

And I slithered off my stool, his two fingers still in the air, bending like bunny ears, and I turned into the sea just as the bartender dropped a new rum and coke where my old one had been. I heard Jack say, "I'll just keep an eye on this," and I thanked him, said I'd see him in a bit, which everybody knows is eternal goodbye.

Whatever Millie had done in the time between the Charley's bathroom and now had wrecked her. The blackout impended; I could smell it. But as I shoved across the crowd, I watched her edge beside that little blond Beta, the one I'd first noticed at Sterling's party, and introduce herself. Total fury, then.

Her and that tininess. An effortless tininess that is all genetics and luck, the gymnast-steroid-virginal look, like she was too small to be penetrated, to be abused, to abuse others, to run, or walk, or do anything except be small, and never-changing, but with a bang-on body, a body impossible.

I watched Beta pretend to listen to Millie, but scan the crowd with a prerogative, and that prerogative was Jack. He was just settling with the bartender, and she angled her body around Millie's, so that it would be available for his viewing.

I couldn't understand why Millie consorted with her, some girl from a rival house. I turned back on myself, and pushed a path to the very far corner of the bar, near the bathrooms, where I ordered a round of tequila from a different bartender, and when she offered up the salt, I shoved the shaker away so aggressively that it knocked over, and formed a grainy mountain. A Sig Mu made a remark about bad luck. I threw back the shots, and Canteen responded as I'd expected it to.

Here was proof that sometimes all you need is a bit of external stimulus, a bit of chemistry to jar the old neurons back into feeling. The bar erupted again, and I barged the dance floor alone, aware of the looks from other girls, who threw fingers in my general direction.

The pack was around me then. Arms linked. Our feet did their thing; the song was not interesting, just rhythmic enough so that our footsteps could conjoin, and we were all a circle. Together we made a pretty picture. This was always something we knew, true and deep. From my place under all those weightless arms, I looked up and saw the glittery, golden faces of so many sisters, peering back with mild interest.

The song broke, and so did our formation. Shots were shoved into my chest, their contents spilling down my shirt. Somebody was buying, somebody male. I could tell by the way the sisters recklessly shoved the liquor around, and then beckoned to shadow figures at the bar for *just a few more, please!*

The nature of a blackout is such that you aren't quite sure when it happens; the only sure thing about it is when it's over. So somewhere in there, I hit that black wall of incomprehension, and when I came back around, it was from the bathroom floor. The sticky yellow plastic of the Canteen women's restroom: here was somewhere I knew. Here was Friday. I felt a spike of pain in my right knee, where I'd gashed it open a few nights before, in my fall at Sterling's. New skin had tried to grow, but the determined grip of my exercise clothing had prevented it, and the scrape re-bloodied every so often, like a budding friend, come to make sure I wasn't completely well. And there was still gravel embedded there. Now, the remaining bits of dirt came loose from the flesh. They left glinting bits of ember on the bathroom floor.

Then there was a voice that I knew, even though I might've never actually heard it: the pinchy sounds of Beta Girl, the teeny bug. When my eyes refocused, my other senses followed, and I felt the vomit in my hair and on my neck.

"Jack?" she squeaked.

I refrained from cutting in, mainly because of Jack's response:

"Yeah? Wait, is that *hair?*"

"Yes," I said. "I'm relaxing." And then there was the kind of thoughtful silence that hangs. I added, "Am I in the middle of something?"

"*Stella?*" Jack was not disgusted; disgust in a man's voice pricks me. It's clinical, that sound, clinical and pungent. And there wasn't disgust there, no, but there might have been amusement.

"What are you doing? This is the girls' room," I said, in the general direction of his voice.

"What are *you* doing?" Beta cut in, toward me. And then— as if I couldn't hear, as if I was not sprawled at their feet, she turned to Jack and said, "Uh. Should we go somewhere else?"

And he heard her, of course.

Except then he did something lovely: he developed, to her, and her only, a deafness. And that was perhaps the first wave of trouble, because I saw—in his pretending—a tiny bit of me, and I admired him like a human, and not like a boy anymore. In his deafness to the other girl, he turned to me, and said, "Stella—what are you doing here? What happened?"

"I have a reason," I told them both.

"We did too," said Beta.

"Look: who the fuck are you?" I turned to her. Rather, I craned my head backwards, and then upward, to get a better view from the ground.

"I just . . . you need some fuckin' help," she stuttered. But she'd already started her retreat, and she turned toward the bathroom door. Her heels banged off, and her voice rang shrill in a loud stream—there were the words *slutty,* and *insane,* and I caught *dead,* or *death.*

So all right, then. She had me understood, or as she'd have wished to understand me.

"She's not wrong," I said, face down again.

I forced out a laugh, which he mimicked, although I imagine that he was between two places about whether it was wise to get involved.

"She's—don't worry about her. You're all right," he said.

"What was she doing here?"

"Well, it's the women's room."

"Then what were *you* doing here?"

"Helping you," he said, and then I felt one of his hands reach toward me, under the stall door.

Never have I so quickly emptied various cavities in and around my head of vomit: under my eye sockets, my ear canals, nostrils, back molars—I spat up rum and phlegm, and slopped a mix of both from all my bodily crevices into the toilet bowl, flushed, flushed again, flicked clean toilet water through my hair, to clear the vomit that still stuck there, flushed again, popped two pieces of gum from my purse, chewed aggressively, spit one into the toilet bowl, flushed again, a quick coat of lip gloss, blotted it with toilet paper.

I opened the door.

"Hi, Jack" I said.

"Are you all right?" he said.

"Yeah," I said. "Why not?"

"Well—you have puke on your top."

"I know," I said, even though I didn't. This was an uncharacteristic lapse.

"I can wear my t-shirt," he said, "And you can have this."

And before I could tell him that, really, this was not an invitation, not even slightly, for him to undress, and that in fact I'd really rather if he didn't, he'd taken off his gray button down and grappled it over my head until it settled on my body. I stood up, put on a face that made him place a hand on the back of his neck.

"That was unnecessary," I said.

"Let me at least walk you ho—"

"I'm fine," I interrupted. "I'm completely fine. Isn't that obvious?" I let out a tortured laugh.

Ah it's so exhausting, pretending all the time, and the night had dragged on for weeks. I gave up, leaned against the bathroom stall, craned my neck to observe the dizzying black and white ceiling tiles, I was no longer drunk and no longer buzzing from the coke. A brutal hangover threatened at the corners.

I guess he could've done anything. He chose to smile. And then he chose to laugh. And I did, too—I laughed.

I should've known then that all of this unnatural laughter meant trouble.

"Should we get out of here?" he asked.

I shrugged, as if maybe I'd like to stay right there, on the Canteen bathroom floor.

"Yes."

Everybody was too drunk by then to notice our escape, or if they did notice, nobody cared. Nobody said goodbye.

I met bits of me back on the sidewalk. Logic, for instance, found me again, and all of the other senses, the real ones that tell you how to act right.

"Where are you from?" I said, and he said "Kentucky," and I laughed and said, "Okay. Bit random." And something else made sense again, like when he'd told me he was of age: there was no coast in him, no California fakeness or tortured cool, and no New York cruelty, the kind of cruelty associated with money and tight spaces.

He lifted a hand, and plucked at the collar of his shirt, laying on my neck. I knew that a Moment had passed, and then he took my hand again. I let it stay.

The grass on the fraternal lawns was bright and groomed.

It had been a whole season and a half since I'd spent the night with somebody else. Since the Spring, anytime I'd gotten close, darkness, and sweating, and claustrophobia had encroached. And so, I simply didn't. And all my nights were still nightmares; but at least I was alone.

But what with the end-of-summer heat, and how it suffocated from the sidewalk, I felt, suddenly and quite surely, that my life might have rewound itself, and begun again in the fall.

Except I had to respect history, which instructed that stupidity here could be catastrophic. And anyway, how good could it be, sleeping with a stranger like this, no matter which way he held my hand?

I wanted to say it lightly, so that he knew it wasn't personal. And I'd been just about to say it: I think, tonight, I'm just going to go home—alone, when he said, so casually, "This is me, then."

We were stopped at the walkway up to Sigma Rho, which was an outline in the dark.

"Oh—so you're . . . goodnight, then."

"It was, wasn't it?"

"Sure. Did you not want to. . . "

"I'd ask you in but . . . not tonight, right?"

It's incredible the range of thoughts that you can have during a kiss. Somewhere I acknowledged that it was a perfectly good kiss, and then I thought intensely about other things.

He'd not asked me inside, nor had he equivocated around coming over to Kappa Alpha. And this was exactly what I'd wanted—not to spend the night.

But why not? What *was* it about me?

Or him? Was it him? Was he gay, or uninterested, or—as the kiss continued, and turned into a series of little ones with gaps in between them—it was *me*, something about how I looked. Specifically, about how my body looked, maybe, in my small top and my tight jeans—too tight—because they showed off every bit of fat that I still had, somehow, despite all the dieting, and running, and throwing up, and Vyvanse, and Ritalin . . . could he feel it, the extra bits of me? And, to him, were they that revolting?

I stopped kissing him, and I said, "That's it?"

He rubbed an open hand on his chin, and his pointer finger twitched across the bottom lip.

"I thought you wouldn't want to—"

"I don't."

His eyebrows crumpled into themselves.

"No," I continued. "Okay. Right—no. Maybe another time."

He nodded, said, "Sure. Us and Kappa Alpha. It's historical. I mean—even if it weren't. I'd still want to—we could always—"

I have a genetic disposition that gives me a good idea of when a night has ended. And that one had. So I offered a silly wave that stifled somewhere around my waist and involved the activity of only three fingers, and then I turned to finish the walk down South University, the end of which is governed by Kappa Alpha.

Well, the night had nearly ended.

As I walked into Kappa Alpha, my mind was in the other place. The Church. I was spooked when I entered the living room and stepped on a human being, who was asleep across the floor. Generally speaking, the living room is meant for aesthetics. It's all marble, with the house crest plastered in unsubtle places. There is no living to be done in the living room.

This creature that I'd bashed into, she'd set up *house*, fluffed up some pillows, a couple of blankets, and a journal lay beside her, with a pen latched onto a middle page. It was as if she slept unaware, in her own private rehabilitation clinic. I gave her a shove with my foot.

"Agh!" she jolted, and I understood that this person was not local. It was in that noise of weakness and disorder, a noise that you'd never hear from the gut of a Kappa Alpha, no matter how weak or disordered she felt. This was not a KA. This was not even a Greek.

"Well," I said. "Sorry. But who the fuck are you?"

She looked up at me. I flicked on a desk lamp just above where she lay, and it corroborated my suspicions. She was strange-looking. The saddest bit of it—I think this now, having known her all that time—was that she'd come so close. One different feature, maybe, or one slightly altered, and she would've been just strange-looking enough to be lovely.

She'd just got unlucky in the genesis of the thing.

Her body had not moved from its den, she was still shapeless, covered by blankets.

"I'm sorry," she said. "I was told I'd be all right here. That I wouldn't be in anybody's way. My friend—uh, Leah?—she told me that nobody really comes here. These pillows are hers?"

She whispered. She was afraid of herself at top volume.

I said, "You know someone here? So why are you not in her room?"

Her head dropped onto a pillow, but then she tossed the blankets off, and sat up.

And it was a body vile. It was not only a body unloved and untouched—I could've cooked with the fat of virginity on her—it was a body abandoned to anybody's will. It was its antiproportions, its unruliness, its guttural attempt to claim space for itself, and thus its pronouncement that it was here—that made it vile. I had not seen such a body here. Oh, they were out there, certainly. In the bottom-tier sororities, and out among the God Damn Independents. I knew one thing for sure: that body was nobody's first choice.

She spoke now.

"Well, Leah . . . she's been busy, is all. She's had boys over or been out. And the bedrooms are small, and Leah just wants some independence, she said."

I knew Leah for the casual moments of my life. I liked a smoke with her because she was unfussy about doing it in the house. I did not seek much else from Leah. She was a fraternity groupie. Specifically, Leah was a Church Groupie. I was always suspicious of a Church Groupie, even though I had been one too, once.

That had been my first identification. Now I was an apostate.

The girl looked at her nails now, and I knew that she resisted the urge to stick one in her mouth, and chew. I remember this only because I had looked at my own in the same instant, and then resisted the urge to chew.

And she said, "I'm sorry. I'm just nervous. What's your name?"

I told her, and sat down. I asked what she was doing here, where she'd come from. And she said that she'd come a long way, from a different college. That she wanted—for once—a good time. To try something brand new. She wanted it badly, she said.

I thought that she could have one—the good time that she sought. It would be ephemeral, whatever amount of it she could scrounge. You can't sustain a good time around here. Because there are reserves of it—the goodness factor—and it's disseminated undemocratically. It's highly subject to fair-weather alliances, unlikely to commit in the long-term to any individual at all.

But I thought that if she did it quick and found whatever it was that she was looking for, she'd make it home by December. And then she could go back to her regular, pedestrian life.

I was briefly fascinated, for reasons that I'm still not entirely sure about.

I said, "Well, we could try. To have a decent time, here."

"Could we? We could?"

"Jesus, sure. I'm always trying, anyway. You could just . . . join in."

"That's—that would be . . . exciting."

"I'll find you soon, then."

"Night, Stella."

I didn't say anything. What I realized much later was that her wishes, and desires, and fears—all of those things that make a person, well, human—actually made her very good-looking, and sometimes beautiful.

I heard her body drift back into place as I climbed the central staircase.

In bed I thought of him, and her. And I felt something that I had not felt since Spring of the previous year, so it took me a little while to determine what it was. When I did, it was simple, and it was only the opposite of something else. As I lay and drifted, I was unlonely.

* * *

UNTIL THE MORNING. I WOKE UP cold and naked, and as I crashed out of bed, a violent hangover overtook everything. And my roommate Elena, who was almost never in our bedroom, was there for some reason, stinking of liquor and anger.

"What happened to you last night?"

I excluded the bit about Penny, and I employed such phrases as *I was so fucked up that I hardly know,* which was in some sense true, and in some sense not. Regardless, the whole hallway was soon dissecting Stella and Jack at Canteen last night, and they looked toward me, and said, nice one, Stella, he's cute, *and* he's a Sigma Rho. His top house membership made him cuter. And I said—he's a pledge, he's not even a brother yet.

"We were drunk," I concluded the conversation. "It won't happen again."

And I sat down to my coffee.

PENNY

I PRETEND NOT TO NOTICE, OR smell, the vomit on her button down, a shirt that is so obviously male. Even though I know nothing of romance personally, she reeks of it. She reeks of romance in the way that those kinds of girls do, whether they like it or not—it haunts her, male attention. I suspect that the shirt belongs to the boyfriend, and that the vomit belongs to her.

I've been here—ah, three, four days—and from the vantage of the living room floor (where I have been miraculously undisturbed, apart from Stella last night), I watch everything. They are so deliberate about *unthinking*. As a result, they are so, so happy. My envy comes and goes, unpredictably.

No one here cares about flimsy things like classic literature, or the future. They rush in and out, and speak only in vagaries. There is a lot of manic laughter, so that it's like a looping background track.

Stella laughs most of all. She has a distinct laugh, twinkly but with a shrieky edge. It makes me think of the fairies in stories from when I was a girl, which makes my stomach tighten up, in a good way.

This morning, she appears downstairs, and looks toward my mouse heap in the corner of the living room. There is a soft smile on her face, and her hair is wet. It itches me. And then she follows the noise coming from the basement, which is where they eat their meals, all together. Smells of hot, sugary breakfasts start floating from the industrial kitchen down there, and soon Leah comes toward me with a backpack over her shoulder, and a single pancake on a plastic plate. Two packets of stevia beside it. A cup of black coffee.

She says, "So, this is for you. I'll be out and about all day."

I say, "Okay. Sure. Where?"

"Just class. And then Church."

I think that nobody, not even the most enthusiastic follower, is going to church on a Wednesday afternoon. And besides, as long as I've known her Leah has never been religious. So I ask, "Church? Which one?"

And she says, "I don't totally know. You don't get it."

Before I can press, Stella comes back upstairs, and walks across the living room in a straight line.

"What's up, Penny?" she says.

I sense confusion from Leah, which gives me a flint of joy.

"You guys know each other?" Leah says.

And I say, "Yeah, of course," like we actually do, and Stella nods.

Leah stands to find God, and Stella takes her place. There is a sharpness in me. And a darkness. They are always here, in some capacity. As Stella sits and looks around the living room, and then at my untouched pancake, the darkness and the sharpness come back hard, like they did the night before, when I'd first seen her. This is envy. This is truer and purer than envy.

I look at myself sometimes, or out at the others; and I think of how interesting it could all be, if only I was somebody else.

She looks at the cup of coffee in my hand. She says, "Could I have that?"

It is abrupt, and it's not really a question. It's only a signal for what we both know to be true, which is that the coffee is hers if she wants it. She takes a sip, and speaks again.

"I wasn't in my, you know . . . best form last night."

And yet she'd been so scarily perfect. The kind of thing created, not born.

Her face is stunning, but unbeautiful. There are different brands of beauty, everybody knows that. The preferred brand, around here, is one of high design and geometric exactitude. Like the sisters learned about proportion, and then implanted it onto their faces with harsh lines and the residue of dewy gloss. They all have the same sort of cheekbone, in the same sort of triangle. Stella's face doesn't configure that way. So rather than convince her features to behave themselves individually, she attacks the overall essence of the thing with harshness and black coal. Black on her eyebrows, and something on her lips like rotting blood. I can't really look away. I sort of want to, and I sort of don't.

She continues, "It was a lapse, Penny. I was with a boy and had a lapse. And then I puked. *On myself.* So, I mean, are you going to judge me?"

"It's all right," I say. "I wouldn't have guessed. And I'm—I'm a whole lapse. My whole life is a lapse. I don't care."

And perhaps I've made people laugh before now; maybe I will after. But I'll remember hers for a long time. It's a laugh that, once earned, you never quite shake off. Through guttural chortles, she repeats, *"My whole life is a—lapse."*

And it's like a redone comedy. I laugh too, a shocked laugh that is unfamiliar with itself. The noise sets her off again. I feel, suddenly, that I am laughing with a gilded butterfly. Then we laugh ourselves into silence, and she finishes the coffee.

"What are we doing today, then?"

With my endurance gathered and my whole heart unready, I say, "Can I go with you?"

And this seems like what she'd wanted.

She places her hands on her thighs in a decided way.

She says, "Let's go upstairs then."

She reaches down, helps me up with two hands. She keeps one hand in hers as I follow. A friendly, girlish type of thing.

Or maybe not.

And upstairs has never been so skyward as it is right now.

It turns out that somebody important lives upstairs.

There is one great God that reigns over Kappa Alpha's drug supply, and her name is Millie.

Stella says, "That's her room, at the very end. So—what do you need?"

My antidepressants have always been a secret. Shelly, my psychiatrist, is the only one who knows. I'm ashamed, disgusted. They signal my deficiencies—they announce to the world that I'm not equipped to deal with things that come so easily to everybody else.

It's as if Stella somehow knows all about the very worst bits of me when she adds, "Listen—it's fine. You can say you need stuff. It's all right if you do. Everybody does. We all go to Millie for it—cause it's so annoying to see the shrinks and stuff. I still see mine. Millie's stuff is better—uh, stronger, you know."

I say, "I'll take whatever she has, if it helps."

Stella knocks, and a voice from inside calls, "Yeah?"

I follow Stella in, and we stop in front of a bed. A girl sits up straight on the comforter, and a boy sleeps beside her. She sucks on a pink vape, and it looks lean and fashionable.

I gaze around. The smoke detector on the ceiling has been viciously disabled.

"What?" asks Millie through the puff of a sticky, bubblegum-scented cloud. "We were asleep."

"Is that Jimmy Crawford?" Stella says in a low voice.

"Yeah. Why?"

"I just thought you weren't a Church follower anymore?"

"I mean, it's just mindless... we don't *talk* to each other."

I understand now in this moment that there is nothing religious about their Churchgoing. Even I can gather what they do with boys when they are not talking together.

"This is my friend, Penny," says Stella.

And then Stella tells Millie about how she's running low at the moment because she's missed her recent psychiatrist appointment, on account of drinking too much the past few nights, and Julie—her psychiatrist—doesn't trust her enough to prescribe over the phone. Although I try to listen, it all gets muddled together, because I'm fixating on that one sentence: *this is my friend, Penny.*

Millie looks at me now. She does not move her eyes from mine as she lifts herself from bed. The boy remains asleep. She goes to her desk, where she pulls open a drawer. Before she takes anything from it, though, she turns on me, and says, "Sorry. Who the fuck are you? Again, sorry—but you can't be in Kappa Alpha. Right?"

Stella steps toward her, and Millie abandons me, shifts toward my friend. Millie has the drugs; but Stella has the power. Stella says, "Stop messing around, Millie."

"You think I'm going to just sell to anybody? Do you know the waitlist I have for these things?"

"And I'm at the top of it."

"And *her?*"

"She's up there with me. And anyway," Stella continues, "She doesn't know anybody. Who would she tell?"

Millie relaxes as she hauls open drawers and drags out handfuls of small yellow bottles, which are taped to sheets of paper with signatures and stamps from several different psychiatric practices.

"Here's Prozac," Millie starts, "But a high dose, so ease in, and Nycadin, and Celeon, Middleish, uh, this one's brand name though—you prefer the high-end shit, I remember. I always remember my clients' needs. Haha! These are generics, so here's the generic of that—and some Addy, but no, because I need that for an exam this week. Ah, but if *you* really need it . . . I could charge you for the inconvenience. A few more Zoloft but they're for Sarah and them, downstairs—and Jesus Christ do they need it. I guess, though, I could charge you if you're willing to match them . . . and anyway, look."

She launches out a new drawer now, and beckons me closer.

"This is some off-brand cheap stuff, which brings you down. Down like calm, you know, for shakes. Because the others might give you shakes. And then, this"—the last drawer, only loose pills, like pick n' mix candy—"is my miscellaneous collection. Some of it is discontinued, and some of it is valuable, and some of it is shitty brand versions of better stuff. I'll down charge. And some of it, to be honest, I don't know. I can't keep track of the loose ones. I'll charge according to what I think."

She waves through the last drawer with one finger. It is a loving gesture, like she is putting them to sleep.

Stella sifts through the drawers. The bottles, I realize, are organized with shocking acuity. They are split up by category according to psychological effect—upper, downer, calmer, hyper, focus, whatever else—and then they are alphabetical, but only within the appropriate differentiation between the generics and the brands, which *themselves* are alphabetized.

Millie speaks to me, "And some coke, too. In the bottom drawer. But . . . you don't strike me as the type."

Stella reaches down to grab a plastic bag from the bottom drawer, and I watch the white powder float around the corners. I think that Stella is so beautiful, and seems so put-together, in a way that's totally unfamiliar to me. I wonder whether it might be okay to be the cocaine type—if she is.

"What'll it be, then?"

"Uh—uppers," I say. "Anti-depress—well, uppers. And could I try a couple of these, uh, different ones? These ones here?" I point toward the drawer of loose pills, which beckon. It is their namelessness that draws me, the silly gamble.

I select a whole lot. And later that day, I watch as Stella swallows a small handful of her own pills, seemingly without much thought. I admire her already, find her so lovely and romantic, and I desperately wonder what it would be like to be her—even for one day. So I do the same—I swallow a few of Millie's pills without thinking about what they do or don't do, and then Stella and I together lay down on my blanket heap in the living room, untouching, and we feel ourselves get happy again.

* * *

I do the same over the next few days, and I feel my worries and my limitations disintegrate, as if they'd never really been there to begin with. I think back to the girl I'd been only a few days prior and think—how pathetic. I feel new, like I'm in a better angle of sunlight.

The worries grow tired of me.

And they leave me with myself.

I get to know her.

And I discover that she isn't so bad, after all.

Stella seems to have decided that my company is decent enough, so we start to do things together. Mainly, we walk. Before, walking felt like a charade. Especially walking in places of natural beauty. I mean: what for? It felt like an ad. An ad for rehab, or Marlboro cigarettes.

But with Stella, I rather like it.

She likes to walk in the Huron Wilderness at the edge of campus, on trails carved by the fit track girls, the types of girls that I envy aggressively. And Stella does too, as it turns out.

It's Friday, and Stella does not have class on Fridays—not ever, she says. We're walking in silence when a blurred cohort of varsity runners, all in blue and yellow, run around us on both sides, and bring us close together in the middle of the narrow trail.

I hate myself for being so unlike them in every way that a woman can hope to be like any other—in looks, in fitness, in status.

Stella agrees. "Ah," she says, and kicks back a bit of gravel that they'd shot toward us. "Fuck that. Just fuck that. What are we really supposed to do, when there's girls like that?"

"What? What do you mean, *we?*"

"Did you not see them, Penny? Jesus."

"I did see them."

"So what are the rest of us supposed to do?"

It surprises me, when Stella worries. And in moments like that, I want to look at her, and tell her that I get it, I do: we are all everybody in some shade of blue.

But I can't. I'm terrified of being mawkish, of sounding glib, of accidentally putting off this exciting and in-the-flesh friend of mine. So, all I say, when Stella speaks so painfully of how beautiful other girls are, is: "Sure. Sure. I guess they are. Perfect, and everything."

Don't you see the greatest strangeness here? So is she. *So is she.*

STELLA

WE'D BEEN GOING ON LONG WALKS, talking about things, and saying a lot of nothing. It was nice.

If Penny could've built a better life from things she wrote in that journal, or read about in silly little novels, I'm sure that she would've been all right. And I could've helped. Because her trouble was all internal. When she escaped her own mind for a bit—really, when I'd introduced her to Millie's drugs—she'd become so lovely and happy.

And Millie's stuff did help. Sometimes I went to her when I missed a session with Julie, or if I ran out of pills early one month, because I'd doubled up, or sold some.

I met Julie due to a combination of factors, one of which happened to be my mother.

Listen: my mother is nothing much. In fact, I have inherited the worst bits of her. Incredible inclination toward alcohol, firstly, and a malignant attraction toward men of suspect character. The difference between me and her, you see, is that I know it all to be true. I see it in me, and I accept it: we've all got flaws. They become more acceptable, though, the more you believe in them. If you walk around with conviction in your own worst traits, people will start to believe that it's all a part of your deliberately cool constitution. And that's the difference: I've got one, an inner constitution. And she hasn't.

However: last Spring, not even my mother could pretend that I was all right. I say Spring; it was winter. It was a perennial Michigan winter. It was an awful winter, and what made it worse: every other American, in every other state, called it Spring so happily, and lost their heads in it.

Not us, not me.

I went home for spring break, cancelled my flight to Cabo last minute, where my pledge class had booked a beach house. I flew back to New York instead. And after a few days, my mother reacted. She hardly ever does that. You've got to see somebody, she'd said. What's wrong with you? What the hell happened to you?

School. School and The Church.

And so, Julie came into my life like a lover.

I sat in front of her then, our midweek appointment. Everything about her middled the scales of attraction: dull tannish hair which was not committed to being dark, nor light, and eyes to match.

She always checks in on me for the first fifteen minutes. Have you been counting calories, she asks, and I say no. And have I been thinking about last Spring, she asks, and I say, I'd almost forgotten about it until you mentioned it! Have I gone off the diet? she asks. Of course, I say. And have I been eating regularly? And I say I eat like a fiend.

This was an especially important session for me because I'd gone into it with a plan. Up until then I'd been on mild doses. Nothing beyond the dull scope of mainstream SSRI's. That stuff helped. Marginally. But I'd tried some of Millie's stronger pills. And I'll tell you something about happiness, real happiness: there is such stuff as dreams are made on. And it's packed tight and chemical, into the right kinds of pills.

Pills which I deserved.

See, I was being treated—Julie's terminology—for what she called an eating disorder.

I detest clinical language. That diagnosis, in particular. It makes me a trope, a standard classification. I become so one-dimensional in that diagnosis, as if I suffer from the romantic and collegiate brand of regular starvation.

And the real trouble with this diagnosis was that it made Julie hell-bent on "talk therapy." And nothing made me want to seek therapy more than participating in talk therapy. Julie was an aggressively average psychiatrist. But her talking skills were abysmal.

So, I'd been studying my Psych 101 textbook. *Inquiry of the Mind* was my golden bough. In the chapter titled "Eating Disorder Treatments and Recovery," I found what I'd expected: only simple drugs, low dosages, and a remarkable array of nonsense including, but not limited to, cognitive behavioral therapy, Jungian technique, art and music therapy, low-grade meditation, and—Heaven help me—mindfulness.

Attempting mindfulness is like praying for the first time at age twenty, and expecting Him to listen. I'd already tried that. Doesn't work. Christ tell me, if you know about mindfulness, if you've got it sorted: *who has the time?*

Julie needed to believe in a different approach. She needed to treat me from a different angle entirely.

What I needed was a new *diagnosis*.

This is how it went:

Julie: How have you been this week, Stella?

Me: It's a struggle every day, but it lately feels like the good days have been outweighing the bad ones. Even when the bad ones come around a good one shortly follows. But who knows how long this'll last.

I looked pensive.

Me: Slippery slope.

Julie: I am so glad to hear that you've been having good days! Our goal here is to have as many of those as possible. Can you identify what could be the trigger point to a bad day?

Me: I find that when I'm particularly stressed or anxious about something, I don't eat. It fucks with my mental.

Me: Excuse my language. It just feels sometimes like I'm a victim to all my worries.

Julie: What are some of the things that worry you the most, and create this negative cycle of thinking?

Me: Schoolwork. I take eighteen credits. Family. I don't much get along with them. Well—you know that. I mean, my *mother*. Julie, according to my mother, if I'm unconnected to a guy, a guy of a certain, how can I say it, breeding, I may as well be a waste. I don't know in which decade they taught that dogma, Julie, but my mother wasn't born in *prehistory*. Still though. To her, I'm not me without somebody else.

Thus far, all of this spoken in truth. Unsurprisingly, Julie absolutely drooled over this particular topic, though it was nothing that I couldn't have found in *Inquiry of the Mind*.

Me: Let's see. I get anxiety about raising my hand in a lecture hall. I start to sweat, you know. And I get anxiety about being late to things. And I get anxiety about being early. Sometimes I worry that when I cross the road, I'll get smashed by a car. Or that if it's snowing, I'll be struck by some freak avalanche, coming down South University. Or that maybe the Earth is on its way out, you know, that it's just so *fucking*—apologies—tired of us, and our *nonsense*. And so maybe we're just, uh, watching it go, sort of burn up, from our chairs on the patio. Oh, and of course: I get nervous, very nervous, about the lack of sunshine in Michigan. It's gray for the vast majority of the year here, you know. And I worry that I'll die young, of course.

Me: Who doesn't?

I smiled.

Julie: Oh, dear.

Me: I don't mean to sound crazy, Julie, but I thought that I should be honest with you.

Julie: And I am glad that you are being honest. Let's not use the word *crazy*. Your anxieties are not unusual for a girl of your age.

Julie: It seems to me that you've got some underlying issues associated with your anorexia nervosa that we need to address in order for you to seek full recovery.

Me: You mean I have *more* issues? What sorts of issues?

Julie: I believe you've got a somewhat serious anxiety disorder and probable general depression.

I looked at her as though witness to the supernatural.

Julie: Do you ever feel as though you'd like to just give up?

I gathered my lips, tried to tie them in a knot, looked around the room, focused on some objects, her pen, her legal pad, her foot, which was pocketed into a gruesome knockoff of a Gucci flat.

Give up? Did I ever want to give up? *Of course I did.*

Julie: Please don't avoid the question, Stella. I'm trying to help you.

Me: Okay. Well, yes. Sometimes I feel it would be easier just to give up. Fling myself off the Kappa Alpha balcony or something. It's just that sometimes these *worries* turn into *whirlwinds*, and then they come crashing down. And I just get so sad. I'm just so . . . I'm loath to use the word *depressed*.

Julie: There is no need to be afraid of the word *depressed*. There is no need to, well, loathe it. It is not an uncommon thing for a young girl like to you to deal with depression.

Me: So. . . do you think this is an *issue*?

Julie: It may be a danger to your health. And we should seek to get you back into a healthy mental state. Your other issues—such as your body image dysmorphia, and your relationship with your mother—will resolve faster if you are mentally healthy.

Me: What do we do then, Julie?

Julie: I believe it would be wise for me to draw up a more robust anxiety and depression treatment plan for you. Now, Stella. This will include incorporations of psychochemical treatment. In short, new prescription medications. Are you comfortable with this?

I forced myself to sing a couple rounds of the chorus of "Waterloo Sunset" in my mind. Dirty old river, must you keep rolling, rolling in through the night. Terry and Julie, cross over the river . . . I sang and sang to myself, and I made my face thoughtful.

Me: Well. I guess if that's the only solution for my, uh, new issues.

Julie: I'm afraid it might be, but of course—prescription treatment is no substitute for talk therapy, which we will be continuing weekly . . . now this plan shall include low dosages of Zozac, as well as an additional medication, which belongs to a group known as the benzonatates—or sedatives—to treat anxieties that may be a side effect of the anti-depressants . . . now with these, we will gradually increase the dosages from mild to more aggressive . . .

I was prom queen again; seventeen, and forever overhead.

Julie: . . . and I highly recommend you begin to keep a journal, which will monitor your new, or improved, feelings whilst on this treatment. And, of course—I repeat—this is all in *conjunction* with talk-therapy . . . and follow-ups every . . .

Eventually, I said, thank you so much, I feel—what's the word—*hopeful*, Julie.

She sent me to the pharmacy equipped with her verified signature, I was legitimate, yes. I was a problem, I needed fixing, and I needed it artificially, and quickly, and aggressively. *Load me up.*

* * *

My pockets jingle-jangled with expensive chemicals.

And it was with a new feeling that I walked off from the pharmacy. The exact feeling is intangible to me, even now; it's never one, and never the other. The sky looked like stained glass from forgotten hometowns, in churches that people go to only out of habit.

I passed The Church on its damp corner. It's got its own cosmic forecast, like a perpetual raincloud. The Church itself didn't bother me so much as the fact that he still lived there. And though I never went anymore, I had intelligence that told me he was the same, unchanged. He was present at all of the Cat Catchers that early fall. *Cat Catchers:* the name used by The Church for their first parties of the schoolyear, in which their members hunt the newest freshmen girls, to make them theirs, and then nobody's.

It was a Friday afternoon. Attending class on Fridays was sacrilege. The Church had set up a pong table, and swaggering around it was a group of boys, hair proudly slept-in, hair that looked like it had had rough sex the night before. They played an apathetic game, red cups stacked in triangle formations.

I'd had friends there once, and some of them were out. Jimmy Crawford, who had druggie and sexual dealings with Millie, saw me go by, just as I'd skipped off the sidewalk to cross away.

"Stella?"

I nodded, kept moving at a diagonal across the road, waved a hand, "What's up?"

I was just about to turn down South University toward home when I looked again toward their pathetic show on the lawn.

Trip Swindle had come out, cig held between his teeth. There was nobody home in his eyes (not even himself), and he wore only boxers and a t-shirt (I recognized the Silverman logo from his internship that summer). I didn't look away in time, because he saw me seeing him, and then both of us pretended otherwise. I rushed home, and got the same old feeling. The one from all of the times that I'd walked away from there before.

I'd hoped to fly through empty skies that afternoon, but my skies had become peopled, and those people had brought their darkness along, like they always did.

Σ

Trip Swindle prided himself on a few different things: the fact that he was a pre-med student who actually knew what sort of doctor he wanted to be (dermatologist), the fact that he could down five Jager bombs in one hour and still function okay, and the fact that he was indelibly handsome.

Most college girls were charmed at the beginning, because he had all the appearance of a content, Illinois-raised schoolboy, gentlemanly to a fault, and sheepish in conversation. But the days have their way with people; good looks make their way out, and other things crowd for space. It took due time, and a good amount of investigation, for some people to realize that Trip Swindle wasn't handsome at all.

At college he lived in a Church. It sat prettily on the corner of South U and Church Street, and nothing had changed of this Church since its creation except for everything inside of it. Gone were the pews, the candles, the illusion of spirituality. Gone was any presence of God, if ever there was one. If you could go into that Church, and feel His spirit anywhere at all, you must be of someplace holier entirely.

* * *

On Friday night, three young women headed there, dressed all in black and skin. Loretta led the triad. She was beautiful in a Midwestern sort of way, with long blond hair that reached past her shoulders, and fluttered sweetly around her face. When she turned to talk to her new friends, her hair swung and grazed the deep dimple in her cheek, which was elevated by a smile of light pink lips and straight white teeth. She was lean and muscular, the body of a girl who used to swim. This is all to say that she was the type of beautiful that everyone mostly forgets about upon college graduation.

But now, on her first night out as an undergraduate, it seemed and felt like what she wanted was hers, and everyone and everything was working in conjunction to ensure that her time here would be terribly good.

She had no trouble getting into The Church, she felt practically recruited there from her place amongst the other wandering freshmen, all of whom would feel like failures if they did not call home next morning with choppy tales of fraternity houses and what-we-did-at-three-AM.

Once inside, few were unaware of her presence. She broke onto the dance floor, which wasn't a task, since the whole floor was the dance floor. The Church fraternity (who had official letters, of course, but preferred the gloating irony of being called simply The Church) had their own established ethos, like all of the fraternities did. And they believed that any floor was a dance floor, if you didn't think too hard about it.

Trip Swindle looked at her three times: once by accident, once on purpose, and once to establish his plan. He watched Loretta lead two other freshmen, neither of whom were graced with the former's proud walk and apparent ease, over to the bar, where the new target held three fingers up to a recent pledge recruit, Sam, who poured three cups of pink wine from a plastic bag. Sam leaned over the bar on his elbows, said something only to her. Trip realized that any time he spent watching, and waiting, and ascertaining, was time enough for somebody else to bag the girl.

The basement of The Church was a place of senseless frenzy in which no one knew exactly who they were talking to, who they'd just finished off talking to, who they were going to go home with later, or where the exit was. It was a dreamscape for Loretta, who thrived off the energy of movement and terrible music. It was all beeps, and boops, and drops, and everybody pretended to understand.

Loretta's two companions followed her around, whenever she switched from the bar to the stairs to the center of it all, which bothered Loretta, because these were the just-hatched, embryonic type of collegiate friends, formed purely out of geographic convenience. They lived just across the hall, but the only thing they shared between them was womanhood, and that was not enough to hold them together.

She burned straight through the middle of the writhing crowd, and her wine sloshed lazily onto her slender fingers. Up her hands went. She might have been on the front page of an advert on the rising quality of the college experience. This was life at wellness capacity.

Fraternity brothers, however, are not so easily entertained. Their attentions darted from the dance floor to the girls, to the bedrooms, which were situated in separate halls, out of the party's entropy. Their shadowy faces moved amongst the party, girls would see one, and target, but then he'd disappear, and where had he gone? In Trip's case, to the bedrooms, with brothers alongside him, and that was where he was now, in a musty room with Jimmy Crawford, and the pledge Sam, who had taken a break from his post at the bar. They carried on there with things as usual; the first party of the semester begged for coke, and some other complements to it which they shoveled out of their pockets, and they sat around in ecstatic stupidity, thinking what a year they were set to have.

When Trip reappeared in the basement, he was still flanked by the other two, who were both mildly handsome but altogether uninteresting. His eyes were glossed red and etched with bright veins, and his smile was slacked, and his walk was swaggered. He zeroed in on the moving target, led his friends on a route that appeared quite random, and as he crossed her, he grinned and laughed at things so empty and stupid that they made you wonder if you'd missed something. You hadn't. Loretta saw that he was good looking enough, but much more important was her abrupt desire to get in on that laughter that seemed to come so easy.

There was trouble with her confidence. Because in her experience, distant male admiration never resulted in much by way of actual approach, which made her think that she might've imagined the admiration to begin with. Because what's attention, without somebody there to prove it? She habitually convinced herself of her own unattractiveness when men's watchful eyes didn't translate to even dull party chit-chat. When Trip walked right up to her, and took her hand above her head to drift her around, she was so restored in confidence that she locked her arms around his neck, and kissed him right there under the lights, and pink wine spilled all down the back of his shirt.

Right about here in the exchange is normally where it becomes apparent that time has stopped for a moment, the world goes still, the present surges toward urgency, hearts fly, thoughts get frenzied, and underarms sweat. All that happened, more or less. Except for the bit about the frenzied thoughts—neither thought much of anything at all.

When she pulled away, he gave her a great, sloppy smile, then grabbed her neck, and directed her back. She eventually gave a laugh that was more like a giggle through her teeth, which she whitened often, and the disco lights reflected from that smile in blue. When he spun her the second time, he stopped her halfway through, and her body folded into his, and then they were dancing.

You get the idea. They were wired off each other's good looks. Others watched, and speculated, and felt their insides dry up with envy. Some can only imagine in private dreams and silly fancies what it is like, to flirt so carelessly like that, and to have those flirts returned so easy.

Her slim waist turned circles. And when it ended, he grabbed her by the elbow, and steered her away, to a darkened basement corner. Their conversation at this point is one of the strongest memories she has of that night. He said, "Don't want you to think I'm rude, you know," and gave a smile that made his eyes crinkle up. "I should have asked your name before all of that. . . " and his fingers grappled at her waist.

"I don't mind," she said. "I had a good time. You're a good dancer, and my name is Loretta—"

"—could've guessed it was Loretta, you know. Would've been my first guess," he interrupted her, with a heavy sigh, "if you had only have given me a chance."

"You would've guessed?"

"Sure. Pretty name. Pretty girl, pretty dancer. . . " and he enveloped her in another kiss, his arms circling around below her waist this time, and she leaned into it, thinking it a pleasant thing that this pleasant boy thought her name pretty, and she even prettier. All of which she already knew, of course, on some subconscious level. But she liked to be reminded.

Their embrace was interrupted.

"Yo, Swind!" shouted Jimmy Crawford, "Smoke something, Swind, let's go! Leave the chi—"

"—Shut the fuck up, man, she's—" said Sam.

"Leave the chick, Swind, for a smoke!"

Trip looked at Loretta, and then back at them, and did some calculations in his head, and eventually came up with results that the girl would be here all night, and the drugs perhaps would not be.

"Really sorry, Loretta," he said, and cast his eyes away from hers, in the direction of his comrades, who made their way out of the basement, and toward the bedrooms. He ran a shaky hand through his blond hair, which was mussed up, as though he'd just awoken, or else been spooked out of a crazy high. He suddenly looked very tired.

"It looks like the guys need me," Trip said. "I'm Risk Manager around here, so I'm responsible for making sure no one screws up too bad. I don't like to talk about it. . . " and he let the thought die, as if ashamed of his own inherent buzzkill.

Her eyes widened. A gentleman.

"Later? Let's meet up later?" she locked her fingers around his neck again.

His smile was sweet, relieved. "Of course. I'll find you before tonight ends. I can't wait." And he kissed her but didn't walk away without giving her a pressing glance, as if to say that he truly missed her.

She galloped back to her acquaintances, who had begun to suggest they ditch the entire scene for a slice of pizza from the shop across the way when Loretta's blond hair cut right across the discussion.

"Saw you in the corner with that guy," one shrieked.

Loretta waved it off, rolled her eyes.

Trip and his brothers escaped, and their steps all fell evenly in line with one another as they swaggered out of the party, up the stairs, and toward a dimly lit hallway of bedrooms, away from the thundering music.

The party in the hallway was different from the one in the basement. It was still a party, but it took itself a bit more seriously, as if it had already started to consider its future. Couples had taken to the walls. Girls stood stacked against the white plaster, boys leaning toward them, pressing bodies, whispering silly things into ears. There was general talk about going home together.

Trip's posse paid no notice to the drunken couples, though many were composed of brothers, and exes, and familiars.

Jimmy Crawford was a tall and lanky boy with a babyish face and a shock of blond hair, which toppled over his forehead deliberately to cover the acne that grew there. He nudged Trip as they entered his bedroom.

"Smokeshow you were with, earlier."

"Yeah, fuckin' smokeshow," Trip said, and he nodded his appreciation toward the direction of the music.

"Later?"

"Well. What would that have been for, then?"

Their hands met in a congratulatory gesture.

They got comfortable on the bed and couch, and flicked on the TV to kill the silence, and Jimmy Crawford brought out a bong, which he packed. A thought came to Trip.

"You sure Mark Brent isn't around here?"

"Yeah. Been asleep since eleven," Jimmy Crawford assured, which was sound enough to Trip, and so he let the peripheral worry of trouble with Brent escape him. The Risk Manager—you couldn't find such a narc in the entire fraternity house. Life here was often caged by his attempts to reestablish order.

Soon, the air in the room was heavy with smoke that smelled so sweet and comfortable, and they each giggled over their own thoughts, all of which had nothing to do with the thoughts of the man beside them.

Weed played funny tricks on Trip's mind, every time. The sound from the television became guitar twangs, and he thought he could've been in the woods, even though he had no interest in walking through natural spaces, and all of that seemed a corporate advertisement, the collegiate obsession with trees and soil, and he'd have sooner crafted his own ad—an ad for what? Girls, he thought. The thought slipped away, and was replaced by equally silly things, until the image of the beautiful girl from earlier drifted slowly back to him, in pieces, until she finally materialized into a full and wonderful face.

He rose from the couch, to slurred objections from his brothers, who didn't care much about whether he stayed or went.

"He's bangin the girl. . . I think. . ." said Crawford to Sam, who sat sleepily beside him, and who responded only with a nod and a deep sigh.

The air outside the bedroom was pure and cold, untainted by the sickly smoke in the bedroom. It shocked Trip's system but didn't really wake him up. He wondered if this strange buzzing sterility, like a dentist's room amidst catastrophe, happened every time he got fucked up. It did.

The basement music reached him again, and the prerogative was to find the girl, because it was nearing early morning, and to be without a girl in his bedroom after a party like this . . . there would be gloating mockery from his brothers, followed by the dull, distant feeling of a false economy, of resources expended without the correct payout.

The party had trickled down, and the couples against the hallway wall had moved to better places with sheets and privacy. But the girls that remained, oh, the girls! Infinite waists, and pink lips, and hands playing in hair. It was systematic. Pornographic. How did they do it, the girls? How did they make it all day and night without succumbing to their own stupid power? How dedicated they were to the cause, the cause of risk, and how relentlessly they toiled at it. He stood there for a moment, basked in all the girls, especially the ones that still danced. Warriors. And he needed one. He specifically needed the one with the swimmer's body.

The trouble was that in all the drugs, and recreation, and the carnival of time in between, his short-term memory was an unreliable narrator. Recall came to him in bits and pieces that seemed only a semblance of something that had actually happened. That girl, she had happened, the blond one in the corner. Had she not? Had her waist not felt so small and ready?

God blessed him with clear vision and facial recognition. She was there still in the center, danced just the same, danced in the way girls do just before they dance themselves into bed. As spotty though his brainpower was, it was her alone that danced in that way, with the circles that sometimes turned into eights. And this power of female recall—this alone was evidence in favor of Trip's religious opinion: God was a man.

He went, crossed the dance floor but ignored the music—time was nasty with its swiftness at this hour, and he had to get on with it—and brushed her mess of blond hair, then grabbed her shoulder.

"What's up, Lo... L... what's up, I'm so glad I found you," and he turned his voice so slick and so soft, just deadened enough from the smoke. How attractive that was, and of course there is always that certain flattery of being found, since it implies that you had been sought to begin with. What man or woman has not lost his or her head over the possibility of that and that alone—being looked for? She wrapped herself easily around him as if to dance, he kissed instead. She let him.

It was simple enough to get her upstairs. She was drunk, and a happy one. The wine made her body fluid and her tongue hot, the rogue type of sexy, makeup and speech both slurred.

He was quick about her nakedness. She was indifferent about his. He rode the high, which made it higher. She looked pale in the night, and graceful, and while it happened, he thought grateful praises of drugs and girls. When it was over, he fell asleep, and she lay there for a little while, neither happy nor sad, but still very drunk, and curious about the name of the boy, and how exactly she'd got from the dance floor, so merry, to the bed, so cold.

* * *

LORETTA ALL THE WHILE SLEPT SOUNDLY in her dorm room bed. She had drunk dreams. The night replayed itself in fragments, and Trip appeared there once or twice. She wasn't particularly bothered that she'd left the party before he'd come back to find her. She had briefly thought that he must have found someone prettier, but she had downed a final drink in response to that suspicion, and headed for home.

"Sleeping at home, then, Loretta?" her friend had asked, with a cocky smile, as they walked away together.

Loretta killed her friend with her happy look.

"He's Risk Manager. He probably had to help a brother. It's a hard job." And she twinkled, which ended the conversation.

Trip awoke some hours later with a fatigue that can come only from being both drunk and high for many hours, accelerated by the girl, and then crashed down afterward. A naked body, a mess of blond hair, lay next to him, and he looked at her for a second, mildly surprised. All he wore were his boxers, and her jeans lay crumpled at the foot of the bed, confused in the sheets.

He'd fucked the smokeshow? The details and specifics were missing, but the evidence before him confirmed his remarkable capacity to score the beauty of the party with such ease that it was almost, he thought, criminal.

As she awoke, he climbed out of bed. What he needed was a smoke, a smoke with his brothers, any kind of smoke, but he normally preferred cigarettes for a hangover, and then weed to get the taste of cigarettes away.

"Morning. . ." she said and looked up at him with a bewildered smile. She was unsure about the progression of this awakening, but she remembered glimpses of the boy coming up to her last night, and treating her like an old friend, which had made her feel special, as if he'd known her all the while.

He looked at her, startled. Girls were always so wise and clever, and with terribly gripping things to say in the nighttime. The trouble always started in daylight, when they tried at conversation.

"Yeah. Morning," he said. "I'm off. Need a smoke. Need a ride?"

"I'm. . . okay." She was not. There was something in his voice, and the way he sporadically glanced around the room and toward the door, that made her think she should've left in the night. She reached for her jeans, and hurried to put them back on.

"Cool. Well. . . I'll see you." And that old sweet twinkle was back in his eye, and he placed one hand on her right knee, which he could reach over the sheets, and gave it a rub, and she felt a bit better, and thought what might happen if she saw him again next weekend.

Trip left and wavered down the hall, in only his boxers still, toward Crawford's room, but Crawford was escorting a pretty ponytailed brunette out the door. Trip watched her go, and gave him a look of respect, before he sank into the couch. He waited alone for his brothers to return from depositing the girls back to wherever they'd come from.

The cigarette smoke gathered and tried to make sense of things. Happy morning—all was sound, and the girls were still pretty, and the cigarettes were still sweet. Some time passed before Crawford returned, this time with Sam, who announced he'd driven the respective girls back to their dwellings.

"Lindsey's home," said Sam. "Nice chick, Trip."

"Yeah thanks. Who?"

"Lindsey. Your girl."

"Right. I know."

He lit another cigarette and thought of what it had felt like in bed with her, before the memory went and left him, and then he thought of not much at all except for prospects of breakfast, and told Sam to get on with cleaning the basement, and imagined all the girls to make his on the weekends, the girls so terrible and wonderful and special.

STELLA

THE NEXT TIME I SAW JULIE, I told her that I'd seen Trip Swindle outside The Church.
And how does that make you feel? she asked.
Well, I'd hoped to never to see him again, obviously, I said. I explained that I'd even skipped a Church party over the weekend. Everybody else went. I knew they'd come back crying and sloppy, that freshmen girls and God Damn Independents would be making shows of themselves and pretending to find The Church boys handsome. I couldn't go—even if I'd wanted to, Trip Swindle had come to despise me, told his brothers and my sisters that I was a crazy bitch—and those whispers came to me in pieces all the time. And yet for some reason I *missed* it there, I explained. Like, I miss it, but I hate it there.
Then she said that that's all very complex and interesting. I wonder whether we should discuss some coping mechanisms for these negative feelings that you have about that fraternity space, she went on. If you once found happiness there and with those people, I believe your next step should be to seek companionship and support elsewhere. Your mother, perhaps. What I mean is—because of what happened last Spring, I believe you should look for comfort in places that are not, uh, *male-centric.* Or, of course, women. Depending on your—what

I mean is, go to low-pressurized places. Find new support in *family*. In *friendships*.

I'd nodded, she did have a point. And romance was so dull and empty then. It was time to reject it, Julie was right. Boys are pretty much always up to no good, and are, ultimately, disappointing.

And so, I decided to walk to Jack's that night, and see what he might be up to.

* * *

JACK HAD BEEN STUDYING, HE SAID, when I came by. Nico opened the great front door; I hadn't knocked. It was pledge season. They were always on guard, watching for the cops, or for the University Admin to drop by under the guise of a friendly welcome-back-to-campus visit. Nico made it seem like he'd only been passing by the front door when I showed up.

Nico had been waiting there, for somebody else.

"Stella."

"Are the pledges busy?"

He looked at me funny, and I knew why. House calls like mine to fraternities were not themselves strange. But it was strange for it to be me, I knew, because I had up until this point been a notorious Church groupie. Nobody knew, yet, about my change of allegiance.

"Nah," Nico said. "Night off. Uh—they're just . . . around. They live on the third floor."

Sigma Rho was one of the few top male houses on campus. One of their perks, because they were well endowed, and alltogether well respected as a general rule, was that every single member could live in the house at any given time; this included pledges, even before they were officially brothers.

But how could they allocate rooms to brand new members, so early on? They dirty rushed.

They were one of the dirtiest, in fact, beat only by The Church. They chose their new recruits well before the start of school in August. They gathered names from coveted lists of future students through links with the admin; they met and recruited through summer internships in the financial districts of New York City and Chicago and Los Angeles; they sought out legacies, interviewed boys whose fathers and grandfathers had been Sigma Rhos long ago, told them in borrowed phrases that they had a spot in the incoming pledge class, if they wanted it.

Sigma Rho never recruited anyone blind. They offered up rooms to their new pledges because they were already guaranteed brotherhood material. All they had to do, after they'd been dirty rushed, was prove themselves during the pledge period.

And that broke some, but not most.

On the third floor there were the garbled sounds of life unwatched. This was life on a nonweekend evening in the fraternity house, and it was a mirror of life in Kappa Alpha, except it felt more charged, and that was the aura of feigned manhood, which realizes itself in simmering anger. Doors were left opened and forgotten; inside some bedrooms, girls clamored either alone or in groups of two or three. They smoked, and they laughed. Their laughs were meticulously designed. They didn't care whether or not anything was funny. But they laughed till they receded to cigarette coughs. That happens: you laugh so much and so often that it gets inside you, and you can't get it out. In some rooms it was silent and dark apart from the noises of pre-sex. And some of them wouldn't shut the door. Some of them wanted to be seen.

Some of the boys simply read books at their desks. There was one that must've been in my class, Psych 101. That class was disproportionately Greek, since no God Damn Independent would throw away four credits on something so elementary. I saw a page of *Inquiry of the Mind* flip over, and in the next room there was the *Principles of Micro* brick, and beside it the slimmer *Principles of Economics*, and then in the next, somebody must've been struggling through Stats . . . and pens blotting, and pages flipping, and words whispering—inflation, deflation, false economy—coalesced with the sounds of sex, and of smoking, and above it all, that terrible laughter rang.

And at the end of the hall Jack was one of the readers. Somewhere I had crafted the idea that Jack might've been having sex, or just about to. And that if he had been, I'd have nothing to say, nothing at all.

"Busy?"

He was unsurprised. He had closed the textbook even before he looked toward the doorway, where I stood.

"How're you?"

I felt, suddenly, like I shouldn't have come—fraternity houses (I'd forgotten) make peaceful matters chaotic. Make me feel unhinged and manic, even when I think I'm doing okay.

"Good."

"I was hoping I'd see you this weeke—"

"I know that it's sort of strange to come by like this, but it's all sort of the same, anyway, I thought. So I thought it would be okay."

"It's fine. I mean, it's nice. Do you want to stay here, or go somewhere? For a drink?"

I wanted badly to go. The fraternity house creeps were all over me. I was flashed with memories of freshman year, and huddled kisses, and feeling like a slut and an idiot in dark bedrooms at The Church and in a Detroit hotel. "Let's stay here," I answer. "This is good."

"I have stuff for mixed drinks. . . ."

"Do you have diet—"

"Yep."

He poured me a rum and diet, although I would've preferred some of the cheap vodka on the corner of his desk. I had the drink in my grip already, and I needed it to have its way with me. I took a sip—a gulp.

"About your shirt—"

"Ah, I already forgot. Let's talk about something else."

Conversation in fraternity bedrooms is circumscribed to the immediate and the real. For instance: if we are sharing a pack, we might discuss the cigarette brand. If a book lay on the desk, we might dissect the class for which it was assigned. We could discern mutual friends in the class, and discuss who they fuck, or who they do not fuck, or who they wish they were fucking. We might then discuss that: fucking. And then we might stop discussing.

That was how it had been with Trip Swindle. Trip Swindle and I had never talked much about anything that wasn't real and true. We spoke in platitudes. And it made sense, to me, because it was easy, and mindless, till it wasn't anymore.

You wonder why such talk had its way with my brain. Why it befuddled my sense and wit, and made my momentum point toward Trip Swindle. I don't know what it was, exactly, but it was something to do with desire: his. This is the type of psychiatric thing that Julie gets off on. But I wonder, now, too. I wonder why and how.

Jack offered a new challenge, one unexplored. Talking about things otherwise.

I scoped my brain for other things. And I said, "Okay. What are your parents like?"

"Oh. I couldn't really ask for better. Uncool, probably. Still. Kentuckians, you know. I'm the first to leave the state for college."

"And they don't mind?"

"Mind? No. Proud. Maybe too proud. A little obsessed with it—with this kind of thing. Big, football-school education. And this—" he moved his chin around and eyeballed the room, and his glance finished on mine—"is completely intriguing to them."

"Sigma Rho?"

"The whole thing. Pledging. Fraternities. Brotherhood . . . service."

We laughed, since Sigma Rho and Kappa Alpha both were notorious for public prevarications about their required services to the community, which is—nationally—the concept through which Greek Life is legitimized. At the end of last year, for instance, President Kathy Van Tassel published a statement claiming that we had raised over ten grand at our "Kappa Alpha Kandy" fundraiser, a statistic which was retracted after the Treasury team discovered that we'd all shown up blasted and eaten, rather than sold, all of the inventory. We'd received a harsh, groupwide scolding at our weekly Chapter meeting the following Sunday, during which I was disgustingly hungover, and removed myself to puke in the back lot. And Sigma Rho's philanthropy was equally unclear; they supported autism alliances and cancer research but rarely formally fundraised, apart from blowout parties during second semester, in which we threw cash to watch boys fight each other in mud baths.

Jack had asked me a question about my parents. I said, "Mom only, really. My dad, he travels. Europe, first. Rome, Verona. And then Denmark—the highlands. Basically, he wants to be able to tell people that he goes hiking. And then Berlin, at one point, for the clubbing. And then Scotland, so he could tell people that he'd gone hiking twice. And now I think he's in Greece; or he was, the last time I talked to him."

After I'd finished this traveler's tale, Jack vacillated. Most people do: they don't know whether they should express their awe over the ex-patriotism of a middle-aged father, or whether they should express sorrow for me, having been so obviously forgotten and left behind.

Jack finished his drink, and rose to pour himself another, and took my empty cup from my hand as he did. I asked for vodka this time, please, and he said, you should've told me that that's what you wanted before.

I said booze is booze. He laughed, I did too. Have you ever had a laugh that matters? What about a kiss? We did that next—we kissed. Only twice. They were small and aware of themselves.

And then I had a new drink, and Jack asked me about my mother.

I concocted my regular lies: "We're just not close," and, "We're very different people." Which both might've been true; but neither were the truth.

The truth, as relayed to Julie alone, was that my mother had forgotten a long time ago that here was my future, right around the corner. And that it was light, and bright, and mine to mess around with.

My mother enjoyed insinuating with cheap euphemisms that perhaps (for instance) I should attempt to attract more nice boys my age or slightly older. Nice boys and men (With Futures). Or, she might suggest that I not eat after seven PM, if I wanted to feel confident in my body, which was another thing that boys (With Futures) found attractive. Or, another, she would imply how very sorry she felt for the neighbor, whose college-aged daughter had just announced the existence of her long-term girlfriend, and how very glad my mother was of me, by contrast. That I was, at the very least, attracted to boys and no one else (boys, With Futures).

I looked at Jack, twenty-one, but with something about him that connoted a decade more. I looked at how he sat. It was the goodness in him, his awareness in how he talked, and drank, and sat there, and his own acceptance of himself—whichever way he was.

He was the type of boy that had a Future, and knew it.

He preferred to talk about other things first.

I was about to offer Jack a trite explanation of Clashing Personalities, my mother and me, when I thought how deranged it was, to lie like that.

Instead I said, "You know, she's a crazy bitch, and she drinks too much. Inveterate drunk; but such light stuff, like watered down rosé and things like that—so that she doesn't get completely belligerent. Just less of a complete person. A total, washed-up ditz, is what I mean. And she can never decide, you know—can't decide a thing for herself. Doesn't know who she is or who she should've been, could've been. So she's left with nothing."

I made sure that a laugh bumped up against my teeth, at the very edge of the whole speech. I caught the melodrama in myself, and I was ready to wave the words away, send them off with a giggle, in case he started to look at me in that very particular way. The way people look at you when they've just decided that you are crazy.

He didn't do that.

Instead, he took a sip. And he said, "I'm glad that you're the way that you are, anyway. That *you* know who you are. And that you've stuck with it."

And I had an urge to tell him that he had it all wrong, that I was still in the process of sorting it out—the reconciliation between who I was and who I purported to be.

Instead, I only asked if he had any music, although I already knew that he did. He had all types of records, and CDs, and hard copies of everything, scattered around and laid out, so that you could see all the cover art. Edgar Allen Poe, Aldous Huxley, a million other men, and a couple of women, looked up at me from the corner of one album, and they wondered what I'd do next. And I might've chosen that one, except for the fact that, by then, I wasn't in any mood for rock n' roll. I'd taken to the blues, you know, they spoke to my hidden sadnesses.

I said, "Do you have the fancy equipment?"

That year the fraternities had all acquired small-scale versions of professional DJ sets with wires, and search tools, and incredible ranges of access, and it felt like the whole world of music rested in their machinery.

Jack had some of the tech, scaled down small, stacked on a bookshelf, where it was plugged into other devices. He nodded toward the systems, and said, "Search for whatever you want, I'm easy . . . I mean that I like everything. Mostly everything."

A statement which often turns out to be false, but which sounded real enough coming from him.

I chose "Me and The Devil Blues," which discusses beating women to satisfaction, verbatim, but is so horribly wonderful to listen to that its thematic shortcomings are neutralized to me. And then, like nothing at all—and with no pain, the song hit us in the chest. And me and the devil were walking side by side—

Also, I was getting drunker. And he was too, I thought, evident by the way that he pressed his lips together briefly after every sip, and the way that he made a gestured point of placing his cup on the floor between larger gulps, as if prohibiting himself from continuing.

One day soon, I thought, we won't have to behave like this, and we won't have to pretend; we won't have to pretend that getting fucked up isn't a hobby, and that we don't love it so softly.

It's a short song. He asked if he could choose next, I took a sip, said, yeah, of course. It's your music, after all.

He went over to those dense mechanics, looked thoughtful, looked at me, asked if I needed another drink (I didn't, but I nodded), he took the cup, took my hand too, released my hand, refilled the cup. Added a little more chaser, this time. He went back to thinking—his bottom teeth gripped his top lip.

In the end, he only replayed the same blues song.

That was how we went into the night together. I played all kinds of blues. And he'd play them back, like he hadn't heard them quite right during the first go around.

So in the first play through, we talked. About mothers (his and mine) and fathers (his). And parties (abstractly, not the ones we went to, but the general thing, the preoccupation with them, and what differentiated a bad one from a good one—the music, we agreed, was the fatal factor), and local bars (the ones that we should go to, he said, together for a drink soon), and other things, like places (such as the Upper Peninsula of Michigan, where Lake Superior is), or Verona (because it was in our brains, my father having gone there himself).

Somewhere in there I suggested that we play a game of Truth, No Dare, and I won't have any disdain for that. Nobody among us is above the use of a drinking game to maximize flirtation and delegate the stress of getting-to-know-you and do-I-like-you-and-how-much to the neutral framework of a preteen game. He said, all right, as if there was nothing of it; he told me to go first.

"Why'd you join? Sigma Rho?"

"Friends," he said. "I had none, coming here. I was recruited from . . . uh. I was recruited early, but it's a somewhat private—process."

I gave him the kind of nod that suggested that I already knew about their dirty rushing, and he gave me one back, which meant that he did not have to speak any more in order for me to understand him.

I drank, though that's not prescribed by the rules of the game.

"And then suddenly you do," he said. "Have friends. Almost too many."

He drank, though also not prescribed, since he'd answered the question truthfully—truthfully to my knowledge.

"Why join Kappa Alpha?" he threw back.

We were both still sitting on the bed, him leaning against the wall with his legs sprawled, one of them stretched across my lap, and well beyond it, and I placed one elbow onto his calf which remained unmoved, and my head into my hand, and the edge of my cup to my lips.

"Same deal," I said. "As you."

But that wasn't the point of Truth, we both knew, although he wouldn't have said so. The point is to discover something that you wouldn't have without the scope of opportunity afforded by booze and free questioning. So, I said, "Lonely. Uh—I just felt really lonely before."

He nodded, moved from his wall to the one that supported me, arm round.

We both drank, unprescribed.

"Like a motherfucker," I added, which elicited laughter, although it wasn't a joke. I'd edged it with a lilt, in case he'd have liked to laugh; and so we did together.

In the repeat playback of the same blues song, we would do no talking, because we were listening. More songs went onward.

"Ah, Stella," he said. "I have to be honest with you, I'm getting dru—"

"I'm already there," I said.

The music played like a third member of our conversation.

But conversations, just like songs, they've got to end, and you can never listen for the very first time again. All of the subsequent listens, and conversations, have to be informed by the one that came before, whether you like it or not. And if you missed it—that blistering chaos of pinnacle happiness from your very first listen to a great song—then you're shit out of luck. You're just shit out of luck. Because you'll never, ever get that first time back again.

The same is true for lots of things.

After a while, we'd lost the rigidity that we both carried, and sank into the bed so that we almost lay, propped up by forgotten limbs. And time passed that way. There was a hand on my knee; and then there was one on my cheek. And there were a couple of small kisses, no tongue.

It was night now. That had happened so suddenly. The sun, it dropped of a heart attack. The music tapered. We let silences sit around for longer, before one of us got up to play a new one, or replay an old one.

Now there was more talk than music, and more silence than talk, and more drinking than silence.

And the silence and the drinking did terrible things to me. There were images of dark Detroit. There were pictures of beds that weren't mine. There were claustrophobic reels, and the feeling of the sidewalk, when you're sitting on it alone in the early morning.

"I've gotta go now," I said, and this was the first mention of the fact that this was a night, and that it was over. He looked at me abruptly, awoken from the stupor that we'd allowed to collect all around.

"Wait—already?"

"I'm not going to, uh, sleep here."

"No—that isn't what I meant."

But what I'd said had already had its way with the mood around us, and there was a shift now, and both of us moved in order to sit up properly, so that there were no more points of mutual touch. The song had ended, and nobody got up to put on a new one.

"I'll walk you back."

I didn't know whether this was the sort of masculine formality that I was meant to reject. Regardless, for everything that I didn't know, there was one thing certain, and it was that I wanted him to walk me home. I said sure, and then he was quiet, and I watched him watch me. He suggested that I should borrow a hoodie, that the Michigan night would have brought cold, and found a black sweatshirt, which I put on.

We walked. The night had lost any pretense of light fall weather. It wanted to remind us. It told us not to get too comfortable.

We talked easily again, now, about the future. Only the immediate one.

"Parents weekend soon," he said. Lit a cigarette, offered it to me. I puffed.

"Yours coming?"

He nodded, lit a second cigarette, the first one was mine now. I puffed.

"Yours?" he said.

I'd been putting off this decision. Julie was on a crusade about Parents Weekend. She believed that it might be the event at which my mother and I concaved like scarecrows, and started to understand each other. And I'd told Julie that the most I'd do, at the moment, was consider. But now I said,

"Yeah. My mom's coming."

I said that because I got the idea, from the way that Jack spoke about his family, that he valued them in the way you read about in happy books.

He nodded, puffed. And then we were at Kappa Alpha. My watch read two, but half the bedroom lights were still on, for the freaks who preferred visible sex, or for the outlier embarked on a late-night, Adderall-fueled study attempt. And through the living room windows I saw all darkness, and I knew that Penny was asleep.

More kissing, small ones.

"Can I see you soon?"

I wanted to see him at the next available opportunity. I half wanted to invite him inside, but nobody goes into Kappa Alpha—in a duo, at quarter-past-two—for unsex.

I thought I'd keep it cool.

"Yeah all right. If you want."

He nodded, one small kiss, turned around to go.

I stood and watched, didn't move. I thought about my mother, her fraudulent dishonesty with herself, and her predilections for booze and insipid conversation. I thought how unhappy I'd become, if my future were composed of white space and shitty muzak.

I called low at first, and then my voice rose.

"Jack, could I see you tomorrow?" I said.

He turned back around, lessened the distance between us.

"Yeah," he said. "Of course."

Empty silence between us now. What to *do* with a boy on a Sunday? God help me if he thought I'd meant *church,* did he attend one, was he a member? Would he pick me up tomorrow, suited, for morning services, and expect me to sing along, and would he be disappointed when I was not subsumed wholly by the Spirit?

"Should we go to the library?" he said.

"Yeah," I said, and he suggested that I meet him outside Sigma Rho. Throughout our arrangements, I spoke as myself. But I was otherwise preoccupied with a buzzy, electronic feeling somewhere below my skin and muscle. Within my ribbing. It told me how very much I'd wanted this, and for how long I'd waited.

I'd been drunk and half-there for so many months, and I realized that it might sober me up considerably—in the mammoth sense of sobriety, the total sense—to go and have a sit in a library, with a good-looking boy who seemed so nice, and normal, and sane, so remarkably un-fucked up in the head.

He felt so instrumental to what I desperately wanted: a sense of comfort, and easy simplicity, and happiness, in the way that I had felt it back in the before times—before the Spring, and even before the sorority itself.

I went inside, and crept into the living room to wake Penny up for a chat. Afterward I slept soundly, and I dreamt of libraries. They came in psychedelic clusters of color and music. The library showed itself as a new place, not within which to do addy under desks, but a place where I might even learn something new, or something that mattered for later.

PENNY

In the mornings, I sometimes wake up to find that the elephant is back on my heart. That's one of the ways that I describe it, to Shelly, and once or twice to my parents. Because they deal better in euphemism, the language of the American adult.

Otherwise, I'd have described it more as it really was: the ferocious deadness in my head, the painful doldrums, which were both vicious and indiscriminate, and that was the worst of it: the fact that my brain was *undecided* on its torture. Sometimes it was a frenzy—just frenzy, frenzy, and back again—berating in non-words. And then just as I might be about to capitalize on the nerves and do something with myself, my brain rejects itself and comes down with the heavy elephant to remind me that I'm no good, and that I've always been no good, and that I'll indefinitely be this way. Then, the hopelessness is ready and waiting. It breeds, and it infects. It spreads right across the parts of me that are still somehow alive.

The elephant comes around in the night, in my medications' off-hours. Which is how I wake in the morning. For a moment, I can't grasp where I am.

The living room, of course. Where I've been for days. Counting is useless, time doesn't seem to work normally in this house. Days fall into one another.

And, if I have to guess, days have fallen now into weeks.

Leah has a way, now rote, of peeking in on me in the mornings, before she goes out to do her thing—alone. She comes in, tosses around pleasantries and some cold coffee from the kitchen, and then she's out the door. Where does she go? It's a mix: the library, class, Church, the Diag, the bar, a different sorority house where she and friends gather to do sorority girl things.

That might've bothered me, before. That might've sent me down gray corridors of self-indulgent miseries, hunting for reasons why I might not be wanted.

But favorable conditions here, which include drugs, unmatched in strength and precision, and the new presence of my friend, bring a peculiar and wholly new realization: I really don't give a fuck whether Leah wants me around or not.

Stella, however, is also vacant this morning. Unlike Leah, she does not make any shows about seeing me, or not seeing me. We are in the practice of joining on the living room floor at night, when Stella comes home from wherever she's been. As far as I know, Stella has never been to Church.

Stella often wears baggy clothing, so that she is an indiscernible mass amongst it. I think this is nonsensical, when she has so carefully built herself into a perfect physical exhibit. She is a gym rat, a jogging rat, a diet rat.

When Stella joined me in the living room last night, I asked her about the boy.

"Is it the same one?" I had asked.

"Hm?"

"The same boy, from a little while ago. The one who gave you the shirt that you puked on."

"Oh," she said. She looked down at the male sweatshirt, as if only just then noticing how it blanketed around her.

"Yes," she said. "The same boy. Yep."

"Do you like him?"

She remained unmoved apart from the two corners of her lips, which irked downward. And then she looked toward me with one black eyebrow arched upward.

"Sure," she said. "Yeah."

"Are you dating him?"

Now both eyebrows met in the middle, and almost became one; I felt abruptly ludicrous.

"Jesus, no," she said.

"Don't you *like* him?" I pressed.

"I do, sure. But come on Penny. Don't be so naive."

And then she added, "I don't know. For right now, you know, he lets me be—when I want to be. He lets me be alone, even when we're together. And he listens to decent music. Or, at least, he pretends to." When I said nothing, she added, "So what more, really, can you ask for?"

* * *

I haven't seen her since last night, and I think she's off making something of her Sunday morning. I'm bored and restless, waiting here, and hoping to see her, even for a moment. Weekends are always unfriendly to me. I spend them in insomnia and half-imagination. To dispel the rising blend of nothingness and anxiety in my stomach, I dry swallow a few of Millie's pills: two of the uppers, along with two of the miscellaneous try-it-and-you'll-see varieties.

I wait here on the floor, and soon enough I remember that the world is behind me, someone is around me, somebody or anybody, and, early morning now, that it is my day to corrupt and malleate, and a deep bright feeling is there, and it is the feeling that here is the day—and there its length, and here its width, and both are mine to walk between.

I start walking away from Kappa Alpha, the way I'd come on that first afternoon. I expect a certain six-feet-under quality across campus. I figure that just coming up toward noon on a Sunday will evoke the natural corollary of sleeping in, and dull hellos, and nothing-to-do-but-nothing.

Not so. Under certain conditions college students can be so loud, and alive, and they can infect their spaces with it. As I get closer to the diagonal walkway that cuts across campus—grassy, colorful, brick and ivy, like a vision or a daydream—I realize that campus and its inhabitants are not only awake, but ready. And they are ready for multiple happenings, all at once.

There is a political function just under the entrance arch, a structure which signals the brooding beginning of the University buildings, stately, and ancient, and imposing, and below it a crowd is gathered. And the crowd cares and cares. They care about all of the issues of the day. They care, in particular, about the environment. This function is concerned with how the environment is on its swift way out; and about how we are encouraging it to go.

I pass by, and am covered in the darkness of the arch, which gives way to the Diag continuing, and open lawns all around it. At the edges of the pavement, where the gray meets the grass, stalls and posters of all different affiliations stand, and their operators search. They shout platitudes about societies, and sports teams, and volunteerism. And they each guarantee, in their own distinct linguistics of persuasion, that they will make our lives worth living.

Naturally, you've got to be careful with that type of promise. One voice, though, comes to me like music. It seems to go unheard by the other students around me.

"Hey! You! You look like someone who likes the great outdoors!" the voice calls.

I don't believe in this type of thing, but if I did, I might think that it's the voice of God. However, it is quite plainly the voice of a regular person, who sits behind a table just away from me, in the grass. A tall girl in hiking clothes. Her table has a board posted up on it, which reads:

Michigan Backpacking Society. Take A Hike! Ain't Life Grand?

And behind those letters somebody has drawn a great mountain range, topped with snow. And there is some artistic reimagination of clouds, and sun, and a moon, and a bit of rain, and birds in flight—all together, and all at once. As if impossibility is an option. On the bottom corner of the picture, it reads:

Grand Teton Mountain Range, Wyoming, Summertime.

The difference between action and passivity is often a matter of how beautiful you wish things were. And I want things to be as beautiful as that impossible drawing on the board. I divert off the paved path and walk over.

"Hello!" she says, and she waves at me, even though I can already hear her. "Welcome to the Michigan Backpacking Society. Are you interested in a flyer?" It doesn't matter, because she grabs two, and offers them to me. "We're recruiting new members. It's a great year to be a Michigan backpacker. We can't wait to meet all the freshme—"

And then she stops speaking, because she notices I'm looking so intently at the drawing beside her.

"You okay?" she asks after a moment. "You look kinda lost."

"I am," I say. "Uh—I was."

"Well," she says, "Listen: we were all lost, once."

"*Were* we?"

"Aren't you interested in joining our crew for spring break this year? Big Bend National Park. Down in Texas land. Have you ever been?"

"Texas? What for?"

"What do you mean 'what for?' All the whole world's down in Texas. It's the American wilds. Ghost towns, and natural springs, and truckers, and El Rio Grande. . . the kids last year even had a real, legit encounter with border patrol, right along the river. They tried to swim over, and—listen, you won't regret it. The mountains are *red*, down there, and we swim at night, and drink music and beer—sorry, we drink beer, and blast music, loud, across the desert. Imagine that for a sec, would you?"

I do. And, like most pictures imagined, it is pretty, it is wonderful, but it is disposable too, and it is bleak around the edges, because the edges know the truth: that I will never go to Texas, that I'll never even try.

"You don't understand," I tell her.

"What's not to understand?"

"*This* is it, for me. This—here—this is my, sort of, peak."

"Dude," she says. "People don't come here to peak. They come here to study themselves stupid, like *robots*. People come to the Midwest to remember why they have to *leave*."

Maybe that is true, and maybe my conceptions of adventure are all wrong, according to the generally accepted idea of the thing. But so far, I am feeling so different here, so new. I see no reason at all why I should ever leave. I don't believe in destiny, not really, but I know deeply that there is nowhere else to go but further in. Leaving here would be something like suicide, only worse. Because there'd be nothing left to do, and I'd be there to witness it.

By now there is an expectant and growing group of other students around the Backpacking Club's table, and the attentions of my original proselytizer dissipate toward them. She has other minds to reach. She says, "Anyway, you'll have a really great time here."

"Thanks," I say, and I believe her because it is easy.

"So, do you want to go to Texas?"

"Yes," I say.

"So, will you?"

"No," I say, and I turn to go, and she has already focused in on a pair of pretty undergraduates with pink and blue hair, and I am forgotten. I take one of the pins from the table, and I stick it through my jacket, so that for the rest of the day I wear a little red circle on my chest, upon which is written "AIN'T LIFE GRAND?" and I hope that it is, or that sometime soon, it might be.

With my new pin, I step back into the crowd that moves along the Diag, and then the walkway opens up to the wide middle of campus, a stone-paved octagon with sides each the size of a small building, and a gold-plated M right in the middle, which, I notice, everybody takes extra care not to walk atop. Sneakers dance around it in careful patterns.

I arrive at the University epicenter. The undergraduate and graduate library stand, imposing. The latter is brick and columned. It had been built in echo of antiquity. The undergraduate library by contrast has been built for the future. It is all glass, high-tech community workspaces, automatic coffee makers, and hyper-focused young people, who are visible through the building's mammoth glass front. And between the two libraries, masses of students travel. They appear perfectly comfortable with the present, and I wonder if they really are. I hop off the pavement again, and my sneakers sink into grass and mud. Here, students have strung up hammocks between trees, and they lay with tangled legs, tangled fingers. And this is collegiate love, I think; it isn't mawkish. It won't translate into grown-up love. Here in its silly present, they believe that it might. And that seems enough for the kids in the hammocks.

There are vacant grass patches, and I sit in one. For once, I am under no impression that people are looking at me offishly, that they are dissecting my body, which is horribly inflated compared to the factory-produced types around me. I do not fret that these people might think I am a grotesque imitation of themselves. Nobody looks. It is so clear, suddenly, how little anybody cares.

And this must be evidence of the pristine execution of Millie's drugs. I know I'm high because I feel like how I did before—before the elephant came around. I have disassociated from myself, and thus disassociated from all of the terrible things about me, the things that make me so insecure and nervous. It's confidence, I suppose, boiled down: this is, I realize, how somebody like Stella operates year-round.

I watch the bodies that move along the Diag.

A pair of white sneakers flashes. They glint, as if they're brand new. Long legs, the type of legs that still carry the memory of high school track and field in careless muscles. And at the hip is a hand, and the hand flicks now against another.

Stella walks along in her white sneakers, and she is vacillating. I watch her hand. It is undecided.

Stella is taller than me, and the boy even taller than her. There is nothing particularly beautiful about him. He is widely built, a wideness that has been halfway transformed into muscle, not slim enough to resemble so many of the boys around here, the ones that have both minimal body fat and maximum muscle mass. His hair is dark, eyes lighter.

And his smile is hers, only bigger, and more gratuitous. It is the kind that occasionally appears uninvited. And it isn't curved so much as slanted; completely imperfect, and it throws off the balance of his otherwise symmetrical face. It is lovely for the same reason hers is: both would be nightmares if on other people.

He smiles now because she's settled on a movement. Her pinky has looped around his.

Then they are gone, walking off toward the south end of college town, where the Greeks make life happen, surrounded by the Huron trees.

* * *

ALL AROUND ME, STUDENTS SIT IN groups or couples or all alone. Broken conversation, and laughter—an infinite deal of it. And music floats around too, pop music. Wherever you sit on the Diag you see the flag raised against the monochrome clouds. It whistles cyclically, like the conversations. We listen to it, gaze up.

And then the pop music crashes back, loud again, from all corners. And the protests return—college environmentalists seize another corner of the campus, and they toss fliers all around, so that it looks like weather.

* * *

EVENTUALLY THE DRUGS WANE. I FEEL them as they go, very precisely, like a hangnail. When the drugs go, they leave behind a rotting ellipses. And they hark up cruel thoughts about how much I do not deserve to be in such a world, with such people in it.

See this is me alone, this is me when the drugs start to go. I can go nowhere, nowhere, nowhere at all, without my neuroses becoming small gods of everything.

I adopt false composure, and move away from my grass patch, walk back toward Greek Row. I repeat Leah's tour, from that very first day, to myself: there's Scholarly Lounge, there's the best pizza in town, there's the upperclassmen apartment building.

There's Sigma Rho, where we have mixers.

I want to be so mixed up in it—to be mixed up in all of it. I stand before Sigma Rho. Silence and an empty front lawn.

It is dead or dying, I think. It is death or dead or dying. Because what's happened? Where are all of the beautiful boys and their beautiful girls, and where is all of the music?

But people are somewhere, and I can feel them.

I creep further, and notice that a blue tarp extends from the house's edges to the carefully curated trees surrounding it; something to block off vast space from creeping people.

Voices now, telling other voices to be quiet. And voices telling other voices to shutthefuckupcunt, and quietpledge, and almostdone.

A rip within the tarp. With one eye I can peak into a back lot. A fast, glowing flash in the early-evening dark, coming from the end of a cigarette. It whips down with the heavy force of human intention, onto the bare shoulder of boy. His skin is seared now, smoking slightly—

Laughter.

Shutthefuckuppledge, youaskedforthis.

I'm mixed up in it, like I want so desperately—but I have to get away now.

* * *

Run run run. The living room is only a living room—but at least I know that it is real.

Every few years, this stuff flashes across national headlines. There was that scandal in Pennsylvania, and the many crises down south, all of which flash aggressively across the public conscious, before they expire softly. There is a communal amnesia which follows fraternity hazing deaths, and injuries, and scandals. This type of thing, it's so textbook. It's so textbook that it's almost funny—but not funny enough to have a laugh about, and not yet. Because I want to ask Stella about the extent of it all. How much burning there is, and how much other madness in the dark. And what I really want to ask, what I really need to know most of all—do the girls do it too?

Does she?

Stella is not in the house. I am alone with my anxieties rising. I am passing the rest of this Sunday night by taking more of Millie's pills and hoping for positive effects. Because new drugs in the evening—it's better, certainly, than no new drugs at all.

I compound the old drugs with new drugs, and I am feeling a bit mad, but it keeps the darkness away.

My Sunday passes.

And I am relieved when Stella comes through the front door on Monday morning. She's wearing the boy's black sweatshirt, and I suspect that she might've slept in it, since now it smells like her: toothpaste, and a not unpleasant touch of plastic, the type of sharp plastic that molds pharmaceutical caps. She nods in my direction then goes upstairs. When she comes back down into the living room, she's changed out of the boy's sweatshirt.

"Should we go for a walk, then?" she says.

* * *

AFTER ONLY A COUPLE OF PACES into the Huron trees, Stella reveals that this walk serves a very particular purpose.

"I'm on a therapeutic assignment," she says.

"What is it?"

"I've been told that I need to reaffirm my personal connections. My nonromantic ones."

We laugh, since this is absurd to us both. I always laugh for longer than her, because I consciously elongate these moments, to the very last possible count. I have a lot of catching up to do, you see.

When I do stop, I say, "So? What's the plan? Who will you reaffirm first?"

"Well," she says. "I think you'll do. And I need to tell you about something terrible that goes on around here."

She says this as if it's an inside joke, but I get the sense that she doesn't actually find it very funny.

"What terrible thing?" I ask.

"There's a story," she says. "It involves a cast, and a setting, and the whole deal. There's an arc."

"Okay. Go on?"

"It's about the Kappa Alpha president, sort of. Partially. Uh, but not really. That—*she*—was never really the problem."

I say nothing.

"No. Kathy Van Tassel was never, *really*, the problem. But it does start with her, in a way. So, I'll start there."

I've heard murmurs of a hierarchy, of a President Elect with a nasty cocaine addiction.

"It was last spring," Stella continues. "It was last spring, in Detroit."

Σ

DATE PARTY: IT LIT UP ANXIETIES that normally simmered elsewhere, which sent them journeying for new and unusual drug concoctions, which wrought new and unusual psychological responses. Because relationships would be shattered; virginities stolen; drugs collected beforehand as if for transborder trade, and protected militantly in the same way, nervous outbreaks of hyper-exercise mounted in the weeks leading up to it. There was a pulsing, manic energy about last Spring. All exacerbated by the distinct fact of this particular Date Party, which was that it was an Overnight.

Kappa Alpha had booked the hotel sixteen weeks in advance.

Freshman year. Winter semester, April. It's called winter semester in Michigan even though a lot of it occurs in the months that any other American might consider Springtime.

Michigan doesn't know Springtime, at least not much of it. Some people say that Spring comes in April or May, no matter what. But to that, Michigan is the exception. There are never any flowers to begin with, and even if there had been once, they would've been false ones, and they would only bring winter, more winter, second February. Here, it's a quarantine of clouds overhead for ages and ages, and they've forgotten what the sky looks like in any other outfit.

Michigan has got the fall semester and the winter one. And this date party was in the latter—Stella had recently gotten through all the hazing, memorized the songs, and vowed to uphold the chapter's social responsibility. And this was to be her reward: the first Date Party as an official member. It was also President Kathy Van Tassel's first as supreme leader. Kathy Van Tassel sought some sort of divine kingmanship; a seat just a cut under the throne of The Lord himself.

On the evening before the Date Party, which would be held at The Dark Room Night Club in Detroit, everybody was busy. They compacted their drugs into small baggies, mainly cocaine, and other uppers like MD, which was starting to become as much a matter of course as the coke. And they tested out suitable hiding places for the drugs, in various pieces of small undergarments, and were pleased with the results.

Stella sat smoking. The weed had firstly been communal, everybody smoking together, till most left the room, and only two remained. The weed calmed Stella's nerves about that sudden twoness. She finished rolling the next joint, lit it, handed it over, he grabbed it, smoked deep and long enough that it was burning violently on the pass back.

"We have a date party tomorrow," she said, lowered the music, which he had chosen, some tuneless remix.

"I heard," he said.

She waited, knowing that he knew. Of course, this was to be expected, having spent plenty of time as this twosome in his room lately, kissing, sometimes naked, usually her more naked, and him less so, but that was okay, because she was happy, then, with how she looked without clothes on.

"You wanna go?" she asked.

Weed had so little effect on their psyches at this point that they treated it as just a hobby, something to do when there wasn't much else, like television. Now he treated it as a way to stall, to think. Date parties were both dangerous and excellent. Excellent because they were normally the most efficient means to sex, especially with a girl that had been holding out. Dangerous because they were also efficient means to getting holed up into something that girls considered *serious*. Ah well. He'd seize his shot.

"Yeah," he said. "What time?"

PENNY

By this point in her monologue, Stella and I have reached the depths of the Huron Valley. We are at Washtenaw Lake, which is really more a creek or a pond. It's only September, but the lake has already become lethargic, and sorry, and frosted over in its shallow corners. Stella and I settle on two human-sized rocks, where sorority girls go to get high or hook up, Stella says.

Once seated, Stella twists her mouth up and looks at the water. She says, "You ever wanna just freeze over in that thing? Just for a few days?"

And I do.

I really do.

Σ

KATHY VAN TASSEL DANCES WITH HER boyfriend. Tim is the president of the top fraternity, and therefore, to Kathy, their relationship is a thing of fated divinity, holy. Even as their dancing becomes gyrating, and then sex-without-fluids, they remain devoted not to each other but to Him.

Man has no good thing under the sun but to drink and be joyful—from Revelations? Which is where Kathy Van Tassel read it last night, or it might've been the night before.

Whatever.

Soon enough, all of those good things under the sun start to feel sort of dull, anyway, sort of weeknight bluesy. Tim fingers her against the wall, in perfect view of everybody else, as if it's just another fraternity party which, they suppose, it sort of is. Kathy Van Tassel feels the eyes of her sisters, and she feels the eyes of God, so she says, "Fuck off, Tim," shoves his hand away. Tim is unmoved by her sudden display of cognizance.

"What the fuck of it?"

"Nothing, the fuck?"

"You're trashed."

"Your treachery will come back to haunt you."

He looks on, into the crowd, and then he wanders off.

She looks around at her disciples. There is the dance floor, an advanced one, unlike the pathetic wreckages of fraternity basements. Around it are booths with high backs, housing couples that are already too wrecked to dance, or have not yet had an upper. Stella whatever-the-fuck-her-last-name-is and her date have been near her the whole time, hidden slightly away by a booth. Kathy looks at them like they are creeps, because he—for one—is.

The Church has been bastardized for years, but the newest pledge class is notoriously the worst. Everyone knows someone who knows someone who has had a half-sketched night there—but most of those someones remember nothing but rumor and fever dream.

Who could really know? Who would *want* to?

Kathy Van Tassel watches Stella, who watches her. Stella's date is alternating between attempts to shout toward her above the music, and efforts to slime his hand along her neck and left ear.

Disgusting heathen kids, Kathy Van Tassel thinks, and her face looks down on all of them, with pungent horror.

She goes in another direction, toward the bar on the other side of the dance floor, which is packed six deep.

These are her young icons. One of them throws a shot of tequila down her esophagus direct, and retches it out just as quickly, along with some other stomach contents. She is a freshman—Millie, the one rumored to have psychoses dense enough to fill an advanced physics textbook. Millie has also come escorted by a member of The Church.

They will all learn soon enough, though their educations will be unpleasant.

Kathy Van Tassel considers a reprimand, but takes a sip of her drink instead. It is a continual struggle to occupy the province of the divine and yet, to walk amongst the people on land. She has not got it all figured out yet.

Stella has watched Kathy Van Tassel recede toward the bar beyond the dance floor, and past Kathy Van Tassel, she sees that Millie has begun already to decide unwisely for herself, as Millie lurches her mouth toward the mouth of a boy who is not her date, though who also belongs to The Church.

Stella leaps at the opportunity to have a laugh, tries to make the scene more amusing than it really is, so that she might distract her date from his pontificating, which has now been fixated on the idea that they might fuck off this shitty party, I mean, the drinks are overpriced anyway, so they may as well just go back to their room in the hotel across the street, which will be—he seems to have come to this realization suddenly and serendipitously—empty, since everybody's here in the club.

"Uh—look at Mil, she's off the walls already. She's been drinking since, you know, four, or something," Stella says. This is an exaggeration, Millie has only been drinking since six, which is when Stella started too.

"She's fucking off Crawford for some late recruit," he says. He doesn't find this funny, not at all. He finds this injurious, as if a blow to his fraternity as a whole.

"Slut," he says.

Stella has been with Millie on nights when they both kiss not just one, not two, but maybe three different boys, either from different fraternities or the same, in two or three different corners of the bar or the basement. And Stella has enjoyed these particular nights, because they leave her in a hangover that features a sort of victory song, something that sounds like power, or like ownership. But her date has strong opinions about what makes a slut so slutty, what makes a slut a whore, how a girl goes from a girl to a slut to a whore. He frequently expresses these opinions, and Stella wonders whether he knows that she, too, was once just a girl, and is now a slut, like the ones he despises.

"Yeah," says Stella. "It's humiliating."

He nods, his hand is back on her ear, he's got this unspoken thing for ears. It feels nice, if repetitive. Stella continues, "I mean, it's like she fucking hates herself."

Millie has now vanished from their sight, probably in search of new prey.

He nods. Yeah. It's almost exactly like that.

* * *

KATHY VAN TASSEL HAS COCAINE TO do, which leads her toward the bathroom.

In order to get there, she's got to move further away from the dance floor and the main bar, through quieter areas, where the richest of the rich boys will order bottle service for a select few. There's a pool hall just past, and there are couples nearly fucking behind the fake bourgeois velvet armchairs. Here, she sees Tim's tie on the ground, and it's recognizable because he's the only one dickish enough to own a vintage Phi Chi embossed item, let alone a *necktie,* but it was an inheritance from his father.

Then she sees Tim's foot, jutted out from the seat of a booth, and it is spinning and twitching, and then after a couple more strides she sees his hand buried in that *slut cunt manic depressive sociopath* Millie's thong.

And of course, what happens next has all been told a thousand different ways, through a thousand different conversations, to any number of people, but the core of the event has always remained the same, no matter who is relaying the rumor.

God has gone deaf to Kathy Van Tassel. This is massive inconvenience, *dude, now of all times?* Millie's face is garbled into fake pleasure—since there is no way in fuck she gets off in that position, and Tim is no good with his hands—but Kathy Van Tassel has been so forgiving of that, of his shortcomings, because *isn't that the whole point, according to Him?* To forgive?

Not tonight. Considering He's apparently out of the office at the moment, anyway. Kathy Van Tassel seizes two glasses which have been gulped free of their vodka/soda/lime proportions, and launches one against the wall above Millie and Tim's conjoined heads (which have now been made aware of their bad luck). There is the blow of the glass against hard surface, and the echoing shards as they arc toward the ground, and all of the glass is rippling, then it settles, and the treacherous take stock of the situation, and find that they are okay. Tim stands, and as he is striding off, he says something which she does not hear, it's something about how she is *so fucking crazy*, and how *much there is wrong with her*, and also about *all of the professional help that she needs.*

Tell me something I don't know, cunt.

Then Kathy has the second emptied glass in her throwing arm, and she aims it at Tim, but he has flighted too far. No matter, he was not the original target. The original target was the freshman girl who is still sitting dumbly on the ground, as if shocked that Kathy Van Tassel's (now ex-) boyfriend has abandoned her in the line of fire.

Kathy Van Tassel lifts the second glass above her head, but that is where God resides too (somewhere up there), and so rather than ruining the idiot girl by smearing her with glass, Kathy Van Tassel merely flings the glass, again, against the wall just behind Millie, where the bits and pieces fly, and one of them grazes Millie on the skin above her eyebrow (that Jesus bitch freak is going to pay for my cosmetic surgery if I get a scar, she says later, to an enraptured audience of sorority members). Kathy Van Tassel leaves Millie quite unclothed amongst the shards.

By this point, Stella has convinced her date to stick around for a few more drinks. Come on, she's said. The party is really okay, I mean the music is sort of shit but isn't this the kind of thing that you, uh, listen to all the time anyway?

"Not *this* shit," he says. "This is just pop dancing shit. I listen to house music—do you even listen when I show you?"

She's tried, but it's dull, lyricless, bridgeless, chorusless, no instruments are involved, but there are a helllllll of a lot of *dope* bass drops, which she has pretended to listen to intently.

"Anyway," Stella says, "it's not awful, the music, we may as well drink a little and dance," and at last he concedes, as if ten-thirty is really such a criminal hour to still be involved at the party.

Having got him to linger, Stella realizes that this involves her drinking more, too, although she doesn't need much now. She almost asks him for just a diet coke, but he is already returning with two vodka/soda/limes (double).

These, and then two more drinks after them, mollify him for a while. But soon enough his hand is back on her ear, and his mouth whispers into it too, cringey epithets, *you are so fucking hot,* and *let's just get out of here.*

Over where the club is darker and quieter, Millie has nursed herself back to vigor after that crazy-ass President bitch Kathy

THE GILDED BUTTERFLY EFFECT

Van Tassel tried to slaughter her. She'll be having a word with the Kappa Alpha Executive Board tomorrow morning, as soon as she figures out who the fuck is on the Kappa Alpha Executive Board, and how the fuck to call them. Now, Millie contemplates. She knows she has to go after *somebody*, and, if she's honest, the President bitch is a whole new level of crazy. There's fighting power in her that only God can give. Not worth it, not tonight.

Instead, she chooses to go after Tim, who should not have abandoned her when she was, firstly, undressed, and secondly, undressed on his account, and thirdly, getting assaulted with liquor-lined glassware. She has never been one for gentlemanly doting, the idea of courtship and sweetness has never persuaded her, nor does she expect much from men generally.

But she has to draw the line somewhere.

She picks up his ugly-ass tie—Jesus, get your head out of your asshole, Tim—and scans the crowd, which has now dissipated, as couples have abandoned their public feigning and retired to their private activities, back in the hotel. Yet still she spots Tim haranguing leftover girls, girls whose dates have found other girls to play with in the hotel rooms. He is asking these loner girls, why not let him buy a round, c'mon girls, tequila on me, why the fuck not, it's still a *party*—

Like fuck it is, dickhead. She appears, dangles the tie before him, begins a tirade, the leftover girls withdraw, the bartender brings the round of tequila shots that Tim has just ordered. Millie grabs two and tosses them in Tim's eyes. Grabs a third, drinks it.

This carries on, Tim is not escaping now—*how fucking dare you almost fuck me then leave me, your ex-girl is a psychopath huh? Huh? A maniac and she nearly fucking killed me, Tim—*

And this will carry on, on, on.

Millie is Stella's hotel mate for the evening. Kappa Alpha booked two couples per room, two beds. Millie and Stella's mutual acceptance of each other, along with the brotherly bond between their dates, made their roommating tonight an easy move.

Millie would realize the following morning that she'd never even gone back to the room that had been allocated to her and Stella, and their plus ones. After tossing the tequila at Tim, who had subsequently cut his losses, and crafted a prolific apology, and declared that Millie should've been his original date, not that *psychopath* Kathy Van Tassel, Millie had decided that that was enough, and gone back to Tim's hotel room to forgive.

And almost immediately after she'd struck Millie with the glass, Kathy Van Tassel had marched up to the concierge and purchased a single room on the Kappa Alpha Executive tab, resolving never to sleep another night with Tim, a heretic.

So now many of them are pocketed back away into the hotel, and The Dark Room Night Club is empty.

Wait—two linger.

Stella has drunk too much. Just as he has almost convinced her to leave—Jesus Stella, the party is over, did you *really, honestly,* bring me here just to stay in this shitty club all night?—she feels her gut abandoning her, and calls out to him to wait one second, she's got to run to the bathroom.

Where she bends over the toilet bowl, sticks two fingers down her throat, come on, come on, come on.

She's had plenty of practice with this—sometimes due to too much booze, and sometimes because, she'll admit, she just finds it so horrible to look at herself in the mirror. But there's hardly any difference in the process. It's about how it makes you *feel*.

For some unknown anatomical reason her stomach won't budge tonight. She sets a cheek on the toilet bowl. Her thoughts are her own, but they come across in hysterical antics. Her date's behavior has grown increasingly erratic this past hour. His hand has not left her ear for ages. She feels it there still, it itches, but she can't scratch it away. He has become so remote that not even banal things that they could normally count on for a laugh, such as watching their mutuals destroy themselves and one another, heralds his interest. He feels not here anymore.

This is what her mother has warned her of, about the dangers of too much fun. She has advised Stella from early on, Watch The Personality. It'll get you into deep trouble, that Personality of yours. It'll get you into trouble with the boys: the recklessness, and the driving around after midnight, and the parking God Knows Where and for how long. And cut out the *jokes,* Stella, people don't know how to react when young women like you turn their words back around to them in laughter. They don't know whether you're laughing at them or with them, and if they're men, they will hate you for either. You think that good men, Men With Futures, want to listen to your talking back while you're driving them around in circles? So cut the Personality. It's too *much,* and it doesn't fit into a house or a home. Her mother speaks to her in a voice that's been written for ages and ages; and all this time ignored. The voice only stops when Stella's nails scrape against the very back of her throat.

She has now failed to throw up three times, and it is time to give up. The effort of trying, as well as the gloomy night, throughout which it has been obvious that he would like to be anywhere else but here, and preferably back in the hotel room, has triggered tears. She looks into the mirror now, wipes her eyes, and pastes some more lipstick on. She stops to think that right now, she is perhaps a high four, on the fraternal spectrum of beauty, out of ten.

She leaves the women's room and sees him near the club exit. She is surprised that he has waited, and this gives her hope that he has come around to a better mood. It is entirely empty but for them.

"Jesus Christ," he says. "What were you doing in there?"

She doesn't say anything but takes off her high heels. The hotel is just across the street, and being barefoot doesn't bother her.

"I mean, I almost left you," he says.

There are no cars on the road, so they cross.

STELLA

Up to that point, Penny had listened to my story with uncompromised attention. I'd told it thus far like a comedy—the drama of the Springtime.

But of course, that's a bit of a lie, isn't it, because that year was perennial winter, and that's all it ever is in Michigan; and the Midwest seemed like a dream to me before, in my earliest months here. That year Springtime never really came, never turned; winter lingered, still does.

She was familiar with the breaking of illusions, certainly. She was a depressive, for God's sake. She dealt in them.

"So, here's the end of the story," I said to Penny.

"There's more?"

"Don't be so naïve. Up until now, it's just been a regular night out."

I ventured on to the bits of it that I'd only told in choppy confessions—to Julie. Now I told it to Penny, and I told it to the end.

Listen:

It was all such a nice time, my first semester of college. It was happiness so pure, and refined, and high-pitched that it was doomed from its very first flight.

Then the Spring came. Or the mockery of it. Something happened when he came, something happened to the order of things, including my headspace.

I'll tell it to you simple and clear.

I'd wanted that Spring so badly to be of the starry-eyed variety. I'd wanted so badly to have something beautiful to talk about with my mother. Boys, and boyfriends, and lovers, and moonlight, and how to catch it, and all of that. Ah, mothers love it. Daughters too. And they love to talk about it together.

My mother had few prerogatives but one of them was perfectly clear, and it was that I find a handsome man who might work downtown in Los Angeles or Chicago or New York City. He'd have a finance internship with Silverman lined up for that summer, he was going to be a senior intern, not even an associate one, and he was a quarter way through his degree in business, and then he would leave his Chicago suburb for the central city, where he would build a life that made sense out of hard work, and money, and fraternal relations across the country, in case he wanted a weekend in New York.

And I was only a hopskipandajump away from ringing my mother with the happy news.

But it happened the other way.

So a quick secret then: I was a virgin before.

Technically, that is. I happen to be a pundit of the camp that believes virginity is all in the mind. It's all in the shoulders, really; how you carry them. If you project your virginity to the world, the world will respond accordingly. I decided to be a reputational slut at age fifteen, and the world responded likewise. But I still had the hymen element of it. I was still a virgin technically.

Somewhere in a dark Detroit hotel, where nobody goes unless they're nineteen and stupid, and nearly dead already, my virginity wanders the halls. And it wonders why it happened like that.

I was drunkenly and fitfully asleep. Sleeping beside him was never restful. He always felt half-awake, like he was waiting for me to make myself available to him in multiple ways; whether as an empty brain against which his empty thoughts could ricochet, or as a body with a few holes to play with, or as hair to tug, or as a set of top-house letters to wave around The Church.

I was asleep and then I wasn't.

We'd had tortured, parochial conversations about it, of course. They'd always begin in the same way: he'd adopt a type of therapeutic concern for me, for my virginity, as if its presence marked some disability.

Here was really the trouble: I thought I might've loved him. I thought I might love him, though all the time I knew he was a person strangely untouchable, inaccessible, a person planned and crafted every morning, and with prerogatives that nobody was in on, he listened to music that was hardly music at all, was a famous womanizer. And yet there were moments that year where we'd be in the dark, and it suited us, together we deserved it—neither of us particularly content or particularly comfortable, and it made a certain sense—when the darkness was so terrible and heavy, and we lay together under it. And then there were the times he'd look over at me and tell me I was beautiful, and he said it like the truth.

I thought I might love him, really, because he seemed to want me, seemed to find me desirable and maybe even lovely—like all of the sisters that I envy so badly. That was enough for me.

And yet I'd wanted to be completely sure before relinquishing my virginity, which I thought of as a sort of endgame, an I've-made-my-choice-and-it's-you type symbol.

But he did it for me.

I woke up to the feeling of intrusion, hardly any real pain, but something entirely worse, I think, than actual blood loss or tearing: the departure of something that had once been mine, and mine only, and somebody else removing it.

I said something like,

what are you doing?

And he said exactly this: "I'm your date, aren't I?"

I lay on my side, and him too, behind me. First, I shuffled forward, and the feeling of intrusion was relinquished; and so I thought it was a cruel misunderstanding, and I felt where my entire dress had hitched up around where my tits hid, soft and uninterested. I maneuvered the dress back down to its proper place, wondered where my Calvins were, wondered if we'd messed around before we'd fallen asleep, if he'd taken them off. Because I knew that I hadn't removed them myself.

Here I at last understood that this was no misunderstanding. And the feeling came back; here now pain too. He said something about, oh shit, I forgot you were a virgin. This had little effect on his next decision. It seemed only to heighten the deliverance of his project.

Somewhere in there I shuffled forward again, and again it ended briefly; and then I was at risk of dropping off the bed, and I thought I'd rather fling myself off of it anyway, and drop the short way downward, than let this continue to happen as it was.

No matter. He gripped me around the waist. I was not going to fall.

It continued.

At some points in there, I *did* protest.

But I'm not going to lie and say that I became righteous.

Because, Penny, you know he'll make you feel disposable, a replicated version of every other girl he's ever fucked—and they were all beautiful—if you really fight, he'll ask what the fuck he came here for then, and then he'll say or insinuate that you're a whore and a prude, both at once, and then there's the stories that he could spin to The Church, the things he could whisper about your body—about how your body looks naked—if you don't let him have his way with it, and he could threaten to flick the lights on and leave you there with everything that's happened, leave you naked with your shitty new reality, and he'd watch you then in the lightness and the brightness, and he'd see you as used, and dirty, and done, and not even good in bed.

You should've thought about this before, he said.

You think you can't black out deliberately. I thought that once, too. Well, I did right then—I blacked out deliberately (it had been creeping along my headspace all night, anyway, the blackout, just waiting, maybe, for me to beg for it).

And when I came to again, he was finished and asleep. A new feeling came to me now: warmth.

Blood.

* * *

HE WOKE UP SOMETIME IN THE extreme early morning, through which I'd remained awake, afraid that he might wake up, and go for another. I was ready for the next time, I would not let it happen again (although, of course, The First Time, the coveted one, was gone forever and always). Regardless I'd lain straight as a board, with my feet flexed, as he slept. My feet were ready to kick.

He didn't do anything when he woke up. He didn't do or say anything at all, apart from when he looked over at me. And when he did, he looked at me like I had a mess of decayed matter where my soul should be. And it was like that matter was putrid; like he never wanted to touch it again.

Somebody looks at you like that—looks into you like that—and there just isn't much else to do except believe him completely.

* * *

I looked at Penny, who had grown increasingly more still, and whose face—you can't make this up, she was a tub of unprocessed emotional refuse—was now fuzzy with pieces of her red sweater, which she'd rubbed across her face in order to conceal the tears.

And I said to Penny, "Listen. I didn't tell you all of that to get your sympathy—I don't need it. I only wanted to try it out, talking to a friend. And now you have sweater on your face."

What I really meant, when I'd said that, was: thank you for listening, and thank you for—you know. Giving A Fuck.

And I think she got the gist.

"What was his name?" she asked after a while of silence.

"It doesn't matter," I said.

I'd left his name out in my storytelling that day—I find it easier to tell it like that, as if the boy doesn't exist anymore. Even when I tell it to myself, I'll call the boy something different, something neutral and unpainful like Joyce, or Kurt.

It helps.

My propensity to erase Trip Swindle's real name from the story must have been one reason why Jack had come along easily, and why I'd slipped, and broken promises that I had made to myself since Detroit, such as: no boyfriends, crushes, kisses, hang-outs, cigarette breaks, walks around the block, study sessions, hey-do-you-know-this-songs, come-over-after-classes, near-sex, considering-sex, next-time-could-be-sex, check-to-see-if-you-brought-a-condom-just-in-case-sex, kisses anywhere including cheeks. With Jack I was suddenly unfrightened of each of those crimes.

I'd long suspected that I didn't have much life left, but plenty of music; and Jack seemed perfectly all right with that, with our sitting around, listening to it, and talking intermittently, and it wasn't casual, not quite, and it wasn't serious, not yet, but it was simple, and clean, and he *let—me—be*.

Unlike the other.

So, after all that, what of me?

It feels a bit like a broken funhouse. At the fall bazaar in your hometown churchyard, where you used to go at thirteen or whatever, to make out with senior boys and feel like you mattered, and it all felt like what you were meant to be doing, and the broken-down funhouse was there to walk through because it was halfway private; except for when you turn to the mirrors, and suddenly there's a thousand visions of yourself, but all you see is the stupid boy's hand on your waist, and then his hand in your jeans—but we're in public and the lights are on—and you see it all come back to you in fat splices, and skinny splices, and halfway-there splices of you, yourself. And you suspect that you're still there somewhere, like you remember; but you can't be sure.

It was a bit like that, afterward, like life in the carnival funhouse; like you can see yourself whenever you'd like; but it's a disgusting and perverted version, a distorted something-else that's been warped a bit by every new fuck-up, and she's come back to remind you of how you look, and how you look is wrong.

People hate these kinds of endings, rightly so. But I may as well end it, truthfully and completely:

I sat alone on the bus ride back to Detroit the following morning, still in my party dress. I'd had this splintered hangover when I woke up, it was a hangover mixed with loneliness that was so real and heavy I could've cooked it in fat and had it for breakfast, and it operated along with a low-grade panic, a panic that refused to acknowledge what exactly it was panicking about. I'd left the room without my toothbrush, without the expensive perfume that I'd brought and forgotten to wear, without the jeans that I'd packed for the bus ride home. And on the bus I was alone again. Somewhere on the highway was a different bus populated with Church boys, and that's where he must've been. Because Trip Swindle certainly wasn't here.

The plastic seat was cold. My dress was short, and I didn't have my underwear on.

I'd left that behind, too.

PENNY

It's amazing how sad Stella has been, and for so long. I'd have never guessed.

When she finishes recounting what happened to her last April, I don't say much for a while.

I'm not versed in this sort of thing. There have been few occasions, so far, which have required my exhibiting true compassion. I have a difficult time, for instance, using my brain to convince my hand to place itself on her shoulder, which is more bone than body, and then further, convincing my lips to open, and telling her in twisted clauses, and stutters, and breaths in the wrong places, that everything's going to be all right.

I manage it anyway.

* * *

Later, we sit on the living room floor, and we don't talk much, but it is not an unhappy silence. Stella eventually jokes about how—maybe—her psychiatrist isn't completely useless, and that this whole psychiatric journey might be worthwhile.

I have a billion questions that I want to ask her. I want to ask her what it felt like with the boy before; whether she had loved him; whether she had said it, *I love you,* and tangentially, what her thoughts were on the girl saying it first, *I love you*, was she into that kind of thing, or was she traditional? Had it really been love or had it been sort of, tricks and false starts? I want to ask whether she's spoken to him since, I want to ask whether she'd press charges, ever, whether she's gone to some higher-up authority. And I want to know what, really, it had felt like, in all of the places that one can hurt; the brain, the heart, and then the obvious places, you know. The bodily ones.

I get the idea, from her silence and the way that she does not look at me quite directly afterward, that conversation on this particular topic is over for the day. And she makes this clear, when she finally does look at me, and asks about my own romantic history.

I know she's doing this as courtesy. It's what we are taught by teachers, friends, parents, television, books, films: we are taught to talk, but not too much, and not exorbitantly. And we're taught that, if we do speak about ourselves at length, it's always common courtesy to ask the listener, next, all about themselves, and to let *them* speak exorbitantly, and to listen listen listen.

I assume that she is only being polite. Either way, there isn't anything to tell, and I tell her so. I hold my hands out in artificial surrender and shake my head. Nothing.

"Not interested?" she says. "I don't blame you."

She is picking at bits of the carpet and watching her fingers. She continues, "I mean look at the shit we have to choose from."

"Not really, Stella. I'm not uninterested."

There is a silence now, in which Stella remembers that I am not a Kappa Alpha, that all of the essences that make me *me* also happen to be undesirable, that my body has a tendency to rebel against its clothes, which have a tendency to get tighter every year, and that my face isn't dewy or symmetrical or interesting. Unlike the Kappa Alphas, who all seem to be projects of the universe's tendency toward beauty and equilibrium, I have been anti-blessed in the aesthetic department.

"I mean, look at me," I say.

And she does; and she remembers.

STELLA

"I have a new friend," I told Julie.

Julie: How wonderful!

Me: Yeah, all right it's not the first moon landing.

Julie: Stella, you should be very proud of all of your achievements, both great and small.

What is her name?

Me: Penny.

Julie wrote this down in her legal pad.

Julie: And why do you value Penny's friendship?

I'd thought about this recently. There was a certain protective element to it, what with Leah—Penny's supposed old best friend—having abandoned her early on. But there was more to it, I suppose.

Me: Because she's nothing like anybody else in my house.

Julie: Would you elaborate?

Me: Sure.

I looked at Julie, and then at both the left and right walls.

Julie: Uh—I meant, would you elaborate *now*?

Me: Oh. Sure. What I mean is, Penny does this thing where she listens to you when you talk, but it's not pretending. It's listening, right. Sort of like what *you* do. Except she's unpaid.

Julie: Now just because I'm *paid* doesn't mean—

Me: Yeah, all right, I'm fooled. Anyway, she listens, and by her listening, you feel like whatever you're saying is worth talking about. Do you get me?

Julie nodded and wrote this down in her notebook as well (did she come back to my stories in the nighttime? Did my recollections and intimate psychoses make good imaginative fodder, like a paperback, and if so, would it be a thriller, or would it be a tragedy?)

Me: She's got bad luck though, Jules. She's got it rough in the head. Bad luck in the mind.

Julie: How do you mean, in terms of the mind?

Me: She's depressed as a motherfucker, Julie.

Julie: Uh, Stella—might I suggest that you might be *deflecting* or *projecting* your own probl—

Me: Okay, Julie. I've read Freud too. But Jesus, Julie. She thinks she's so worthless. She wishes she were wallpaper.

Julie: And you believe otherwise because you value her friendship?

Me: Sure. Not that I'd ever tell her so.

PENNY

THERE ARE PARENTS COMING THIS WEEKEND. They supposedly always come around this time. Stella has decided to invite her mother, although she says that she isn't sure why.

If I had to make a guess, it has something to do with the boy. The new boy, that is. Not the one from her story. I want to ask more about him as we sit in the living room one evening. While we sit, girls come and go. Stella tells me their stories, their crushes, their problems, their preferred drugs. She talks about them as if they're different from us—as if it's us two together, and them somewhere different, and that makes me feel lovely, as if I am slowly morphing into somebody just like Stella. As she talks, I play around with my drug stash, move the pills here and there on the couch, into different piles and rows, based on color, and size, and effect. I restocked earlier today, visited Millie and grabbed a new handful. I no longer really care about asking for anything specific, and I find that my experimentation leads to all sorts of random energy bursts, and moments of joy and clarity. Even moments in which I feel I might be a genius. Now, I grab two pills and pop them.

"Toss me one," Stella requests, and I do. Like me, she is unconcerned with the specific effect of the thing, so long as it has one.

THE GILDED BUTTERFLY EFFECT

Stella has also lately acquired a high dosage of Vyvaid from her licensed professional. She got the drug, she says, after weeks of artifice. You should hear this woman, she says. She still—*still*, Penny—believes in the advanced prolonged benefits of *talk therapy*. Gimme a break.

She has the Vyvaid nonetheless; traditionally used on children that suffer from concentration deficit, but Stella had gone through the depths of the Psychiatry stacks in the Graduate Library, and unearthed trials which suggested that the drug addressed forms of depression that realized themselves in lethargy, and irritability, and lack of motivation, and general despair. She'd gone to Julie full of lethargy, and lacking motivation, and general despair. She tells me that this drug is her holy grail. It destroys my appetite, she says. I feel like I'm running off air. It's amazing.

She swallows a pill with black coffee, which is the only thing she's been interested in consuming lately, besides alcohol, and other drugs.

None of which seems delinquent to me, or even problematic. Because of the way that she talks about it: like it is the only thing to do, and like it really helps.

So why not?

After we swallow, I change the subject. "Are you going to introduce your mom to your boyfriend when she comes to visit this weekend?"

She shakes her head.

"*Boyfriend*. God, Penny. It's the modern *day*. The modern *fucking* day."

I smile, shrug.

She continues, "I mean—who has that kind of time?"

Σ

THE THING ABOUT MOTIONS IS THAT parents love to go through them.

When Mini Harrison's plane landed in Detroit, she took two Prozac, and some deep breaths, and then thought about something that Crin at the Westchester Country Club had told her a few days ago, after Mini had told the ladies that she was off to Michigan for Parents Weekend.

"The problem with Stella," Mini had said, "is that she hates me. And you know what? She can be a real bitch."

"It may seem like she hates you," Crin had said, "but sometimes kids act like that when it's an expression of love, you know? It's, like, the Oedipus Complex."

Crin had a way of talking about things as if she knew them, which made her easy to believe.

"You don't know Stella," Mini said. "She tricks people. She's been *seeing* someone at school. You know—someone certified in . . . the *mental infirmities*. Which I thought would help. But now she's on a whole therapeutic plan. She says it might turn out to be a *five-year plan*. She says to send payments to her account for these appointments, always to send her payments. She says it might take a very long time to right herself. What good can come of all that?"

"A few pills? God, Mini. Everybody's on them. All the kids. Not just kids! It helps, don't you see?" Crin said.

"Sure. It helps with *what?*" asked Mini, who purchased her Prozac and whatever else happened to be in vogue at the time from Crin. Mini's extreme and probing self-consciousness whispered to her often, and told her that any real doctor would only think she was a wasted, middle-age failure. And anyway, Crin always seemed to have extra, and Crin didn't require an appointment.

Crin thought about this, realized she needed to draw an important conclusion.

"For," said Crin triumphantly, "the modern condition."

"Yes," said Mini. She nodded toward every other nodding head in the circle, each of which nodded back, and this went on for some seconds before their necks threatened to unhinge.

"Of course," Mini said. "The modern—state. Well. Like you said. The condition."

More nods toward her now, this support felt good, this was comradery, and these women understood her better than anyone, better certainly than her conniving ex who'd committed perfidy and bummed to Europe. And these women were, plainly, better company than her daughter, who spoke in tortuous colloquialisms designed to frustrate her mother, and who was so beautiful and yet so full of guile, of counterfeit, of ploy and laughter, false laughter, laughter at *her*. I mean, she was just a *freak*, sometimes, the girl was, what with how severe and morose she was occasionally, and hysterical and happy otherwise. These behaviors had started last April and morphed her daughter all through the following summer, which had forced Mini into paying for her psychiatrist.

Who, Mini thought, should've fixed her daughter by now. It had been long enough. Stella should be righted—herself again.

"Yes," Mini said again, over the ballooning murmurs of the hats around her. She spoke into her rosé and watched the last ice cube start to go in the heat.

"The modern condition. Of course."

"How else to deal with it?"

* * *

REGGIE SWINDLE WAS HARDLY HANDSOME, BUT money has a way with bad looks, makes them better. He had women in constant rotation, conveyer belt style, in all of the corners of the American Midwest, throughout which he travelled as a Senior Associate at a company whose crowning achievement was a high-power vacuum, debuted at the turn of the century. He had nothing to do with the vacuums nor any of the other household products; for the past twenty years he had headed its financial investments division. And all day long he thought about stocks, and bonds, and depressions, and booms, and how to go about speaking of it all in such a way as to keep women interested.

Reggie Swindle sipped his second drink at the Delta Terminal Bar in Detroit Metropolitan Airport. His dinner plans with his son slid around his brain and clinked into his ice cubes.

He was sitting next to Karen, who had just revealed to him over her own drink (on him) that she dreaded Parents Weekend, and that she'd be on the first flight home after the Saturday tailgate this year. Her daughter, she'd said, was a Kappa Alpha, just like Karen had been once.

Karen had nasty premonitions about this weekend, considering the events of the year prior, which had included her own blackout as well as her daughter's. Once her daughter had succumbed to the liquor, she had swung a determined but poorly aimed fist at Karen, amidst a remarkable slew of pejoratives and warnings to never, ever return to Michigan.

Before all went dark for both parent and child.

Reggie and Karen were getting along fine at the bar.

"You seem nervous," Reggie said.

"I am," Karen sighed. It was a magnificent sigh, mouth wide, molars available for viewing, a gesture that suggested they might stay a while here, please.

"Can I buy you another drink?" he asked, and before she said anything the gold card was on the bar and two fingers held up, so Karen stayed a while.

* * *

Trip sat in his Church bedroom.

He thought that if he stared long enough at the spot just above his desk, he might experience a sense of calm.

Football Saturday was a weekly pandemonium even without the addition of Reggie's arrival. It was the outlying middle ground of the Greek social calendar, the one day of the week during which caste was degraded, and the bottom tier sluts came to The Church to tailgate, whereas on a regular night they'd never be allowed even a piss in The Church backyard. And the top tier girls acted even stranger and more coked out, and you never knew what kind of trouble you'd get into, with all of them gathered here at once. You get the two top houses together in such close proximity like this (Kappa

Alpha, top as always, and Beta, who'd recently clawed their way up), and funny things can happen.

Trip remembered the catfights of past Saturdays, girls in clothes that were hugely spirited and as teeny as he could dream, rolling around and spitting at one another, and he remembered the girls sneaking around, stealing drugs from pockets and purses, sniffing, snorting, crying, whining, calling to him: where have you *been*, Trip, and why haven't I *seen* you, Trip. And even worse were the remnant girls he'd been with in the past, who looked at him with artistry both deadened and practiced, which made him feel altogether cold and wrong.

They shouldn't come around here if they were going to make him feel like that.

But never mind. Reggie was a sobering force.

He'd be arriving soon from the airport, in a rental car too luxurious for a two nights' stay in a college town, and he'd be in that gray suit, his casual Friday suit. Because they had reservations—an hour away, now—for The Chop House. Trip had booked these, back at the end of August, almost right when he'd got back to school for the fall, since already (he'd heard) Parents Weekend dinner reservations were booked up.

After last year's Ruth Chris dinner failure—when Reggie called his son to say that, unfortunately, he'd been to the Ruth Chris in Minneapolis only just a few days ago on business, sorry son, I'll pass tonight, but you can go on, and grab something on my card—Trip had felt he should seize their table at The Chop House, early and secure.

Since Chop House was a small business, local to Ann Arbor, and Dad couldn't have possibly patronized one recently.

* * *

THE GILDED BUTTERFLY EFFECT

LATELY, PENNY HAD EXPERIENCED SOMETHING OF a status elevation. Apparently, consorts with Stella, and dealings with Millie, made her a commodity.

Leah suddenly wanted to be a part of the crew.

Penny's old friend had even offered up her own bedroom floor, in case Penny wanted to abandon her mess in the living room. It seemed like a good idea now, Leah had said, for the two girls to do some catching up.

They had been so close back in high school, after all.

Nobody was much bothered by these recent developments, although Leah quietly registered the abrupt manner in which Stella addressed her. Leah suspected this might have something to do with Stella's lack of affinity. Stella, who had once been the domineering alpha dog of the Kappa Alpha Church Groupies, back when she had pseudo-dated one of them (tough luck, bitch), had broken off her ties this year. Leah had done the opposite, and remained deeply hooked on their fraternal religion, and even suspected that she might've fallen in love, or in like—at the very least—with a member of The Church.

Whilst Stella, it had been whispered, had a new affiliation—with a SigRho pledge.

With that going on, and Stella's mother coming for the weekend, Penny had little else to do but feign fascination with Leah's garrulous chit-chat.

Leah's parents were not coming; after last year they had quietly decided that perhaps visitation should occur infrequently.

Early on Football Saturday morning, before the mother-were due to meet their Kappa Alphas at the house prior to their walk to fraternity tailgates, Penny wished Stella good luck with her mother. And Leah gave a disinterested wave, before she and Penny stepped into the masked and struggling sunlight of Ann Arbor, to get breakfast in town.

Stella watched them go from the Kappa Alpha balcony, where she'd also watched Penny come in on her very first day—she remembered it exactly. And then she sat, and waited, and lit a cigarette, and she didn't stop lighting them till her mother's hired car came along down the road and parked before the house—so that her mother was perfectly clear on Stella's active and determined destruction, from her insides out.

* * *

THIS YEAR, REGGIE SWINDLE HAD NOT bothered to call. Trip accepted this quietly when ten o' clock arrived with no word, and The Chop House was closing up anyway, with its last reservations at nine. Trip went to bed without brushing his teeth, or changing his clothes, or taking off his socks, or having a sip of water, since none of it could've mattered less.

* * *

NO ONE KNEW ANYTHING, EXCEPT FOR the fact that Michigan on a Football Saturday was as close to heaven as anyone knew.

On Friday afternoon the liquor stores went dry. The local dealers were also tapped out, and anybody that wanted something would've had to get it midweek, unless you had some kind of special connection. Coke was reserved for the Greeks, who were willing to pay for it; the God Damn Independents were barterers, they begged for extra coke on Saturdays, begged, and cried and pleaded, in pathetic shows of reverence.

The consumption was science more than art. Weed too early would knock you out, you'd miss it all. Coke flew anytime, except for right before sleep, or else you'd be hyperactive till July. And the ideal equilibrium between beer and liquor was a craft inaccessible to those unedified. It took countless errors before mastery; one shot too many, one half of a Key Stone Light too much, and—just like that—you're undressed on some elevated surface, singing the Christmas song that ended four minutes ago, asking everybody around you whether they'd heard that crazy fucking drop, and if not, could the DJ please replay it from the beginning?

There weren't any DJ's, not really. Rather, it often seemed that the songs you most desired came on just in time to remind you that they still existed.

And the music was so critical to everything.

A thought to turn anyone dancing: these days were the best days of their lives. That's right—the best days *ever*.

The only trouble was that no one could seem to remember them afterward.

* * *

STELLA, MINI, KAREN, AND MILLIE WALKED to The Church. Millie was fueled by Cheerios and orange Svedka, and Stella by coffee and orange Svedka. Mixed.

Stella was not one of those girls who was enlightened about the beer and liquor balance. It had never seemed worth her while to learn—blackouts weren't so bad, once they were over.

She had struggled with Millie against their visit to The Church. But it was inevitable, she knew. The Church hosted the best tailgate, and even Sigma Rho was invited, though the two houses were rivals—which meant that, even though the Swindles would be there, so too would be the Jacks.

Which also meant that by the time they'd rounded The Church Street corner, Stella's vodka/coffee mix, which she'd brought in a disguised plastic cup to keep her going throughout the day, was empty.

Her mother was dressed in an outfit built for attracting sex and male attention. It was strappy, and short, and bright gold (sequined), and navy blue.

But worse than the outfit was the silly grin attached to the bottom half of Mini's face. It was the sort of grin that only stuck around because the rest of the body, and the face, did not know how to respond to outside stimuli.

As the group neared The Church, Stella lagged behind and her mother dropped back too. For the first time that morning, Stella looked over at her mother squarely and wished she had not.

Mini's skinniness was beginning to look like frailty. She was impossibly fit, impossibly small, and not even just for a middle-aged mother—she was tiny even for a girl; could compete with the loveliest of them. Stella thought about this often, especially when she looked in her bedroom mirror. Genetics had done an evil thing to Stella. How could it be that she had inherited her mother's affinity for booze, her capacity to choose men badly, but not her mother's boniness, the absolute lack of space required by her body? There had been unjust genetic mutations somewhere during Stella's conception. These had warped into additional muscle, which had guided Stella into semi-stardom in high school track. But who the fuck cared about past high school athletics when they meant that her mother's birdiness, the way that she looked she might presently drop dead, or else disappear into flight, were altogether inaccessible?

Stella was better, she had tried so hard to be better this year—with a better boy, a better friend.

And yet her mother had all the blessings.

And now Mini took Stella's silence as conversational invitation. Mini thought she might ask about the one thing that, she knew, all young and beautiful college women were interested in.

"So, Stella," she said. "Who is your boyfriend at the moment?"

Stella sped onward toward The Church. Mini quickened after her.

Stella said, "You know, mom. I have other things going on. I have a new friend, who I really like. And I have a perfect grade in English 270."

Stella had rehearsed this in her bathroom mirror the previous night, in accord with Julie's prescriptive, behavioral guidelines for the day. These included: give your mother the benefit of the doubt; open up the conversation to things that *you* care about; practice what you might say, in case things begin to go south.

"Okay—who is your new friend? Is she a Kappa Alpha?"

"She's—a GDI, I guess. She's not Greek."

Mini pasted another inappropriate grin across her face, slowed down her walk.

Stella took this to be genuine interest, and slowed down her walk, too.

Mini felt that she had stopped living upon her own college graduation. She'd studied something that she had not cared about, nor, it seemed, did any potential employers. Her own sorority sisters had similar disillusionments, and similar ways of dealing with them. Those sisters were the only ones, really, that understood—them and the ladies at the Country Club, who'd all been sisters at different schools once, too.

There was a hereditary, selective, arcane, elite, powerful, beautiful, genetically favorable, almost-imperceptible, fun-loving essence about sorority women that you could not find in other crevices of the working, professional, nine-to-five, grotesque world in either city or suburb.

Which is why Mini was flummoxed at this development in her daughter's life. She tried to exercise a tone of sympathy and care—under previous advice from Crin—when she said, "Why would you do such a thing, Stella?"

Which Stella should've expected, but the booze had dulled her inherent suspicions, and she'd forgotten that her mother was like a bit of plastic, with no original thoughts or feelings.

"Fuck's sake," she said.

What else was there?

When she looked again at her mother there was something else there, and it was vicious: Mini was looking back at Stella as if curious about her original reason for birthing her in the first place.

So Stella said, "I guess there's a boy, too."

The gruesome look slipped off of Mini's face and was replaced with one of optimism. Mini gripped Stella's shoulder and said,

"Tell me more."

* * *

REGGIE SWINDLE ARRIVED AT THE CHURCH just before the sororities were due to show. He gave Trip a handshake, pumped twice.

"Apologies for last night. You got yourself some dinner?"

Trip nodded. He'd had Cheerios.

The boys fiddled around with the music, songs stopped, and started, and stopped again. At this early hour, nobody was drunk enough yet to know how to handle it: the sons wanted to dance, but not under the gaze of their parents, and the parents wanted to want to dance, but could not remember how to begin.

Reggie went to the bar and brought back two Key Stones in each hand.

"Listen, son," he said, and brought his head closer to Trip's.

Trip readied himself to forgive his father for forgetting about their dinner reservations last night; it was always easier to forgive.

Reggie said, "Do not be a lightweight today. That would embarrass me."

And he handed Trip two of the beers, one of which Trip cracked, took a sip. Nodded.

"Remember," continued Reggie. "I'm an alum of this chapter. My reputation here matters."

He smiled at a passerby.

Trip felt a touch of gratitude that his father was not drunk yet, that he'd not yet turned hellish, that he'd thought to keep his voice down through the course of these admonishments.

"I remember," Trip said.

* * *

THE MORNING HAD DRAWN TOWARD TEN o'clock, which meant the party was well into itself. Tailgates were held outside in The Churchyard, in order to accommodate the huge influx of bodies. The mass crowds meant that patrons were crammed into spaces so tight that one might find it inhumane under different circumstances, and immobility meant that everybody itched to get elsewhere, higher. Students sought high places, jumped onto them, and then leapt off, just to see if they'd make it down. They danced on top of the bar, on top of the roof, on top of each other. Cigarettes passed freely, drugs passed quietly.

Millie and Stella were not prepared to waste away the greatest day of the week by following their dated mothers around like schoolchildren. It was lucky that Karen and Mini got along stunningly, immediate likenesses, it's the old school Kappa Alpha quality, Mini had shrieked too loudly. At that, Karen had got a glazed doughnut look about her, as if she could've been anywhere at all, and it would hardly make a difference.

Millie and Stella slithered away, grabbed two bottles of liquor off the bar, some Church pledge called out that they had to take a cup, not the whole thing, those are for *sharing*, and each girl threw up a middle finger.

And although they were technically together, both began to silently and separately approach the tedious process of getting so drunk that they could not remember who they were.

It took only a smidgeon of the bottle before Stella was atop a surface, with little idea how or when she'd made that climb, but there was nothing unfavorable about this position, she realized. Up here she could never be caught unprepared, since she had eyes on everybody.

And it was for everybody that she looked.

Trip Swindle and his buddies were trying to snort something over near the DJ booth. There were no parents in their immediate vicinity. Stella had tried to ask Trip, once, about his parents, and the strain of the air between them afterward was so tangible that Stella never brought it up again, nor anything that might've been conceivably connected to a life outside The Church.

Kathy Van Tassel, maniac preacher, crept toward the circle of Trips, and tried to look both sexy and furtive. She had some stealing to do—at a moment when the boys were collectively and loudly in love with themselves, which resulted in some strange dance that involved bouncing off one another, shoving and hardening each other's frail egos, Kathy Van Tassel slipped a pointer finger across the bar, where a baggie waited to be emptied of its coke.

Her cross, which today was gold and diamond-encrusted, laughed in the sun as Kathy Van Tassel made off.

Stella felt a splash of beer on her ankle, a failed shotgun between an unfamiliar dad and son, and the sticky feeling of warm Coors in her maize socks. She was just about to turn around and have a word, when she saw that Penny had made it here too. She was entering the lot just behind Leah, who must wield some type of high school nostalgia-induced power. That was the only way that Penny could've been convinced to join such an event.

Leah was also under the false pretense that a certain Church member, Jimmy Crawford, was en route to announce his boyfriendship to her. Leah, who spoke rarely to Millie, was unaware that Jimmy Crawford spent half of every week asleep in Millie's dealership chamber.

This information would remain hidden. Leah broke into the circle of Church boys to hook an arm around Jimmy Crawford's neck, which forced the boys around him into stifled laughter and raillery toward their friend, who was *pussy whipped, what a fuckin' laugh, who would've thought that Crawford would be out here kissing his girl, is that your girl, Crawford, sure it is, look at em go.*

Stella had no patience for the guileless girls that trusted The Church, who wanted to be Church girls forever, who came to college and immediately turned religious, and would remain as such till the boys' artifice wore off, and then just like that it's a decade after graduation, and nobody knows where the boys have gone, but they're certainly not with you. No, Stella was keener on Penny's movements, it was time to get her out of that mess, out of *this* mess. They could go home, have a coffee and sober up, and Stella could go to Jack's later on, assuming he too was done with the tailgate early, and assuming he too had abandoned his parents.

But Penny was just as much drawn into The Church pack as Leah was.

She'd followed Leah into the encroach of boys, who continued to drink, smoke, laugh, and some of whom had now abandoned their teasing to speak charmingly to Leah, and to Penny by proxy.

Something entirely unrelated to alcohol began to warp in Stella's body, made her sick.

She leapt off the surface, and swerved into the crowd, and knocked some kids over, shouted false apologies behind her, buzzed toward the corner where she'd seen Penny and the boys, but her momentum was interrupted by Karen and Mini in her path, passing a full bottle of liquor between them. They remained upright with considerable concentration.

And Stella decided that Penny would be all right—just for now, just for the hour—as she turned off in the other direction.

Then Jack was there before her so suddenly, had seen her leap off the surface, he said. He gripped her by the elbows, which she held tightly around her body, the only sort of embrace that the limited space allowed.

"Stella!" he said. "Aren't your parents here?"

"No," she said. "I don't have parents. Why do you ask?"

She gestured to a nearby pledge to toss her a beer from the box that he carried around like a weapon, and he did, and Stella opened it with her tooth.

"What the hell?"

"What, the beer?"

"No, the parents."

"What about 'em?"

"You've talked about your mom—look, never mind. It's all right. Mine are right over there. Do you want to come meet—say hello?"

He pointed. They were tall, and pale, and they smiled around themselves, as if not witness to near-sex, near-overdose, and theft of all sorts of things, from hearts to horse tranquilizer. They were perfectly fine, *it* was perfectly fine, because after all it's a family affair.

They were the types of parents that told you that they understood, and that you could call them if you wanted to. The types of parents that wore sunscreen on family vacation, made sure that you did too.

"Jack, let's—you know, we can get out of here."

"*Why?* Are you okay? They wanted to—is it wrong, that I've mentioned you?"

Questions of rightness and wrongness were beyond her, on account of the liquor. She knew two things, only: she needed a bump, and she could not meet Jack's parents.

She'd never met parents that were Parents, parents that were like those in films, the ones who vouched for you, and who stood by your side, no matter how intensely you proved yourself deserving of standing alone. How to speak to them, what to say?

And what if it went off without a problem?

What of her and Jack then? Would it be Saturday brunch with the 'rents, and babysitting for free, and phone calls on Sunday evenings, and road trips to Kentucky?

As she thought about it in half of a half of a moment, it struck her as being a wonderful condition—Jack, parents, brunch—

Next she felt the need to vomit.

"Uh—I'd—you know. I just don't know any parents," she said. "*Many* parents, I meant. Many. So. . . later. Let's do later. I'll come by. Uh, brunch?"

She swiveled around and walked away, left him quite alone, just as his parents had come up on both of his shoulders, curious about the pretty girl, and why the rapid escape.

Where to, Jack?

Difficult to tell; the crowd had done its camouflage, and Stella was gone.

She had reeled off to the corner of the lot, where she'd first seen Penny consorting with the pack of fraternal men, and where the cement was lined with bushes. Here she placed her hands on her knees, bent at an angle, waited for the coffee and the orange liquor to flow out of her.

But it didn't come. Just wasn't its time, yet.

Millie wandered up, and Stella straightened, turned to her drug dealer, and said, "Where are our mothers?"

"Long gone," said Millie, sucked at a fresh cigarette.

No matter. Favorable news, in fact, to be rid of the dead weight.

"What do we do?" Stella asked, held out her hand for a cigarette, to which Millie complied, grabbed one from a pocket.

Millie said, "What else is there? I'll die if I drink more."

"Well, I could use a beer, do you want me to get you one?" Stella said.

"Yeah, why not."

Stella walked behind a bar that had been abandoned, its position unfit for the direction of the crowd, which preferred to prance and gather at the dead center of the lot. She grabbed two cans from behind it, tossed one to Millie, and joined her again.

Stella said, "I guess we could go watch the football."

There was a silence. And then an eruption of laughter. Stella sat down on a bit of loose gravel, didn't care anymore that she was wearing light yellow pants. They drank.

"I'm nervous," Millie said.

Stella's Saturday had turned to talk therapy on The Church ground. This alarmed her; it was not a traditional element of her and Millie's relationship, which revolved almost exclusively around the temperamental and expensive business of achieving an ideal high, something that wasn't prescribed but fought for, earned.

When Stella responded with nothing, Millie said, "Can't I tell you why?"

"If you need to."

Millie drank, lit a new cigarette, didn't offer another to Stella. Stella said, "What is it then? Tell me, for God's sake, so I can help you."

"Jimmy Crawford is in The Church," Millie said, and passed over her new cigarette.

Stella took it, meant to kill it, and Millie said, "He saw me. He didn't even say hello. We hooked up *last night*."

"Did you say hello to him?"

Millie let her mouth fall to hell. "Are you fucking crazy?"

Millie just didn't get it, Stella knew. And if she didn't get it now, she never would. Because Millie was under the misimpression that now that he'd seen her naked, there was talking still left to do, and that he'd want to go conversational, want to get to know her, and to know the dark bits too.

Now that he had seen her naked, Millie felt that he might want to speak and walk with her in the daylight. And that was Millie's worst idiocy.

"Who the fuck cares about some idiot in The Church? Who really cares, Millie?"

"Yeah? Who the fuck cares about some *Church* idiot? *You* avoid Trip Swindle like a fucking—do you ignore him, or does he ignore you? *You* care about boys in The Church, Stella."

Stella stopped smoking. There was a decent song on, which she hummed along to, pretending to be consumed by it.

"Stella, I *said,* you avoid Trip Sw—"

Stella leaned her face close to Millie's, almost as if to kiss her. Millie recoiled, "What the fuck?"

"How about you give a shit where your drunk mother is? How about you stop chatting bullshit, and worry about what's important?"

"I *do* give a sh—"

"Clearly not. I'm going to find Mini."

Stella rose and returned to the nearby bar. One more beer would trump the new edge of Millie's attack. What was it about this place that turned girls toward hysterics? *What was the draw?* She'd felt it too, back then. She'd groped blindly through its appeal, had reveled at The Church, had craved the elitism of being sought after by its occupants.

Millie came up behind her at the bar, and nudged Stella as she grabbed a new beer from the tumbling pile.

"You're looking for your mom," Millie said. "And I found her."

She wore a stupid, teasing smile, which told Stella that her mother had been found someplace wrong.

"There," Millie pointed. She pointed *up*, up toward where the kids all danced high on stages, where Stella had been— where Stella had *just* been, it seemed. How long, how long? Stella's brain went to beehives when Millie pointed up there.

Her mother's hair had come undone from its neat ponytail and swung all around her head as she danced like a popstar or a maniac, or perhaps most accurately, like a nineteen-year-old girl: all hips.

"No."

Mini's hands were in the air and her foot banged out of time with the music. And her *company*. Mini had somehow wrangled every single parent from this erratic crowd, every single parent that was a washed-up, middle-aged, faded-but-trying, addicted-but-recovering, parent-but-child, would-be-frat star, would-be-sorority-bitch, pig-bellied-exec, failed-self-help-novelist, trust-fund-depleted imitation of a human, and together they stood in misplaced pride, in what might only be considered a *squad* of squashed dreams.

And they had an audience.

Divorcees swapped booze and tongue; they wrestled in kissing so involved that it made their progeny seem abstinent. A man in a morbid gray suit danced beside Mini—oh Christ, danced *on* Mini—till Karen grabbed Mini to pull her around, swap places.

Still they raged. A plastic bag of brilliant pink wine started a circulation, and Mini took a long pull once it reached her, but shoved it from her lips without locking the spout; wine spilled all across the front of her lacey t-shirt, seeped rapidly through its negligent material. She looked down at the mess, and then pulled the shirt up and over her head, and threw it wildly to the ground, revealing a skeletal stomach, and a MICHIGAN patterned maize and blue bra.

All without sacrificing the beat of the song in the percussion of her frail hips.

They watched one another.

Stella was drawn forward, toward the stage. She did not know what she would do, or to whom. She could not bear this, it had finally become too much.

Stella shoved a path, and made it to the edge of the surface where Mini's sneakers were planted, sneakers that were too young for her, and expensive, and white. Stella reached out to grab a foot, any diversion tactic would do.

With one arm outstretched, Stella gazed through the storm of spotted, hairy, lumpy, anorexic legs planted on the surface, but stopped when her gaze was matched from the other side.

Trip Swindle watched her so briefly that it might've been the booze, and then he returned to stare up through the legs, and toward the mess of arms that reached for clouds, clouds, clouds, and she saw that his hand had reached out too, out toward a dress shoe that was connected to an idiot in a poorly fitting suit. But Trip Swindle retracted his reach abruptly and looked back across at Stella—and a half grin slipped across his face.

But then he turned, Jimmy Crawford had appeared at his shoulder, and together they looked up at the pack of parents, and then joined in a stupid, boyish handshake.

Stella took a deep drink from her beer and went off, having never made contact with her mother at all.

As she left the lot, she saw Millie sitting in the gravel, crying now, she was no better than all those other pathetic bitches that came here looking for the greatest time of their lives. She turned back and saw Mini dancing on a new man, somehow the surface had opened up to spawn more identical parents. *How many were there, just like them?*

Stella looked around at the hundreds of kids swarming, and realized: there were plenty, plenty. And they'd be replaced at a constant rate, even after they were all six-feet-under.

Aggressive solitude came to Stella. It rang and laughed. This happened to her, these colossal moments of nothing, in the gloating middle of what should've been an excellent and opportune party, when she'd be suddenly, aggressively alone. And nobody told you about that bit of it, when you accepted your bid to Kappa Alpha.

Somebody could help, she thought, if she could find him. Where had Jack Ellis gone?

Where had *all* of Sigma Rho gone?

This party had died ages ago, that was her tragic mistake, that she'd trusted a dead party to remain ever-fun. He was at Sigma Rho, had to be, unless he was in some other sorority house, in some other bitch's bed—no, well, maybe. There was no *law*, but surely there was some type of mutual agreement, what with all the extracurricular time they'd spent, all of the talking and the music. But who could say, around here? *Who could possibly predict?*

Stella walked quickly, and made good pace back down South University, until she stopped on the sidewalk near 7/11, where she leaned forward into some bushes, and vomited a lovely projectile, before she continued on her way.

She approached Sigma Rho. If they had had a tailgate at all, it was an unsuccessful one. There was no evidence around of a good time. The dead fraternity matched Stella in feeling. This crash was unlike any other she'd thus far felt from day-drinking, it was so *difficult,* so uninteresting and doldrum, to walk down this road and to home, after such a failed day.

But this misery, she spun it out of nothing, there was no proof or promise that it had to end like this, the day didn't have to be over, it wasn't even *noon,* Football Saturday didn't end till at least kick-off, and that must be ages away.

She went up to Sigma Rho.

That day so many people had reminded her why human beings were such shit company, why you couldn't count on them for any type of reassurance. Mothers, they were the original good company, the very first that are supposed to be versed and learned in all of those classic maneuvers that had to do with support, and togetherness, and not feeling like you're lonely. And Mini failed today, unsurprisingly. And what about the boys? They too were constantly failing at it, at human reassurance. When was the last time she had been able to put her head on somebody's shoulder, and allowed them to make her feel deeply okay?

Trip Swindle hadn't even come close.

But with Jack it was closer, the closest. And he should be here now.

A girl was passed out on the lawn just outside the Sigma Rho front door; Stella wondered if she was dead, left her there. You really can't help them all. And some of them were so intent on ruining themselves to capacity.

She knocked on the great front door and hoped that someone she knew would answer, but no one came, so she went around to the back lot. The plastic tarp that hid the backyard and empty land had been strung up, but this, she thought, was just meant to keep the police out. She moved it aside at one corner and bent her head under.

But she shouldn't have. She should've just gone home, shouldn't have sought a cleaner conclusion. She should've known when the day was wrecked and given up on it.

She'd walked into something wrong. Nico was the Sigma Rho Pledge Master this semester, and he stood, now, in the center of a circle of freshmen, all of them shirtless.

"Thirty pushups," he shouted, and they flattened to the ground. Nico paced, and put his foot on their backs, pounded them to the ground, where they waited quietly.

"Back up again," he shouted, and they did.

When they stood, she saw that they all had one fifth of cheap vodka taped to each hand.

"Now," Nico shouted, "no one's done here until both those fifths are finished," and the pledges started to drink, and then they started to retch.

Stella found Jack. He quietly tried to down one of his fifths. The brother next to him vomited some onto the asphalt, and some onto another half-naked body.

She thought that her tendency to forget the unique situations of other members of the world was a disease, a deficiency. Of course he was still just a pledge, *of course* he had to be hazed, and yet she had rarely asked. Did she not care?

Did she, like her mother, have not a single maternal, compassionate, empathic limb, not even etched into the top bit of her runty toe?

She dropped the tarp and headed back for home, alone again.

There seemed little point, now, in parents and in boys, because at the end of it all she was always alone again.

Football Saturday ended a few hours later, and the game started. The stands were half-empty, it was a nothing game, some school from the West come to be defeated, and everyone was in bed, too hungover or too busy thinking of the person beside them, or vomiting into toilets, or still getting hazed, or sitting at their desks making crafty concoctions of their remaining drugs, like Stella chose to do.

Some unlucky ones had been purged by the Ann Arbor police, and their parents were on the way to pay the bail, but drinking underage was only a misdemeanor in Michigan, the incidents could be wiped clean, a blank slate for Sunday.

Somewhere toward the south side of Ann Arbor, a touchdown was scored. And then another, and the game was won, but none of them were there to watch it. They'd hear about it tomorrow, and pretend to care, but would be distracted by the lingering hangover from yesterday, and the sad silence of the coming week, and how miserable and doldrum everything would be until the next time came back again.

* * *

MINI AWOKE WITH A SLITHERING HANGOVER in an empty child's bedroom. No—a teenager's bedroom. Wait—a teenage *girl's* bedroom. A photo of a mountain range, with mangled descriptions of some past Total Solar Eclipse, had been blown up, and taped to the wall. It was a lopsided job.

Judgement day? *Judgement Day?*
Was this the Afterlife?

Not bad, she thought.

The floof of the bed overwhelmed her, but not unpleasantly. The owner of the bed had gathered every feathered, pom-pommed, velveteen piece of cushion, pillow, and blanket that must have been available within the town's limits. And for a reason that Mini could not now recall, she had fallen asleep here, amongst the floof. Fallen so deeply asleep that she had traipsed into death.

Something indiscernible had happened between the booze and this hangover, it had involved faceless strangers. This must be the end, she figured. The tailgate had been her Way Out.

It was comfortable here.

It was comfortable and quiet, and it all made her feel like a lovely sorority girl once again, lean, and bright, and desirable. She felt that unquantifiable essence of older childhood, or new adulthood; where fluff matters, and so too does the appearance of the posters on your wall.

So if this had been her deserved exit, all right, then.

No matter.

Worse things, certainly.

She slept on.

* * *

TRIP AWOKE IN COMPANY.

He was inundated with his final recall of the tailgate before he'd pitched to nothing. There had been his father, up there, his father so ugly and boorish, but somehow still kingly, surrounded by older women that were beautiful and cadaverous. And there had been Stella across the way. Stella, wide-eyed, and nymphic, and dark-haired, and—he gave her this begrudgingly—still good-looking, well above the median around here.

But not worth it, not worth it, her dramas and her spectacles.

There had been some raillery in the corner, followed by cocaine, followed by some betting, and they'd bet with cocaine, so there was more cocaine. And then there was a bit of discomfort on account of the cocaine, so they'd done more betting to distract from it, but they only had cocaine to gamble, and so they did more, all around, more cocaine.

Trip could not gather what they'd bet on.

Until he peered over at his company.

Karen wasn't surprised to see Trip Swindle looking back at her. Nor was she remorseful; she could've done far worse.

Regardless of the tickling pride that laced her, now that a handsome—*young*—face had proved her still worthy of male attention, Karen felt no inclination to sit around and get to know each other.

Which was well and good for Trip, who gazed fondly upon Karen's wordless redressing, the grabbing of her sunglasses, and the hunting of a toppled bottle of prescription somethings, and then her exit. How marvelously and totally free of histrionics. How elegant and economical—not even a beg for a morning fumble, a premeditated kiss. This was sex and women; this was women of class and decorum, this swiftness, and totalitarianism of choice, and departure.

This was *older women*. He fell asleep as the door clicked shut behind her.

Once out in the hallway, Karen saw that all the bedrooms, and walls, and empty spaces inside The Church were plastered with their Greek letters, and arcane flags, mottled with insignias. Many years ago, she'd been known for her perfection of the swift fraternal exit in the very early hours of the morning. So, this was nineteen again, and how wonderful it was. They could not understand how wonderful it was.

Back then, she would steal from the fraternities, and bring items back to her own sorority house, show her prizes off like fascinating treasure. She'd come home with old composites, those professional photos of each pledge class. And her own pledge class would sit in a reverent circle around the photo, and circle with dark marker the faces that they'd fucked; and they'd vandalize the faces of the boys that had fucked them.

She'd had a boyfriend in a fraternity once, thought she'd marry him after graduation. Now, as she left The Church and turned down a quiet street, she tried to recall him. There had been no breakup. Not that she could remember, at least. He'd gone to New York, she believed; gone to the stocks, and she'd waited awhile. She'd waited awhile, till he was nothing again, and she was only mildly curious, now, as to whether he had ever existed at all.

* * *

REGGIE SWINDLE SHOWED NO SIGNS OF having ever been to the demolishing, collegiate party that had incapacitated everybody with hangover.

As he flew over Metro Detroit, he thought about his son.

About how his son had pixelated throughout the day, how Trip had started the morning as a handsome, complete, Middle-Western kid with a propensity to drink, and a firm handshake, and a desire to please his father, which had not made Reggie Swindle proud *per se* but which suggested that one day he might feel something akin to it.

But how his son had pixelated! From a man to a boy, surrounded by hoodlums that were too tall for themselves, in the corner taking drugs as if nobody could see, and neglecting his father, and the impressive time that his father was having up on the stage, surrounded by heartbreakingly good-looking women, women good-looking *in general,* not *for their age.* As Reggie had gyrated with the rest of them, he had watched his son. He had watched his son be unwatchful toward his father. And here was Reggie, *setting the example.* But what did Trip care, as bent as he was on petty drugs with short half-lives, and on strutting around in his pack of silly sophomores, as if the place was *his,* and not *passed down?*

Trip's attention to Reggie was in a deficit. It was as though Trip believed that he could've made it into the school's top fraternity house without the influence of his legacy father, who'd once served as President, and Rush Chair, and now, Alumni Board Member. Reggie had set the example. Without that, his son would be nobody. Worse—his son would be a GDI.

Which had elicited in Reggie such a white anger, an anger so crystal and sure, that he had shoved off the tall woman, Kelly, Karol, *whoever,* and swaggered home, back to the motel.

He had not said goodbye, and he would not call.

He would not be back next fall.

* * *

MINI WAS MARGINALLY DISAPPOINTED TO DISCOVER that she was, in fact, alive.

This fact revealed itself in the form of a girl, a girl of about Stella's age, but far less beautiful. The girl entered the bedroom, half of her body occupied by her smile.

"Hiya," she said.

When Mini only stared, the girl continued, "You must be a little confused. Let me explain: this is Delta Mu Phi. A sorority here at the University. Part of our philanthropy is to ensure the safety of members of the Greek community on high-risk nights—and days.

"We found you quite inebriated at *The Church,* where you agreed that it might be best for you to sleep it off here. In the comfort of kind women. We call ourselves the Wellness Fairies," the girl finished.

She sat on a stool and faced Mini.

Mini looked into what she believed could be the homely mask of a psychopath.

"Delta *Mu Phi?*" she said back to the girl.

"The one and only."

Heaven's sake, the bottom of the bottom tier. No wonder they got off on philanthropy, and no wonder their charity was such a dearth of pleasure and youth, no wonder this bedroom resembled the inside of a girl-baby's Heaven. Delta Mu Phi was the dead last of the lot. Mini now recalled her own Bid Day—decades ago—when a bid from Delta Mu Phi would trigger not only immediate tears and sobs from the recipient but college years thereafter which were marked by the worst type of ostracization, the very worst form, particularly to a young woman: the ostracization of being *ignored.*

The girl herself was worse than ugly. She was not ugly, nor beautiful. The girl was so typical, so benignly average, that she was doomed to reign over nothing and nobody, and to confine her opinions to her brain, and to seek any type of worthwhile romance either in post-grad, or amongst the God

Damn Independents who, at least, operated across a fairly even playing field of aggressively unarresting looks.

This all came to Mini the moment her gaze moved from the specimen in front of her to the poster on the wall. All Mini could say, through the new shame of being physically inside of Delta Mu Phi, was, "Okay. Good poster."

"Thanks," said the girl, as if she believed it earnestly. "I don't know what Eclipse it references. I liked the color scheme."

And that's it, Mini realized. The life of the condemned plays itself out in sickly rooms like this one, in which not even the bright life of sorority membership can save you.

If she did not break free, she too would be amongst them in their hellscape.

She assembled her escape route. She located her sneakers, they were set neatly at the door, and she momentarily wondered where her top had got to, but discounted its absence as a fluke. She did not knock the possibility of physically altercating with the girl, should the girl—or her condemned sisters—attempt to obstruct her way. She shifted herself in the bed and geared her feet to leap.

She leapt.

Out the bedroom door, down the front stairwell, out the front door, across the green lawn, onto the sidewalk.

Nobody followed. Nobody shouted, and nobody called the police.

It was like she hadn't left, or like she'd never come.

The ecstasy of freedom from the worst social stratification on campus showed itself through Mini's body, and she briefly felt young again, did a twisty dance right there on the sidewalk.

But then came the shakes. The shakes brought their friends, the illnesses of hangover.

And Mini Harrison crouched on the concrete, one sneaker still in hand, and vomited rainbows into the shrubbery.

STELLA

MY MOTHER HAD ASKED ME WHY I'd be friends with somebody like Penny, and I'd had no response.

But then I did my thinking about it, and what I came up with is simple: I liked her.

Recently, she had become more attractive, you know—humor, and earnestness, and wit have their way with bad looks, make them better. And we laughed a lot together. We laughed till phantoms went to bed, sometimes.

Which is why it might seem counterintuitive that I had avoided her since the tailgate. Listen: it wasn't Penny so much as it was *Leah*. Leah had an affinity for The Church that was—maybe still *is*—near to obsessive. She's deeply at risk of becoming a conglomerate of all of the things that the boys have said, and done, and told her about. You can see it in the precision of her movements, the way every single act is coordinated across the flimsy plane of male attention. It is best not to associate with someone who's forgotten who she was before—before all of the mixing with fraternities, before we all started to become images of other people, girls who live for boys. We're all at risk of it here, of forgetting who we were and who we'd wanted to be; and The Church is the worst catalyst to it, they sort of get inside you and re-wire, so that you crave a brother's arm-around-waist or come-for-a-drink or let-me-fuck-you-in-the-afternoon. I was like that, for a while. And I'd rather not catch it again.

I had almost forgotten to watch out for fraternity groupies, in those nice weeks with Jack and Penny. And I'd almost forgotten—or else suppressed (Julie would love a bit of textbook suppression, she would cling to it like an amphetamine) — how much I detested The Church, and its affiliates.

That charming and insipid half-grin on Trip's face at the Tailgate had reminded me of my principles. And I could not wholly trust my sisters, the ones that still fed into it—so long as there were girls to feed into The Church ego, it would breed, and grow, and thrive. That had all never been an issue, with Leah—because she didn't present much by way of friendship value, anyway.

But Penny, too, had gloried in it. She'd giggled like a real girl, even though I knew that her laugh was a stifled chortle, an ugly noise. Giggling like a woman in love is not in Penny's pot of tricks—yet when she'd been with the boys and Leah, there had been a light in her unfamiliar, a light that is only aroused by the attention of men who you believe are handsome, good, wealthy.

So—there was a bit of me that distrusted her, in a nagging way. A suspicion—small and deviant—which pestered me about the fact that I had confided in her. Confided my Springtime story, my most painful secret.

And there was a bit inside of me that worried that she might've not believed it.

But I reminded myself that Penny had almost cried, for God's sake; Penny had reached across my shoulders, told me that everything was all right—

That everything's okay, and everything will be all right.

In the few days after the tailgate, I'd attempted to expel my new suspicions of her, and I wanted now to reach her again as my friend, and to tell her about my mother's strange disappearance, and lack of contact since Saturday—something which was not a negative development, only remarkable.

All of which was why I'd decided, on Wednesday night, to catch her around.

I knew she would be at Slounge, because Leah had sniveled her way back in, and would drag Penny out to the bars tonight.

I even told Jack that I wanted him to meet my new friend.

I'd spent the past few nights with him, having returned to Sigma Rho late on Saturday night, and found him unkilled from the hazing that he did not know I had witnessed.

And I did not tell him.

On Wednesday night, I returned to Sigma Rho to wait outside for him, on my route to Slounge. He came outside, gave me a kiss. He had little aversion to doing that in public. He invited me inside, for a drink first, and I declined, said that I wanted to get out soon, wanted to see if my friend was all right, she didn't go out much, she barely even drank.

Which was true. But I couldn't go inside for another reason, which was that I'd spent the past few nights there and hadn't done anything more than get undressed to my underwear. And the same went for him.

And I knew how these things went, knew how they progressed steadily, and then revolted into decrepit nothingness once the progress stultified. I knew what he wanted, the same as what everybody wanted. Yet it had been so long—since last Spring.

And I believe that there is a trend nowadays. Once a boy has seen you with your clothes off, and done what he desires with that, he has very little interest in continuing to get to know you.

Often there is little conversation thereafter.

I liked talking to Jack, simply enough—about music, books (titles and summaries borrowed from Penny and supplemented with some of my own knowledge), his family, minor witticisms about their provincial Kentuckyness, and he had a good head for alcohol, in that he managed to match my state of intoxication and then he *let me be*.

But once he saw me with all my clothes off and did what he wanted with it, there'd be nothing left to talk about.

We walked to Slounge, held hands.

PENNY

In English class, Professor Peterson used to call these turning points. Now that I'm actually involved in my life as the lead character—someone who can leave, someone undiluted—rather than as an expendable side-friend, I seem to be experiencing them too—turning points.

When all of the parents came, it triggered something in Leah that reminded her how we were friends, once. And suddenly, to her, I am worthwhile again.

Meanwhile Stella has a new boyfriend, whether she admits it or not. She's spent the past few nights at his house, and I haven't seen her at all, since the parents came to school.

I'm sure that she has spent these nights with him. I don't know what they do together, but I do know that it's got to be more entertaining than sitting with me on the living room floor.

And that's okay. I've never been in love, but I've read plenty of books.

I get the idea.

This all means that Leah is interested in having me around, and that I have time to be around with her. The interesting thing about the lifting of depression is how much Day there turns out to be, when you're not spending lethargic hours—blurred, listless hours that feel so dead and wasted—with

THE GILDED BUTTERFLY EFFECT

heavy animals on your chest, and when you're not speaking to yourself in silly poetry about the deep dark sadness and how it births, grows, breeds, dies, and comes back again—it turns out there is loads of daytime within which to do other things.

I cannot bear to consider all of the hours of daylight, in summers and good weather, that I've passed up for heavy quarantines of my own creation.

Anyway, what matters is that the heaviness has receded. And I've been invited to attend a "bar night." Wednesdays, I've been told, are for the bars. Specifically, to hop them. I've got no fake ID; Leah assures me that I won't be asked, says that Kappa Alpha has special relations with all the bouncers at the bars on South University.

In Leah's bedroom, we have two fifths of vodka. I've not dabbled much in alcohol, because the newness of myself obtained from Millie's drugs had been so far sufficient. But this is what they do here; it would be an incomplete night out, Leah says, if I consume *nothing*.

She pours me a bit into a red cup, follows it with sugar-free and calorie-free lemonade.

I start to feel like I've never really realized what, exactly, it takes to be a girl—a real one, a worthy one.

Leah says cheers and welcomes me to the Real World. She says that I look great, that her shirt suits me, and that her mascara is working wonders; the first part, I know, is a lie. Her sheer golden top hangs on me all wrong, accentuates everything hanging, and flapping, and out of proportion. She says that this is what everybody will be wearing.

"And the music," Leah is saying, "is bang on. At Slounge, it's just bang on, Penny."

"What kind of music?"

"Popular," she says.

I like music that was popular a long time ago. I like music that not just escapes clean and free, but that also shoots you on its exit, and you say *thank you* anyway. Music that grins and then snickers. It gets to the punchline first and it makes all the girls laugh. It's all wonderful to me, before around the 1980s, when everybody and everything started to become new again. And it's just so exhausting, all of that trying, all of that newness, when things were so good before.

I told this to a boy in high school, once. I thought he had asked me the question—*so, what kind of music do you listen to?*—out of flirtation, so I'd told him the truth. Early rock, skiffle, I just really like *guitars*—

He told me that I was a snob, and that I only feigned it so that he and the other members of our class would think me unique, and that kids our age have to—to some degree—like, if not love, the music of our own time. He had said, "Why, Penny? *Why?* Why do you pretend to like that stuff?"

"I'm not pretending. It's just about how it makes me feel."

And he'd only shrugged—"Whatever with the metaphysical shit, Penny"—and dropped me off back home again.

"It's pop music mainly, pretty much," Leah is saying. "But, like, remixed. Because pop is for radio, and *this* is for the party more. Do you get me?"

I nod, take a sip of my concoction, wince as it flashes through my stomach.

"Yeah," I say. "My favorite."

* * *

ALL ALONG SOUTH UNIVERSITY, GIRLS WALK. They are more fawn than woman; they flop and trip down the road, as though walking on new legs. And as the girls grow flopsier, the boys grow in confidence, and their swaggers kickstart, their helping hands linger longer on female waists and smalls of backs, and it seems, for the boys at least, that the soundtrack of their tailgates plays louder now, and in their heads.

The Svedka and lemonade mixture has made me feel good. Things seem all well and good, everything around me sounds like laughter, and where-are-we-off-to-first.

Outside of Scholarly Lounge—Slounge—there is a line around the corner, but not for us.

Go right ahead, ladies.

Then there is an elevator ride to the underground. In the box, we're all squished and breathless. Everybody seems either drunk or pretending. Leah nudges me and sips from her drink, which she has disguised in an old Gatorade bottle. She's done the same for me, and as she sips I do too, because that's what feels right.

"This always works really quickly," she says. "This type of drink."

She spots her cohort when the elevator doors open to a dark, crowded bar with a packed dance floor to one side. I recognize Kappa Alphas, they are monopolizing the far corner of the bar, and Leah drags me to them, throws two fingers up into the air at nobody, but somebody somehow catches the signal, responds, and two shots are in our hands.

I look around for Stella, this is certainly where she'd be, and I want to ask her about where she's been, how things went when her mom came to visit. And I wonder whether I'll meet her boy, the one she has chosen.

I don't' see her anywhere, and then Leah is with me again, carrying two new shots, and there is a boy beside her. I feel like I know him somehow.

She waves at the air between me and the boy, and says, "Penny, this is Jimmy."

I remember him through *Millie*. Isn't this Millie's boyfriend, the one that I see so often in her bed, when I go upstairs to collect more pills?

"Hi, Jimmy," I say.

He doesn't recognize me, doesn't realize how many times we've met before. Doesn't even really look at me properly, and I feel suddenly so stupid and gargantuan in Leah's tight sheer top, all flecked in gold and glimmer. Nobody realizes how badly I'm trying to be beautiful like them.

Of course they don't.

* * *

LEAH IS THROWING UP IN THE Slounge bathroom. I've watched her down four shots of tequila without a problem, but the fifth hit back. She had grabbed me around the waist suddenly, said it was an emergency, and we cut all of the other girls in the bathroom line just before she hurled all of the tequila up. It splashed into the toilet, and some of it flew out again and landed in her hair.

She rests a cheek on the seat, I fill my now-empty Gatorade bottle with tap water, hand it to her. She has no interest. Instead, says, "Fuck, I'm worried, Penny."

"It's okay. I'll take you home."

"Not about *this*. I'm staying."

"I—okay. What are you worried about, then?"

"Jimmy's told me something terrible."

"He's not worth it," I say, which is a statement that I used to read in novels from when I was a girl, when those types of fraught romance stories gripped me.

"Terrible game," she says. "It's a terrible game that they're playing this year. For rush."

I can't understand what this really means, but I wonder whether it has something to do with him sleeping around with so many girls—sisters. I can't empathize, not directly. But I can understand the loneliness that she might feel. And I can pick loneliness apart with expert tools.

"Well—you could do better," I say, another bit that I learned from girlish stories.

It seems to mean something to her, anyway.

She says, "Do you seriously mean that?"

"Of course," I say.

And I mean it.

They all could.

* * *

Leah drinks water, pops gum, revives herself. We're back at the bar then. And Leah wraps an arm back around Jimmy Crawford. I look for Millie, think that this might set her off, but Millie isn't here yet. I want her to be around, because I think that Stella might be around with her.

There is a presence beside me, and it says hello.

He looks like a minor celebrity. Blond and blue-eyed. A cliché in every sense of the term.

And I realize why clichés persist—why we are obsessed with them, against our own judgement. Clichés can be so beautiful. And this one has come in the shape of a boy.

He smiles easily toward me and stands just far enough so that we don't touch, but close enough so that I can feel him. He looks away, back toward the bartender.

"Can I get you a drink?"

You've no idea the colossal acreage of pages that this particular line, in all its many forms, has taken up in my personal reading. This is the question that starts the novel which will become beautiful, and which will throw its beauty toward an ending so happy that it's almost disgusting, almost suspicious. Or it could be the question that comes at the middle of an upward climb, and then sends everybody through turmoil.

At least in what I've read up till now.

You've no idea what it's like to finally feel as though you're your own character in your own fiction, and that the fiction is real.

So I say, "Yeah. Of course,"

And the drink is already on its way.

STELLA

MILLIE HAD BEEN WAITING FOR ME outside of the Slounge elevator, on the upper floor. She collapsed toward us as soon as we walked in and shoved us into the tiny box when the doors opened. As we jolted downward, she acknowledged Jack with a nod, and he put his arm around my shoulders, which felt new and good.

"I've got to talk to you," said Millie again.

We reached the underground bar and Jack steered us away from the open elevator doors. A stampeding mix of overeager nobodies and deliberately aloof somebodies all rushed into the thick of things.

"I have to talk to you," said Millie. She looked at Jack, still beside me. "Alone," she added.

"Jack, would you—"

"I'll get drinks," he said, and left us for the near side of the bar, where the Sigma Rho boys had established their formal order. Across the dance floor, at the bar's other side, the Kappa Alphas were congregated, and I was unsurprised to see that they'd closed themselves off there, along with all of the boys from The Church.

"You realize you might've called that a date that you just interru—"

"We don't *date*, Stella. Listen. Do whatever you want. I have a plan. Well nearly. I have a plan, or it has me. Do you get it?"

Millie's mind is confusing and erratic. It gets worse when she's on coke or speed, and right then I could tell that she was probably on both, or something else entirely.

"Yeah, I'm listening, but can you listen for a second? Do you know how fucked up you are right now?"

"Yeah, that too. I hear you, sister."

The music raged around us. I saw that Jack was in conversation with the (female) bartender. It was time to join him again.

Millie continued, "You've got Ellis. Jack. The boy, as in—you've got him, and I need him."

"What the fu—I'm *here* with him."

"Not like that, fuck me—no. See: the boys need *me*. What I have. They want to buy, see, and I want to sell."

"They have plenty, if you mean cocaine."

"Right, but they need it in *mass*. For rush. I need to sell, and Jack can tell Nico who can tell Trip that I'm loaded, that I've got *tons*—"

"Like fuck I'm getting involved with Trip Swindle."

"What, you want a cut?"

"Of what? Well, *no*, anyway."

"Just introduce me to Ellis."

And I said, "He's still a pledge anyway, he has no influence—find somebody else."

Millie was already gone and smashing through the crowd toward the other Kappa Alphas and The Church. I turned away and found Jack with his pledge class and the rest of Sigma Rho. He handed me my drink, vodka and diet coke, and I felt like he really knew me as I was, for a second.

Sigma Rho is a top house, but it is generally considered more attuned to social refinement and overall good manners, especially compared to The Church, which is its rival house, also at the top. The Church is known for recruiting drug dealers and horrifyingly good-looking boys with lots of money and coke habits. I've always had the sense that Church boys hate girls in an elemental way. I felt this even when I was with Trip Swindle for that brief time last Spring.

It was nice being around Sigma Rho for a change. Jack put a light arm around my shoulders, handed me my drink, and then I was greeted by pledges and sophomores, some of whom introduced themselves. I congratulated the pledges for almost finishing their pledge period, which everybody knew must've been coming to its annual close. I'm sure it's been hellish, I said. A round on me. I smashed my card against the bar, ordered shots for all of them.

A friend of Jack's, another pledge called Bleis, shoved in and grabbed a shot off the bar. Before he threw it back, he looked at me.

"Thanks, Stella. But it's not over yet. We still have Hell Week, and a few things left still to—"

And then Jack shoved him against the bar, and jolted his head erratically toward me, and then toward Nico, who held court just beside us with the Sigma Rho upperclassmen.

"He'll hear," he said, and Bleis shrugged but nodded, grabbed another shot, handed one to the both of us.

At the time, I thought it was just blackout nonsense. Hell Week would come and go, like it always did, and the boys would be all right, like they always were. And we were not supposed to ask, never meant to pry—outsiders shouldn't know about the details of rush and Hell Week. Because the more people know, the more it'll all leak out, spiral outside of their control.

And if the administration hears about the hazing, Greek Life is dead.

Some think that it is already dying.

Most of those people are God Damn Independents.

Bleis went off and the shots were all taken. Jack called for two more mixed drinks. I watched two God Damn Independent girls, who had taken the dance floor. I looked away, trained to treat them like furniture. In my scan, I spotted Penny across the bar, right in the mix of The Church and a group of Kappa Alphas. She held a drink in that boastful way that a girl holds a drink that has been bought for her by a boy. She was alone, for now, in a shirt that was not hers, and that fit too tightly. She smiled to herself.

Like this had been the point all along.

PENNY

THE BOY BUYS ME A DRINK, and then promptly goes off to the bathroom. He goes with Jimmy Crawford, and a wake of other boys, who all look like variants of himself.

I didn't know what to order when he'd asked, so I requested the same drink that the Kappa Alpha beside me had just ordered, which was: vodka/soda/lime.

And the boy had said,

"Two, please."

And now the boy is back.

I get smiles from him, and all of his followers, when they return. It seems like Jimmy Crawford has recognized me now, what with the knowing look of acknowledgment that passes between me, and him, and this good-looking boy beside me. So maybe he is okay after all.

And that's when this boy introduces himself as Trip, but never mind that, he says, *enough about me, tell me about you, where are you from?*

He squeezes the lime into his drink and tosses it to the ground.

I say, "I, uh, am from the Northeast. A small town in New York? You don't know it. Well, unless you do. Well, it's upstate, New York. Not the city, is what I mean. Maybe one day."

I'm mortified by the nonsense spewing from me, so I take a long sip of my drink, and it feels like it goes straight from my tongue to my stomach to my brain.

"Yeah, sure," he says. "Near Albany? No, yeah. My dad's done business out there. Years ago." He takes a dainty sip of his drink and says,

"Nice area."

It isn't especially nice, and it isn't anywhere near Albany.

But still, I nod. He nods too, which gives me a strong sense of warmth, and reassurance.

"Another one?" he says, and then a second drink—he asks for a double, this time—is on the bar before me.

"But I'm sure you like it better here," he says.

I nod twice.

STELLA

JACK WAS KISSING ME AT THE bar. It was not the slight, puckish kiss that sometimes happened in brief moments of quiet, when we felt unsure of what else to do or say. This kiss was efficacious; it lingered, and then it lasted even longer; and then it hung around for the after-party.

Jack leaned against the bar, and me against Jack.

When I broke off the kiss, I felt I was myself again. *Myself:* the version of me that made herself available around Jack, and around *my* new friend in Penny. I thought—drunk thoughts—that myself, she was all right, when she was with all right people. She was tolerable, you know. She was smart, too; she had that going for her, although she frequently forgot.

But he is like depression. Trip Swindle just won't fuck off, and he pops up in the most problematic moments, such as, for instance, when you're out at a party, and you've just forgotten all about the—well, about the depression. And I saw him now, through the darting bartenders, and the grabbing hands, and the singles thrown like pennies toward the cash registers. I saw two doubles as they landed before him.

Trip Swindle was not alone tonight.

He had found himself a girl.

And she seemed to be having a marvelous time.

I watched as Penny clinked her vodka soda (I can't remember when she'd started to drink that) with Trip's glass. They both took too-long sips and looked not-quite at one another.

I'd notify her. I'd notify her tonight, I'd come clean. *That* was the boy, the real subject of my terrible story. I would tell her that she shouldn't entertain him, that his darkness was hidden by his whispers, compliments, flimsy platitudes that he'd got from Shakespeare 101. I'd warn her and we'd right this; and we, together, would figure out a way to create a small hell for him here.

Then there was a change across the bar.

Trip Swindle reached a claw up to Penny's earlobe, stroked it, and his hand lingered there. Everything tonight was lingering. And then her hand joined his on her face which, I saw now, had been made-up. It didn't look right, like that—she was a clownish imitation of herself, a pathetic and botched attempt at replicating the easy beauty of the Kappa Alphas all around her.

Their fingers intertwined on flesh of her earlobe. Ears, and particularly the lobes of them, got him off like speed. If they were not already fucking, I realized, they shortly would be.

And I watched her stand there beside him. I watched her stand there, becoming happy again.

She'd been lying—about her loyalty, about her sympathy. She'd put a false hand on my shoulder, told me through jeering teeth that everything would be all right, sister. She'd lied, and lied, and lied, listened to my story and laughed to herself, all for her own entertainment, my wrecked reality of no use to her. All while I had been off, thinking about how amazing it was, the power of friendship true and real, the catharsis of telling your horror story to a nonhorror girl, thinking it amazing—uncanny—how things can start to look up so suddenly in the fall.

PENNY

My heart starts talking when our hands touch on my face. And it tells me that this is the right thing for me now. That it is *lovely*. Here is something I've never done, something no one has ever done to me—touched me like this, around the face, in a way that implies that I am somehow special.

But my head says other things. It's always going off and doing that, of its very own volition.

Yet this time, it might be onto something—it tells me that this is not quite right, not quite logical. Something here is unsound.

Boys like this do not approach girls like me in the bar; buy them drinks; touch them on the face.

I drop his hand.

There is a silence, but he flashes up two more fingers. The bartender begins to fix, and I say,

"I think I've had enou—"

"We've just started to get to know each other."

Maybe I'm misjudging, misreading the situation. I have had a lot to drink, tonight. I just say, "Okay, all right."

One more.

While the bartender mixes, he asks me where I'm from. I wonder whether I might be going crazy.

"Uh," I say. "Upstate New York?"

He throws another lime onto the ground. I watch it fall and realize that he is throwing them all onto the same spot and resting his shoe upon the stack.

"Right," he says. Nods. "Near Albany."

I nod once.

STELLA

INCREDIBLE HOW QUICKLY THINGS BECAME CLEAR. My sudden clarity derived from a ferocity that I'd worked hard to suppress, curtesy of Julie, Jack, Penny, alcohol, drugs, music, on and on. It still surfaced, sometimes. Even now, I feel it in the mornings, in those two or three seconds after wake-up when my mind is blank and vulnerable, and memories become available briefly; I shake them off. But right then it all came back at once.

I grabbed Jack, asked if he might want to go home, sorry about this, but isn't it sort of, well, shit? Isn't the music just sort of bad, Jack, and hasn't it been since we got here, and I think they're watering down the drinks, do you feel that too? It's dense in here, it's sweaty, even just a *walk*—

"I've been wanting to get out of here, anyway," he said, found his jacket from where he'd stashed it below a table. Right then I was pissed off in its cleanest, sharpest, most implacable form, and yet I still felt something that might've been like comfort—because he knew what to do and what to say, even when he didn't know why.

We waited for the elevator to ding.

But before it did, Millie erupted before us.

"I struck a deal," she shrieked. "With the boys. Listen, don't tell anybody. Yet. Swindle was practically begging, he says I'm the best around—you'd know, Stella. You'd know, with Trip, right?"

She said this in jest, like it was an inside joke about some random ex, some nobody that I fucked and forgot.

But the line between humor and fury is a very fine one indeed, and it often hinges directly upon the thing that happened to you just prior to the joke.

Fury came, and I realized I still carried my drink, empty now. It looked back at me, the glass, and then it was obvious that there was only one available option, which was to smash the drink at Millie's feet.

I imagined that they were Trip's eyeballs.

"What the *fu*—SECURITY! Get this *motherfu*—"

The elevator dinged, and I shoved past Jack, who stood still. I knew that he wouldn't follow me.

He lacked temper; was passionate only on the positive end of the spectrum, didn't often experience disarray, wasn't addicted to any prescriptions, handled his booze, didn't swear at his mother or father, didn't throw punches, harassed nobody, spoke in earnestness.

The Myself that presented around him was similar to that, and she was who I wanted to be.

She was just so frequently otherwise engaged.

The elevator was empty. I knelt in the corner.

You always see girls, mainly GDIs or bottom tier Greeks, crying in these elevators. They cry more than they talk, and certainly more than they laugh—and it's always about a boy. I would not cry. Because it was fury, and spite, and vindication. I wanted to spit, to crack something. Sure. Somewhere in there was sadness, somewhere below my heart—it begged for me to listen. I wasn't in. I just wasn't there to pay it any attention.

I knelt, watched the floor, saw nothing. And then there was Jack's shoe holding the elevator door open, giving him extra time to slide through. He tapped Level One, pulled me up from the corner.

"It's all right," he said.

It wasn't; but he said it like the truth.

PENNY

THERE IS SOMETHING PECULIAR ABOUT THE way the boy stands, throwing limes beneath his dress shoe with militant precision. I slurp at my drink for a while, and I wonder whether it is my turn, now, to buy him one. We haven't said much. I can feel the eyes of his fraternity brothers upon us, and it does not feel like a compliment.

If this is the start of my romantic tale, I am disappointed to find that it has the unexpected eeriness of a contorted flirtation. There is an offish feeling that you get every so often, like when you've wound up in the darkened halls of your high school alone at night, or when you dream that you're at the senior prom, and you're watching everybody have their best day ever, and you wonder whether you are, in fact, really there. Whether you can really be there at all, if nobody sees you.

The boy is looking at me plenty, looking at my face, and my ears, and my body. I get the sense that he isn't seeing much at all.

And then a force breaks everything. This strange feeling of being fictional shatters when Millie crashes toward us, flinging her body around as if to shake off a pest that only she can see. She zones in on The Church boys, then leers around the silenced crowd—a crowd which is silent for only a glimpse of a glimpse of a second, before it returns to its buzz buzz buzz of conversation and music. Yet I watch Millie, still, and she can feel it. She comes toward me and the boy. I turn away from him, and his emptied glass, and his stack of limes below his foot, and ask Millie what had happened, and was she all right. And I add, "Have you seen Stella?"

Her eyes roll. She doesn't focus on anything in particular.

"Have I *seen* Stella. Like fuck I have. More, Stella's seen me."

"Are you—what are you *on* Millie?"

"Are you not?"

"Okay—is Stella here?"

All her movements cease. And when she looks at me next, it is out of closed windows, nothing and nobody present, all animation cut off. Millie has nothing left to say tonight. I turn around again, to tell the boy that I have to go, and that I am sorry (I'm not sure whether I really am or not).

The boy is gone. Nobody stands beside me anymore. His empty glass remains on the bar—this is my evidence. My evidence that the flirtation, no matter its dim quality, is nonfiction.

As I move away from the bar and toward the elevator, Millie summons her last breath to call out after me, "She's gone, gone, gone," before there is the thump of her body dropped to the floor, amidst the dancing sneakers.

STELLA

Back in his bedroom now, Jack undressed first, which was different.

And when it came down to my undressing, he did it so slowly that I said For God's Sake, off with it.

It was simple, and peaceful, and dark. It was quiet, for the most part. Till the end.

So, if you wanted fireworks or something similar, you are shit out of luck.

It was better than that.

* * *

When it was all over, we talked.

Which was also different.

Because nowadays in America, especially amongst the young, we have such a sad time together; we reserve only half moments for conversation, and getting-to-know-you, and what-does-your-heart/soul-look-like-when-your-T-shirt-is-off—we skimp on all of that, now, to get right down to it. Sophistication, and the rules of the day, and fast paces, and a general lack of human reassurance, all demand that there is little talking and more of everything else. Nobody wants to talk, after they've seen you naked.

And yet afterward, we talked.

His hand was on my stomach, I wondered if he felt the fat there. I wondered only briefly; he didn't. He wasn't looking for it.

He threw on some music, "Me and The Devil Blues," I'd shown him this song ages ago, it felt like, and songs just like it, in all of our heretofore inconclusive nights.

"I love this," he said.

"What, the music?"

"Yeah."

I asked him what had taken so long, hoped he knew what I meant.

"But who's—what's the rush?"

I didn't say anything, having assumed up till then that there must be a rush somewhere, and to someplace.

We were getting older.

I told him that I needed a cigarette, he reached into his pledge pack, which he was required to carry around with him. That was something that we rarely talked about, his pledge status, on account of the fact that nobody ever wanted to recollect it, and because of its utmost secrecy.

I broke our silence on the topic and said, "Are you almost finished?"

He knew what I meant, and said, "Almost."

The song ended. I'd have normally leapt to throw on a different one, because silence busted me up and gave me the twitches, its unproductivity made me ache—especially in a state of nakedness. Now I let the silence fall, watched it sit. It was unaggressive; lay dying softly.

I lit the cig, passed it, he waved it away, lit his own.

And then all the way through the morning—which was my fastest morning ever witnessed, and I still hold that there must've been an astronomical phenomenon which caused the immense rush between one o'clock and six o'clock, some kind of Total Solar Eclipse—there was talk that vacillated between noncommittal and heightened, and then we slept one hour between six and seven, and the smoke sat still and everywhere.

* * *

AND YOU'D THINK IT'D BE ALL rainbows now, wouldn't you? You'd think it'd be all rainbows, but with the bright colors only, in with the yellow, out with the blue.

That's how it's meant to go, with these kinds of stories. There's the commotion and the drugs. After all of that, there's the bit that makes sense, the bit right at the end. That bit is meant to be the silky retreat into domestic bliss, after the couple have finally sorted it, got through their romantic muck, commemorated their copular reality—once they've fucked.

You have it wrong.

Brief highlights: not rushing, clothes came off in equal parts, conversation before, conversation after, a little laughter in the middle, the feeling that somewhere in my body the rain had ceased for a second.

What more could I want?

Please. It's the twenty-first century—a sweet caress, a morning fumble, and a dead night conversation, that's all well and good—and would I do it with him for ages? *Of course I would*—but we aren't really so simple, so easily tempered. The boy was secured; the boy was kind; the boy respected me.

But satisfaction in the romantic realm—that's not satisfaction *terminus*. You can't really think—what with all this we've had to deal with, what with the world that's been left behind for us—that it's the silly security of the boy; that that is *enough*?

No, I was content, I was reeling, I was fine. I was wildly enamored with Jack, in fact.

Yet while the end of the night was lovely, the middle had been so long. The middle had dragged on—and on, again.

The middle had revealed the exact places I had slipped.

And it all came back to the girl on the living room floor. She slept there now, coming up to nine in the morning—the same morning as last night, when Jack and I had slept only briefly.

It had been two very different days.

I told myself to breathe. I told myself to read. I listened to music. I journaled. I wrote a *letter to myself*. I wrote a *letter to Penny*, which I destroyed. I got on the floor and did one hundred crunches. I listened to music, again. I read a poem called *Wind*, by Ted Hughes, which depicted nature as an uncontrollable storm. I tried to think about motifs in poetics. I read another poem, by Maya Angelou, which actually did make me feel better. Far better than the nonsense about personified weather. I tapped my foot to a song that I tried to *write myself*. I paced, then did jumping jacks, then checked my belly in the mirror. I did one hundred and fifty crunches.

I did every single cognitive behavioral technique that Julie had enlisted, for exactly such situations. Situations in which my rhyme and my reason were pummeled by crystalline anger.

And it took about two hours for me to exhaust every psychological coping mechanism that Julie droned on about, when she was trying to divert my attention away from Vyvaid, Celein, and infinitely higher dosages.

And I'll tell you something for free.
That shit just doesn't work.

* * *

I CHECKED MY CALENDAR. I WASN'T set to see Julie for another six days. I put on a sweatshirt, Jack's, and crashed upstairs into Millie's room without knocking.

"Give me benzos and speeds," I said.

"I saw you last night," she answered.

Something that rushed back now: I'd smashed a glass at the feet of my drug dealer.

"Listen to me: I have cash. No, listen, Millie: I'm *sorry*."

"What?"

"I shouldn't have—wait, what?"

"I saw you with Jack, last night. I wanted to ask you how that was going. With him? Since their Hell Week is almost here—I mean, I heard. About Hell Week?"

"You—wait. What did you get up to last night?"

She fell straight back into bed, hair all swarmed against one side of her face. I saw now that she had leftover vomit caked against one cheek, and that the hair had dried into it.

"Fuck knows," she said.

"Uh—do you want to talk about it?"

She put two hands over her face.

Millie is difficult to like, both when she is sober and drunk. But when she is badly hungover, when she barely knows where she is or what she's done or with whom she's done it, and when she starts crying over her blackout and the empty space of the night—as she was then—I actually quite like Millie.

"No," she moaned.

"Ah, this might not be a good ti—"

Something seized her and she thrashed upward, a perfect right angle now, and she swung both legs (so skinny, so stupidly skinny, I never saw the girl eat, and I envied her), landed and keeled over before she buzzed toward me. The smell of her own vomit reeking from her hair consumed the whole space. She glowered at me now, shorter but somehow bigger, it's the drugs, it's the drugs that make people so beyond themselves. There was nothing about her to contend with, till you gave her drugs; then there was everything to worry about.

She started to pace, two steps back and forth in each direction, and said, "I'm striking big. Or I'm about to. I'm *funding*. I'm a *donor*. What's the word, Stella. What's the word, it's—philanthropy. Jesus, fuck that's me."

"You've lost it. I have cash. Just tell me what you have and go to bed."

"That's the thing!"

"That's—*what is?*"

"I'm clean out. I'm empty. I've struck *deals*, Stella. Do you have any idea what season it is?"

"October."

"It's Hell season."

"Fuck off, Millie, *what do you have?*"

"It's gone to the fraternities. Bought out. In preparation, Stella. What Nico told me. And Trip. They've told me—and I should be honored. *You have no fucking clue how much money I've just made—*"

"You're dealing to Tri—you've sold him *everything?* Millie—look at me. Look. You're clean? You're *dry?*"

"I'm rich!"

"But are you dry? Are you *sober?*"

"I'm *rich.*"

Then, a perfectly geometrical arc of vomit roared from her lips and triggered my evacuation to the doorway. From there I watched her place her hands on her knees and gaze at the orange mass that was congealing on her carpet. It would fester there.

She retreated into a tight little ball on the floor and went quiet.

I wondered if she were dead or merely comatose, but I couldn't convince myself to check either way, because my preoccupations guided me swiftly downstairs, to consider this new horror.

Millie was, of course, not my only dealer; and I had, of course, back-up stashes of all types of uppers, and downers, and in-betweeners. But when you've been playing for so long at it you start to build favorites; you start to operate at your very best at a particular conjunction of affectations; you start to develop pet preferences in drugs, and you start to reject, and revolt, and comedown if you lose them. I had all types of miscellanies hidden around my room, and there was Julie, of course, for the bimonthly supply (but God the effort, the drama, the smoke and mirrors, for just one stupid script), but Millie alone carried the cleanest cuts. It was all the stupid fuckers who wrote her so many strong scripts, the ones who had identified her as a serious malady.

Something was changing, something fraternal. If Millie was beginning to deal in mass to The Church, then the boys must've been deficient. They were deficient, or they were *growing*, building an arsenal. It is not unusual for houses to group up together, to deal and buy wholesale, pawn off certain material amongst themselves prior to big tailgates, benders, spring breaks—particularly the stuff labeled

Short Term Use Only, benzos and valium, crazy-strong derivatives of both, hospital-type shit that's become party-type shit, the kinds of drugs that you don't go to therapy for—the kinds of drugs that you go to Millie for. And the fraternities needed more of it. I knew, somewhere, that it must be something to do with pledge season.

And anyway, I could not consider fraternities then, because fraternities made me consider him, and then it's all types of spirals, and a spiral was one thing that I could not afford, what with Millie's absence now from the ring, and immediate relief suddenly unavailable. I retreated to my own bedroom, popped some whatevers—uppers, I think—which were well beyond expiry but still shoved into a pillowcase, and I waited solemnly for my salvation.

PENNY

THERE HAS TO BE MORE TO me than just sitting here in limbo. I wait now, as I have been since Slounge last night—or was it two nights ago now, yes, two—for my friend. I'm waiting for Stella to come down the stairs, for her to smile and hand me some coffee.

I'm waiting for somebody else, too.

I'm waiting for the boy from the bar to come by and reveal himself. Because isn't that the next forward motion? People don't just approach others in the bar, buy them two drinks (doubles!), and talk about hometowns for a while, without some kind of reason or purpose.

Right?

Right?

I sit around and I wait.

I've also got a new endeavor, which I decided upon somewhere in my fourteenth hour of waiting for other people.

I've decided to enact a minor experiment.

What I seek is a simple thing, or it should be. I want to get to the root of the depression that I've shed here in Michigan. I want answers real and researched. Because here, there has been something foreign and something great: friendship, and excitement, and even moments of calm. Even moments of happiness.

I've embarked on a process-of-elimination-type science. Thus far, I have emptied my pockets of the remaining pills that I bought from Millie last week. And my plan is basic: I'll stick with *one* color pill for a while, and gauge how it sits. And then the other colors, by themselves too. And once I've cracked it, that one chemical that lets me participate, and habituate, and speculate throughout the world just like everybody else—then I'll return to Millie and buy that wonderdrug in mass, and do away with all of my private manias, which might be keeping me from—me.

And one day, I will deliver my answer to a psychiatrist, who will help me forever. One day, I will have it in legal abundance, and things will make sense.

And once I do, waiting will no longer be my only extracurricular. Once I do, I will never wait around again for other people to make things make sense.

Instead, people will wait around for me—and I'll be off doing better things.

STELLA

I called Julie.

I told her to write me in for the very next day.

Clear your schedule if you must, please, Julie. Things have turned dark, and frankly, Julie, I just think you might be the only one that gets it.

It's astounding, the threat of a major depressive episode. Julie offered to see me right away.

I sat before her in that stoic room. This felt like my final performance, like all of my cameo roles and bit parts had served to prepare me for my Big Break.

But hold your applause till the end.

I don't know how to say this, I started.

Julie: This is a safe space.

Me: Safety is a spectrum.

Julie: Er.

Me: I guess I'll just come out with it.

Julie: Take your time.

Me: Well, I've only paid for an hour.

Julie: Well, take your time within the hour.

Me: All right. Here it is: I am starting to lose my will to live.

Julie: Yes. A classic symptom of acute depression.

Me: Let me rephrase. I am gaining my will to die.

Julie paused here, but I wanted on with it.

Me: What I mean is, Julie, I am seriously considering ending my life.

Julie: Have you been having suicidal thoughts?

Me: That's what I've just said, Julie.

Julie: Yes, I see. Let's work through these feelings, and I also want to give you the name of a hotline number, which you can call anytime . . .

I knew the hotline number. It was practically tattooed onto me by the school administration when I went officially Greek.

Julie's voice drifted back.

Julie: What I am trying to tell you, is—life is short.

Me: Only if you're having a good time.

Julie: Er.

Me: Listen, Julie. I've researched treatments that are meant to remove people from dire spirals. Such as the one I'm in now.

Julie: Like what? I am happy to reconsider your current dosages. I wonder if the Vyvaid has been truly working?

Me: Julie, let's not mess with the Vyvaid anymore, all right. Because honestly. There have been remarkable studies on the effectiveness of intranasal Esketamine. In the NMDA receptor agnostics family. I've read studies.

Julie: Stella, those trials are only in the very early stages. The FDA has only just approved the intranasal application.

Me: Reports of success have been outstanding. Actually, a research group is performing trials on it right here at the University.

Julie: Yes, I do believe I've heard of that.

Me: Julie, I have tried everything. Yesterday I meditated for two hours. I did what you told me. When I had an invasive thought, I pretended I was on a train. And I pretended to get off the train and leave the thought behind.

Julie: And this tactic was unhelpful?

Me: Yes. The intrusive thought just followed me off the train and asked where we were off to next.

Julie: You seem to have taken the process of mental visualization as a means of coping very, er, literally.

Me: I've got an active imagination.

Julie: Did you not mention something about a boy, a few weeks ago? Is it your relationship with him, perhaps, that is triggering this state?

Me: Yes. My deep dark sadness, it haunts me, right, it sits on my chest. I'm its doormat—I don't know when exactly it's coming, but when it does it stomps on me, and then it breaks in. It goes through all of me, rummages around, and then everything goes deflated—and yes, it's all due to a boy crush. We've cracked it.

I swear to fuck Julie almost popped the champagne.

Stella: It has nothing to do with a boy, Julie.

Julie: Might I suggest that you are using sarcasm as a defense mechanism?

Me: Julie, the thoughts follow me. And they are telling me to do terrible things.

There was another pause but this one wasn't heavy, and I knew from that, and from her little nod, and the way she picked up the pen and big notepad, that I'd got it. And I *had*. She told me all about it, wrote the prescription—no refills, Julie's not a complete nimrod, although she edges the line—told me to call her after the first use. It's a one-off type of drug, meant to make you remember yourself again, and then set you up to settle comfortably back into mainstream antidepressants, the regular kinds of pills that every American everywhere pops like Ibuprofen—it's only meant to elevate you just enough for a day or two, to remember what life is like when it's worthwhile. Julie rattled on: precautions, side effects, come-back-in-a-week.

I did not know yet whether I'd be the one to enjoy it. What I did know was that things were tottering at Kappa Alpha. Millie had gone corporate, gone fraternal; her new operations, whatever they really were, would supersede her side-jobs throughout our home, and precautions had to be taken.

I had currency now. I had ways in which I might use it.

I left for the pharmacy. They work fast. The prescription was sent over, ready under my name, like personal shopping, and I have excellent taste.

And that is how I obtained prescription ketamine.

PENNY

SPEED IS A REMARKABLE THING, BECAUSE it is a cut above what they call *downers*, what Shelly-the-psychiatrist calls *antidepressants*. Speed is remarkable because it doesn't just remind you how, and why, to be happy once again; it holds your hand and sprints off and away, you're pulled along with it. Speed sort of shoves you, lurches you around, till you haven't got a choice, to be happy—though the happy is edgy, it is cagey, it is temperamental.
Energetic.
On speed unadulterated, there is a frantic note to my happiness that arrives alarmingly quickly, and my urge is to temper, to temper off the excess ecstasy, which might, by accident, turn into mania. But I can't do that, because what if speed is the ticket? What if this particular thing, which I believe is known, medically, as an *atypical* treatment, gives me the kind of lightness and freedom from myself that I crave so badly? It's a craving that is painful, because the lightness is so close; it is a craving that hurts so dearly, because I am the only thing keeping it away.
So, on speed and speed alone, I jump up in the morning and already that makes all the difference, to jump, and not to dally, and—as if I am nothing, nothing at all—I crash outside, where the ground is warm. The sun is out—and it may or may

be, really; but it is to me. No looking back at the door, or waiting for company, waiting for reassurance. Don't need it, and what do I care? What does anybody? I start toward campus, in a combination of a skip/run/jog, and I am out of breath now, but even these footsteps down South U are rhythmic, with their own fine beat. The beat from a rock song stripped of amplification and gimmick, so that all you hear is the lead singer's shoe-tap and the drummer's unconscious clapping. And that's how my sneakers go and how they pound, pound, pound, pound, but that could also be my heart. It is bent on making itself heard today, but that's no problem, there is something to be said for hearing your heart, hearing it stuck in your neck and everywhere. Reminds you that it's there, that it's still working. I am now on campus, and I recognize that it is beautiful, more beautiful than ever, except somehow less so, because all of the greenery is fuzzy around the edges. Speed (right, speed, that's the drug of the hour, the drug of the day) has that effect. You feel it sparkling in your eyelids, your corneas, your hairline, and the gap beneath your pinky toenail.

Now in the center of campus. There is the flag half-mast again (they are either always mourning somebody or else have forgotten how to stop) and at the hour, the classes are released. A general giddiness of escape, you'd think they'd been jailed or muted, that's the joviality with which they are released onto the green campus. Nobody looking my way (how lovely for them to think me unthinkable). There is a difference between anonymity and belonging. Both involve the comfort of being a non-spectacle, both involve your being around other people without other people being around you, and yet for now—for once—I feel belonging. And I walk first here, then there, and here the sun hits me, and I could hit it back, and it would say nothing.

On campus it is as though my thoughts are starving and eating one another—none of them have enough room to form completely, and then the next comes stomping in, leaping around. There is an energy; it is hard to tell whether it is happiness, or whether it's just adrenaline.

They might be the same thing, in the end.

There is the library. I sit in a familiar spot in the grass, I've been here before, on my previous trip into the thick of it. And then I'm walking around just like other people, like normal people do. Because it's okay, it's all right, to have a presence, to leave bits of yourself behind wherever you go.

For one of the first times in all this time there is a very clear aspect about it all, and I flex my hands, and breathe full and clean, and plant my sneakers again, and they're off, pound, pound, pound. I establish a song in my head (one of those songs, perfect for the moment), I point my eyes up to singing skies and, in true happiness, I rise.

STELLA

THE SNORTABLE KETAMINE WATCHED ME FROM its high horse. It watched, taunted, and laughed, rotating around me, and gloating about my indecision. It called to me like a seasonal sale.

For the first few days, I hurried past the living room to the front door. I did not want her to suck me back into her warped confessions about her depressions, about how tired and sad her life was on the everyday, how *insecure* she felt all the time, how *beautiful* everybody was here, and how *if only* she—

I'd pass by her den and peek in, and I'd find it vacant. And I knew where she was.

The Church. Where she was getting off with a sociopath.

I journaled.

I asked myself questions.

Such as,

should you try and ascertain this situation logically?

And,

is this the type of person you are, the type of person you want to be?

And,

how will your next decision impact your future, whether positively or negatively?

Optional Pros and Cons list may be helpful.

These were all Talk Therapy Techniques that had been shoved at me unwanted. The trouble was that when I sat down to consider the questions, with a clean sheet of printer paper and a steady pen, the answers that I arrived at were not as Julie might have hoped.

For instance, my answers to the above questions read:

likely.

And,

I've not got it sorted who I am, but I'll get on that once I've sorted *this* out.

And,

well, I won't know until I've done it, will I? And like *fuck* I'm drawing a chart.

The trouble with talk therapy, which nowadays comes suited up in marketable terms like cognitive behavioral jibber jabber, and Paradigms of Thoughts, and Feelings, and Actions, is that it assumes that you've got the desire to change. It assumes that you want badly enough to be somebody else, badly enough to fuck off your hobbies, and your glitches, and your little private manias, to burn time etching out pros and cons lists about decisions that you're going to make eventually anyway. I haven't got those types of desires; I haven't got it in me to look at my thoughts and have a chat with them and ask them whether or not they're rooted in reality, whether or not they're worth all the wreckage.

My logic tried to tell me that she was a friend. That she was confused. That she'd never belonged here, she was only an error in the system, a complete fluke. She came in like water, and everything short-circuited.

And she'd not known. She'd not known his name.

At first all of my problems, they seemed so dissonant, so unrelated to one another. My confusion over Penny's allegiance was detached from my real life, because Penny never belonged here to begin with; and the ketamine—when to take it or how much, or why I'd so desperately wanted it to begin with—felt like a problem for another girl, a girl far crazier, a girl like Millie—and somewhere in there I felt frantic to become worse, crazier, off-the-deep-end-mad. And somewhere in there, I was frantic that I might've been already.

And other problems, they clambered around underneath, they popped up as I made those therapeutic lists, as I practiced my deep-breathing. There was Trip's invisible hand over it all, or so it felt—somehow, like a contagion, he'd gotten in everywhere. The drugs, the girl. And me—he'd got into me. I'd not seen Jack for a few days, and logic tried to prevail too, because I knew that something was happening in the fraternities, something that kept the fraternities away from us, something to do with pledges. Then I thought back again to the ket; and I thought—maybe *it could help everything.*

I must've paced around like a caged beast all day. I remember chain smoking. Threw something at the smoke detector in my bedroom, it made a horrible crash, but I remember lots of chain smoking after that. And more thinking—a horrible habit, which I want to eradicate. Then I stopped, the room sort of turning, and the ket stood solid on its shelf. I lifted it, I looked at it square. I said to it—yes, indeed, I *spoke* to the motherfucker—I said to it, I deserve you, me alone, I deserve your loveliness, your horrible comedown, and your path (that therapists love to speak about, warn about) of no return, the gateway of hard and unfriendly drugs, drugs factory-produced not to help out or guide your transistors but to shatter them and rewrite them anew.

I held the tip of the bottle to my nose, and it smelled of empty bedrooms. I wanted it directly.

However.

The problem wasn't me, not entirely. It wasn't even Penny or Jack or Trip, at face-value. It was all about who they'd become—who they would become, when I wasn't looking.

If Penny were Penny, like I knew her to be, then she wouldn't touch ketamine, it just wasn't her style. She was not about parties, about fun. She was about treatment. She wanted to get well forever, not fly through one quick, sunny day. But if it had got into her, got inside her—that ineffable quality throughout this house, the quality of a Kappa Alpha that makes you shut the fuck up when she's talking, when she's walking, when she's kissing the boy that you think you might love—then she'd break her spine for more drugs, for one more night of party. That's all they ever do around here, right; more drugs, constant pleasure. And maybe her too.

Or maybe not.

If she had rerouted herself, morphed into some off-brand rendition of me and everybody else around here, then shouldn't she take it? Shouldn't she take it, and see how it feels, to crash like drowned clouds, and believe in your life forever, till your lonelinesses come back—come back so sudden, to feed again?

Adversity is pivotal in the development of strong and attractive young women.

Which was something that my mother said to me, once.

* * *

I REACHED MY CONCLUSION A COUPLE of days after I snagged it, and it was this: I'd let her decide for herself. And that would be the ultimate gamble—if she'd morphed irrevocably into a strangled version of herself, into a version of herself that looked like one of us, she'd welcome the stuff, and so she'd deserve its high and then its horrendous comedown, like the greatest and most tragic crash you've ever seen, like the biblical crash (who really remembers which book, which edition?) where the devil does not merely fall back to America but startles the whole planet and pitfalls into the middle of the earth itself—that's the ket crash, that's the calamity of a ketamine drop. And if she didn't take it, if she was herself, and herself, and herself, without all of the extracurricular nonsense (if she was, most importantly, without *him*), then she'd yammer on, and she would babble about her nerves and her near-hysteria, and she'd start on how pharmaceuticals are all well and good but the party drugs, the real drugs for real people, those are bad news, bad news *really*, and shouldn't she just stick with the generics approved for humans by the FDA? The pretty stuff in the pretty bottle, in the pretty drawer, in the pretty dealer's den?

I would see then, I would know. A simple maneuver, and nobody would lose. Because if she didn't want it, I would take it gladly. Take it or sell it. Because, to be frank, I was getting a bit scared. Even back then—there was a loneliness, see. There was this sense of nobody there, and nobody to tell it to.

It is quite possible that I myself was experiencing a bit of a crack-up. It was starting to feel like there was nobody left at the sober table.

Perhaps the ket would help—like obliteration, starting over.

On with it. What happened was this: I woke up and coughed down some miscellany and washed it down with water that tasted suspiciously like vodka, and it was a weekend morning, or it may as well have been, since nobody was awake or else nobody was sober, and hanging around the house was that stale air of discomfort and what-or-who-did-I-do-last-night? that haunts in the early hours after a big night out. On the first floor I peeked around the corner, found the living room was empty.

Apart from Penny, who was sitting up and watching, or waiting.

And right then I saw her again as I'd seen her on that very first night. She was a Goodwill advertisement, decked in other people's ill-fitting clothes. One lumpy leg was tucked under her lumpy ass, and the other one stuck out at a pathetic angle, the deformed stretch of a girl who didn't exercise, didn't go to yoga, didn't care to be nimble or muscly. Her clunky hands worked over the off-brand Moleskin that she used to "detail her experiences," as she'd explained to me once.

Experiences. Experiences that she was now experiencing with him.

Or was she?

Or was she?

I instructed myself to smile as I crossed the floor. But it stretched a bit, made me feel unhinged and overeager, so I softened to a close-lipped mask, and then arched the right corner upward, for friendliness.

All of this in the moment it took Penny to realize that I was approaching, at which point she leapt up and grinned.

"*Stella,* I've been sort of, getting worried. I know you spend a lot of time at your boyfr— at that guy's, but it's been—it's been a *while,* hasn't it? I knocked, but you haven't been around. I've been, uh, walking, a lot. More. Around campus."

I settled down beside her nest, and she mirrored me, but continued to yabble.

"Do you want to, uh, walk today? Are you busy?"

"I've been worried about you too, Penny," I said.

"Excu—I've been all right. As all right as I can—"

I could not entertain her pontifications. I had to know who or what she was now, and whether she was gone for good. I looked into the round face, sort of moonish, craters and hills and nobbles where cheekbones should've been, and a smile that slanted even in its off-hours. There was nothing beautiful about it—but did she know? Or had he told her otherwise? Had she not got around to the later bit yet, the bit where she feels like every beautiful element about herself has been sapped out or stolen?

I said, "No, listen, Penny. I think you're losing it."

"I—well, it's not *impossib*—"

"You're crashing into the, you know, depths. They're saying."

"Why? Who would say that?"

"Psychiatrists and the girls, the other girls."

"Are you all right, Stella? Listen—I'm trying something new. That's true. Yes. But I'm not, I wouldn't say I'm *losing it*, and I wouldn't say. . . well. What I will say is that I haven't *lost* it. Wait—are *you* okay?"

That struck me intensely, for some reason—are you okay? Because of the gall, the presumption. I *was* okay. I am.

Or maybe not. But I can trust my brain. It's gotten me around to plenty of bright places.

Plenty of dark ones.

(I was on some silly off-brand speed then, so I was focused more on my inners than what Penny was really saying, or what she might've meant).

I felt her dense hand, which she'd shifted from her lap and placed on my shoulder. I said, "*I'm* all right, Penny. It's *you* that we should be worried about."

"But I haven't even seen you in days—is there something—is there something going on?"

"Ah, sure. But listen—"

Whatever I'd taken was starting to buzz. On speed, my sweat begins in my armpits, and now I felt it travel quietly from its nest down toward my belly, where it went cold, and I told myself not to fixate. I centered again on her deadish face and thought about my ketamine; about how badly I wanted it for myself—and already my original reasoning was fuzzy to me, a dizzy spin of decision-making that felt almost like I'd not been present at all.

As far as the drug goes, its commercial purpose as factory-farm horse tranquilizer is its most unbecoming quality—otherwise, its permanent damage on humans is minimal. It only harks up the chaos that is already there, you see. It doesn't really come up with anything original, like LSD does—it only digs into the very back of the refrigerator, for things that you should've tossed out ages ago. First it tricks you, with pure euphoria. Then it dives deep and roots around. It sits down at the kitchen table, and it starts to chat with you about all kinds of things that you'd told yourself you'd forgotten. And the worst bit is that it convinces you that that's all there is left, really, the rotting decay that's left behind, all decomposing with the thoughts that you don't let yourself think before bed. It's a highly addictive thing, ket. And the crash is like death—with the additional flaw of consciousness.

No time had passed, by the way. The fixations of speed allow thoughts to come and go with remarkable dexterity, and Penny still watched me with these unfocused, unlit eyes.

"I thought that you might want to try this new script—I just got it," I said. "It's excellent, this med. I use it now, to deal with it."

"To deal with *what*, Stella?"

"All of it. This whole thing that we all deal with. Together."

And I grabbed the little bottle—only big enough to contain one amazing high or two decent ones—from my pocket, laid it flat on my palm. She looked but did not touch.

"Is that—I'm not sure I should—it's a delicate thing. Stella, listen. Like I was saying before. I'm trying something new, with all of this."

"So? So what? It's just a bit of fun."

An unplucked eyebrow twitched, and the foot that was connected to her stretched-out leg gave a kick beside me.

"Hey," I said. "I'll just leave it. I'll just leave it in my desk drawer, how about that? And you can—I'll save it. And you can have it, if you want."

"Thank you, Stella."

"Let's catch up later," I said.

"Yeah," she said, and I rose from the blankets.

"Goodnight."

"Yeah. Goodnight."

We hugged.

All before ten o'clock in the morning.

PENNY

My private experiment has reached a standstill. The speed is too speedy, and the valiums and the benzos are too depressive without any speed to energize them. But I hope (incredible that I still hope) that there might be some perfect drug for me. I can't be the only one with such afflictions; I can't be a medical anomaly; in all this whole country there must be a drug floating around for people like me. Somewhere, somewhere there must be people like me—and if they're anywhere, I'd guess that they might be here. Stella blurs out the front door, and I think about her offer. What if it works? What if it really, really does?

But first, I go upstairs.

Millie looks out her bedroom window.

"What? What is it?" she says.

"I—uh . . . I'm trying to find a new medication," I tell her. "One. Just one. One that works. And I'm trying to stick with it."

"Yeah? Well, where's your shadow?"

"My—"

"I mean, who the fuck are you? Listen—who the fuck *are* you, by yourself? Are you even *Greek?* Even Greek remotely? Who are you, legitimately? Without her? And it doesn't matter. I'm not selling to girls anymore. I'm all tied up—selling to the boys for rush."

That can't be right. There can't be *me*, I think, without Millie's drugs. She goes on, "It's Hell Week right now. And you can't understand because you *don't get it*. It's Hell for other people right now—and they're buying it all. Some people need them. What do you need? What the fuck is wrong with you, seriously? Get out. Get *out!*"

"Millie—I—listen: what happened? I can't—you don't understand. I need these . . . for medical purposes. They're prescribed, Millie. Can't I—you must have something left. You've sold *all of it?*"

"I don't know anything about your prescriptions. And even if I did—what of it? What of them? It's medical for everybody, and the boys too. Aren't you listening? It's medical for all of us!"

And yet my diagnoses alone feel real, feel intrusive, like a fundamental part of me.

"Fucking delusional!" she is screeching now. "All of us! Why should you get any special treatment? Why should I sell to *you?* When there's real people in need? You don't even live here! *Fucking psycho—*"

Now each word is complemented by the movement of one of her limbs downward, as she hops from her top bunk.

"You better get the hell out now," she says.

I move backwards into the hallway, where long-haired heads peek out of bedrooms and then retreat again.

In her doorway, I stop and turn back. This makes no sense, I should shout. You'd had *so much*.

Now she paces around the room like a caged animal. She pauses at her desk and grabs a textbook. Winds up to throw.

And finally, in the vision of her winding up to hurl the thing in my direction, I understand the severity of my situation—something has gone terribly wrong. Something has gone terribly wrong with my supply chain.

I go back downstairs. My hysterias have been waiting backstage, and now they crawl up from their nethers, through my lips and my forehead. Still, I am running downward. I'm no longer involved with myself, really—I seem to be watching from somewhere far away. I see myself as I shove my face into the garbage bin on the first-floor landing, near the front door.

Because this is the place. This is the place of my crucial error. This is where, in the fervor of delusional self-improvement, I discarded my remaining pills of all colors, all the ones which only worked in combination with the others. I'd been so arrogant in this pharmaceutical plan, so wrong.

And I continue to watch myself as I hang my head in pathetic regret, and gaze at the inners of the garbage bin. The Kappa Alpha Kleaners—the name of the service that mops up the vomit, and the pissed-in corners, and the residues of sex, and the tears all matted in carpet—have been around already.

And the bin is empty.

STELLA

I HAD CLASS, OFFICIALLY. I WENT to Jack's instead.

I'd spent more time there since that night at Slounge. It had been a combination of enjoying his company, liking him as a person, and attempts to avoid Penny.

And yeah. The sex.

I knocked on the Sigma Rho door. Smashed it, really. It's ginormous, and you have to stampede yourself against it, in order to be heard from the inside.

And then Nico slithered out, closed the door behind him, and stood before me like a bouncer.

"You have to come back later," he said.

I went to shuffle around him.

"Fuck off, Nic—"

"Stand back, Stella. Stand back."

"All right. What the fuck?"

"Come on—Jesus, Stella. Come on. Think."

"What, it's—is it Hell Week, now?"

His non-answer was enough. The Sigma Rho pledge master would never say that phrase himself, especially not to some girl from Kappa Alpha with a crush.

There was no noise coming from the house—dead silent. I turned away, and the door slammed shut behind me.

I went to class instead.

Which stimulated daydreams.

I thought about hypotheticals. My hypotheticals were fueled by emerging notes of anxiety—about what I had offered her. About drugs in general. It was going haywire; sobriety was coming, I thought, and it felt so suddenly like there was nobody around to help, like I'd been abandoned way, way, way up high, at the pinnacle of things—but that it was going downward fast.

Control was slipping. I'd gotten too comfortable, and my control was slipping, or it was gone already.

* * *

WHEN CLASS GOT OUT, I HUNG about on campus like a God Damn Independent. I saw Kappa Alphas wander around, in packs of only themselves.

There's an American flag that looks over campus, right in the middle of the Diag. It was at half-mast.

I don't know who for.

Hadn't been paying attention.

I thought about ketamine, thought about its abilities. Then I thought about dinner.

And I thought about how hungry I felt.

I had some strong Ritalin in my backpack. The last of Millie's speeds. Millie's Ritalin made you forget everything you've ever wanted or hoped for, in a very uplifting way. Even more importantly, it would make you despise food. It's like poison. A few days on it melts my flesh and shrinks me up and makes me beautiful again.

Ritalin kept me from the terror of abjection, because the worst thing that a girl can be around here—worse than being dumb, or slutty, or distrustful—is bad-looking. But experience lately had proved that my control was false, or it was imagined. My inability to eat, my capacity to stay small and pretty, was victim to the whims of other people, who could cut off my chains of access.

I couldn't wait around for other people to take everything from me, everything that mattered.

I did not wish to be ranked, in the scary history that I feared I might be writing, amongst those girls around me who were winning—but whose successes were pyrrhic.

I was a *woman*.

So, I'd do it on my own.

* * *

THAT WAS WHY, WHEN I WENT back around to Sigma Rho on my way home that evening, my backpack was emptied of all of its pharmaceuticals. And I did not have more waiting for me at home—the ketamine had been Julie's solitary gift, with express instructions *not to mix*.

Sigma Rho was back to its regular cacophonic conditions. There is a wired atmosphere around the place—an atmosphere that flattens under the weight of attempted description: "It's just, I don't know, *really fun* there."

The only odd thing that evening was the number of shut bedroom doors on Jack's hallway. There were more of them now, and I thought that everybody must've been asleep.

Jack wasn't. He said Nico had told him I'd been by.

And that he'd waited up.

He asked how I was, still maintained silly pleasantries. Jack had such a relaxed certainty about himself—like he had decided, a long time ago, who he wanted to be, and so that's who he became. And like he was okay with that.

I told him that I was fine.

I'd never told him much about Penny. Never got around to it. We so rarely talked about Greek people, about our social life, although it was the same life between us. We spoke of Other Things: other people, like mothers and fathers. He still had to call his, every Sunday. Or other hobbies, like reading. I'd been trying to do more of that—Penny had said that it exercised empathy. And there was of course the other music. Music that didn't drop. Music that hurt, you know. Painlessly.

Other moods—like unhurried and looking forward to tomorrow.

One day though, once Penny and I had cleared the air and had a laugh, I'd tell Jack about her, and they'd meet.

But that night I just kicked off my sneakers, looked toward the pillow, touched the edge of his t-shirt. And then his socks were off, and talking became whispers, and then whispers became other things.

PENNY

I run to Leah's bedroom on the first floor, knock viciously.

"Shit," she says. "You're up?"

"It's ten o'clock."

"I had a *breakup* last night, Penny. Jesus. Yeah, I'm fine. Thanks. Thanks for asking."

"Uh—Jimmy broke up with you?"

"Jesus, Penny, *nice assumption,* no. I broke up with him. Fucking—hellish, you know. The hazing tactics. I can't deal. Not this year."

"I'm sorry. That's awful."

She nods, and then her face plummets to her pillow.

"I—Leah, I am so sorry. I . . . have a serious issue."

"*As if a breakup isn't serious?*"

"Leah—listen. I'm out of medication. I'm out of it and my—uh, Millie stopped. She's stopped selling, I think. Leah, do you know anybody?"

She gazes at the ceiling. There's a pervasive stillness in the room. Then she snaps her eyes to mine.

"Do what everybody else does," she says. "Hello? Just go to the source. They're waiting for people like you to show up. All you have to do is ask. It's not *difficult,* Penny. Jesus. Do you really think that these psychiatrists care? At all? It's just a phone call."

"And besides," she adds. "You could do with some professional help, anyway."

* * *

I HAVE TO BE SQUARE WITH myself. My supply chain is hijacked. I have nothing left to take, not even a single SSRI pill.

Paranoia comes around and tells me how much it's missed me. It asks where it can hang up its jacket.

I creep downstairs to the basement living room, where the sorority's Executive Committee maintains a bulletin board plastered with announcements and infographics. Flyers with emergency hotlines, who-to-contact, where-to-go, and how-to-recognize-the-signs.

I choose the first phone number listed on the campus mental health hotline sheet and type it into the communal house phone. I enter my birthday when it prompts, press 1, yes I can wait on hold, ninth in line, eighth in line, seventh in line, Jesus Christ, sixth in line.

Without speed, I am prone to falling asleep whenever I have nothing better to do. And I am *completely out of speed*—

"Campus Mental Health, this is Laura speaking. How can I help?"

"Hi, Laura."

"How can I help?"

"I'd like an appointment?"

"Who with, please?"

"Er—therapy, and psychiatry. Somebody who is—who can do both?"

Laura is silent for a moment.

"I have a lot going on," I say.

"Certainly. Are you an undergraduate?"

"I am."

"Wonderful. The University has a network of on-campus therapy and psychiatry professionals who are ready to help. The wait time, at the moment, to schedule an initial consultation, is six to eight weeks."

"I'm sorry?"

"The wait time, at the moment, to schedule an initial—"

"Nothing sooner? Nobody?"

"I'm afraid that the University health systems are overwhelmed with undergraduates seeking initial consultations at the moment."

"But where am I supposed to go in the meantime?"

"The University is committed to offering its students as many avenues of help as possible, and we have connections with reputable providers in the area who you may be able to reach for a more immediate consultation, but these providers will be out-of-network and may not take insurance."

"What are their—could I have a phone number, please?"

She starts to read out contacts for Ann Arbor healthcare providers. The first one, she says, is called Brennan Private Psychiatric Services, a small company run by a woman who specializes in "women's issues" across the college population. Laura disconnects the call when I thank her, so I punch in the new number.

"Dr. Brennan speaking. How can I help?"

"Dr. Brennan? Hi. I'd like—I need an initial consultation. I struggle with a variety of—women's issues, I guess . . . mental health, women's issues. I need to talk to somebody at first opportunity—Hi, Dr. Brennan, are you there?"

"Please call me Julie," she says. "Who's speaking?"

"Penny. It's Penny."

"Thank you for reaching out, Penny. I'm the in-house psychiatrist for Brennan Private—

"What's your availability, uh, for tomorrow, or this week, Julie?"

"—And I am not accepting new clients at the moment."

How wrongly have I presented myself to this woman? How have I so quickly asserted that I am not worthy, that I am not fixable, that I am not an attractive candidate for her prescription-writing? Even over the phone, I am bodiless and faceless, I am unsuitable.

Never the right time, for me.

Julie doesn't say anything else, but she stays on the phone. Do I need to *demand* an appointment, burst through the doors of her practice, prove my hopelessness hopeless enough?

"I wish you the best of luck with your search," she says.

Click.

Time passes. I feign interest in the bulletin board before me, a wall of chances and opportunities, internships, and research, and clubs, and trips abroad. I know right then that I'll never have my go at any of it. That has been my greatest problem: how much time there is, and how little I know what to do with it.

There isn't anything left, really. Only one more option. I walk upstairs as if dragged by necessity which, I guess, I am. This will be professional drugs, for professional women. Even before I retrieve it—and it is right where she'd said it would be, in her desk drawer—I see myself in a few hours: I'll relent to the day, and let time perform its sorry little show, and wait quietly to feel something.

Σ

THE PLEDGES OF THE CHURCH AND the pledges of Sigma Rho were gathered together in the Sigma Rho basement, along with their respective Pledge Masters. The pledges were blindfolded. The Masters paced.

Sigma Rho rivaled The Church for everything: girls, parties, looks, musical taste, grade point averages.

It was really about the girls.

Jack Ellis was not one of the unlucky few who'd also been handcuffed. He touched the silver cross around his neck. He heard one of the Masters pacing around him, but he couldn't tell if it was Nico, or somebody else.

Trip Swindle, The Church's Pledge Master, stood still at the back of the basement. Suddenly he shouted, "Up! Everybody."

And everybody leapt to their feet. Those in handcuffs struggled more, but everybody stayed quiet.

Trip was the keeper of the goods. He retrieved the stash—from the dumbass girl, the dumbest girl on Greek row, the only idiot who would offer up such strong pills in such mass quantities, and then leave a *greeting card* taped to the bag, *XOXO, Love, Millie*. Trip placed pills in open palms and the pledges knew not to wait, washed them down quickly with half-drunk fifths of clear liquor, a bottle of which was duct-taped to each of their left hands.

THE GILDED BUTTERFLY EFFECT

This served several purposes: the use of concentrated speed was essential to one of the tenets of Hell Week: sleeplessness. This fed the pledges' delirium, which made Hell Week tasks more difficult, and also provided some entertainment to the Pledge Masters. Some of the other pills, which Trip handed out now indiscriminately, like the benzos, and the valiums, and the party drugs like Molly, provided additional obstacles for the pledges.

This would be a particular kind of Hell, the Masters had explained. Because it's all in good fun, in the end. All for your benefit, Trip had added. After Hell Week you become real men—Sigma Rhos and Church Members—and then you'll be drowning in girls, and drugs, and everything will be great. It builds character, Nico had tuned in. And it builds Brotherhood. *Next year we'll laugh about it and watch the new pledges go through it themselves.* The Masters had laughed into the dark, then—it had been a riot, for instance, when they'd watched the pledges take SAT tests in the dark, just as they were starting to roll on Molly.

Time passed. Nico and Trip waited for them to get speedier, could feel new atoms atomizing. Trip stowed away the bag, looked toward Nico. They had flipped a coin over who got the glory of this announcement. Nico had won the honor.

It had been decided weeks ago, this final task. It represented all that the brotherhoods stood for: social navigation, control, sacrifice. Power, mostly—especially.

This year's Hell Week agenda brought Trip joy unlike much else. It was a joy that felt like religion. And Trip had used his early intel for personal gain. He'd spent these past weeks scouting for pigs, establishing his prey.

Nico began, "Welcome, pledges, to your final initiative."

Nods and murmurs across the group, but Trip was glad to see that his boys stayed perfectly still.

"You might've heard rumors, whispers, stories, lore."

They were all smart enough not to nod.

"Now, though, you receive your final task. And once completed—once proof is established, and then that proof *burned*—you are a brother, a brother fully initiated."

Heads rose. They couldn't have a clue.

It was too genius.

"Welcome, pledges," Nico repeated. And this was the cue for the Pledge Master Secondaries to go around and untie the blindfolds, so that the boys could witness their Masters pronouncing their fates in real-time.

Blindfolds dropped.

Nico continued, "Boys, it'll be disgusting, and degrading. You won't like it—I promise you. But it's about teamwork, and loyalty, and knowing that your fellow brothers are going through this nasty hell right beside you.

"You're to find pigs—piggish girls, pledges—and roast them. Make them love you, that kind of shit. It shouldn't be that hard. Fuck them, too. Close your eyes if you have to. Roast the pigs and photograph the evidence. We'll count it all at the end, see which house really has the stamina, the bravery, the dedication. And if you make it through this, boys, if you become initiated brothers, you'll have all of the girls that you want, whichever ones and whenever. Wait until you see the top-tier girls that we have for you, if you make it through. They'll seem like angels after this. And you can do whatever you want to them.

"Welcome dear pledges," Nico finished, "to the Pig Roast."

PENNY

I MARK THIS DAY. I MARK it as the happiest that I have ever been. This is life at its uppermost—and all I am doing is sitting on the living room floor, watching the wall be still.

STELLA

IN THE DAYS THAT HAD FOLLOWED my throwing out those last few pills, I'd been excluded from Sigma Rho. Jack had warned me that this would happen—Hell Week meant that outside visitors were treated as intruders. And he said he was sorry—but that meant me, too.

It would be over soon, he said. Finally.

I had still not been down to see Penny.

That was a critical error.

I'd not been to see anybody, really. I was experiencing a malignant crash, the kind of comedown that follows weeks and weeks of misuse of prescriptions that should've never been prescribed to me at all. I'd used speed for its ability to suppress the appetite. I'd also got daily jolts from it, nothing to do with hunger. I'd become accustomed to it. Julie might even dare to say *addicted*. Because those jolts tapped into something so lovely: hope, and enthusiasm for the day-to-day, which makes you remember that you're still alive, and that you may as well keep it that way.

So now, I felt inadept at being an alive woman. Lethargy crept and coddled. No therapeutic technique or visualized train or letter-writing-to-nobody could fix the unshakeable *tired* that dogged me. I sat in my bedroom, and slept, and thought about what would happen if I didn't exist anymore.

I could not risk wrecking my remaining sanity to go see Penny now. Penny, who'd once been my friend.

Maybe. Or maybe not.

I did have to go to Chapter, however.

Early Sunday evenings, every week, all two hundred members of Kappa Alpha meet together in one room. We flop down in the ornate great hall of the sorority house, there in white dresses, and we wear our pins on our lapels. We chat so much bullshit with one another that it feels like we might really be sisters.

Till we all go back to whatever we'd been doing before, by ourselves.

The Executives force us to wait outside the house until six o' clock on the dot, at which point they bust open the doors, and their song reaches us. The song then catches on, all the way down the line like an echo.

And I'm always at the back, so I normally only get in one verse. We hold hands, sing our Song of Rituals in soft voices, and file inward:

> *Oh, you can't get to Heaven*
> *Without a key*
> *It won't unlock,*
> *That door you see!*
> *You can't get to heaven*
> *Without a key*
> *Which you will see*
> *When you pledge Oh, Kappa A!*
>
> *Oh, you can't get to Heaven*
> *Without a kite*
> *You'll sail right by,*
> *That shining light*

But with KA,
I'll see the light and proudly be,
A worthy sister, of Kappa A!

Each girl conducts the handshake with the Rituals Master at the door before she is allowed entry. It's a conjoining of the fingers in two *O*s, and then some crawly maneuvers that involve feather-light fingers running over your own. As we do the shake, we whisper the password, which is *fos*, the Greek word for *light*. The Rituals Master makes us perform the ridiculous show until we get it just right, she waits for some imagined click or spark between our hands; and you're standing there in your white dress, while these haunting girls are humming and singing all round you, and the desired effect is achieved. You feel like somebody is watching, somebody not human, or maybe it's just you, yourself—watching, and thinking, what the fuck is this all about?

That night, I fumbled the process. The Rituals Master gave me a look of disappointment and made me go through it again. I was singing all the while.

Oh you can't go to Heaven without a—

We stopped the song as soon as the doors slammed shut behind us, and then the Rituals Master make a show of flicking the lock.

I sat near Millie, both of us hidden away toward the back of the group.

There were all two hundred of us present, and we were only marginally quieted by Kathy Van Tassel's whacking of the gavel on the wall. She had to use the wall, since she had no podium. She began her opening remarks over the remaining whispers.

"Every week, we meet in our formal attire and sing our Rituals Song to honor our Founders and to be reminded of the bond that brought us here, a familial connection. We use this time to understand our sisterhood in a new and bright light..."

It always started off with some variant of this.

I opened *Inquiry of the Mind*, to start the following week's reading. Since I'd cleansed my own drug stash and decided to face the day unadulterated, I'd begun to take Psych 101 seriously. My desire to live through my comedown hinged on my understanding of the inner-workings of the mind. I had been studying a section titled *Other Approaches: What To Do When Medication Fails,* which was bent on nonsense about habit-building, and positive-affirmations, and manifesting, and all this other optimistic, God-save-thou-from-thyself bullshit. As I read, I realized that Millie was glowering at me.

"What?" I said.

"Your friend is wrecked."

I kept my eyes on the book, and my face placid. Over Kathy Van Tassel's yarble, I said, "Don't exaggerate, Millie."

The following silence was filled by the President, whose powers of lectureship increased as her disciples' attention fled.

Kathy Van Tassel was saying, "We want to use the next few minutes to emphasize and redefine certain aspects of our Kappa Alpha *social responsibility.*"

She glared at the conglomerate and let that sentence seep, then continued, "It is thus our duty as your Elected Executive Board, to publicly flag an upcoming Questionable Event. This Event may infringe upon our exceptionally high standard of social responsibility, behavior, and —uh—*aesthetic,* that we fastidiously establish, as a national chapter. As many of you know, the Fraternity pledge period is drawing to a close for the semester..."

Every fall, they are required to berate us on the dangers of hazing. The University feeds them these lines in fruitless efforts at reform. I turned back to Millie, and said, "Penny? She's always been wrecked. What of it? *You're* wrecked, too. I mean, Jesus fuck—you can't even remember your last blackout, out of your fucking mind at Slounge."

"I can. Most of it—not all. With her it's a different form of wreckage. *Wrecked*. She wants some magic fucking pill. She's in for, like, actual stability. Not for fun. That's unhinged behavior, Stella—she wants *treatment*."

"What the fuck are you talking about?"

"She wants some magic pill—because she's *so fucking wrecked*—"

"*You're* wrecked, you're talking nonsense!"

"It's you! It's *you* and the nonsense, bringing madwomen around to buy, even though you know I'm short, I'm dried out, I don't even have for myself right now, it's *wrecking everybody*—"

I ticked my eyes over to where Kathy Van Tassel still spoke, tried to feign attention. Millie persisted, "You think she's like us? Just the odd benzo, and she's off swimming? No. She's *deep-rooted*. She talks about *diagnoses*. Her comedown—her comedown isn't about falling from, like, height. It's about *dropping*."

"You're hysterical. I've seen her stash, speeds and SSRI's. You're losing your fucking mind over your new deals—"

"Please. Like she's not been using all kinds of other shit, since that very first day? The second she tried Percolin—chose it herself—she's been obsessed. It's bad."

I forced my eyes away from her and she still pestered on, on, on, on, about Penny's comedown. And now Kathy Van

THE GILDED BUTTERFLY EFFECT

Tassel was making her closing remarks: "Kappa Alphas. We urge you all to stay carefully away from the Pledges in fraternities that we associate with at present, which is to say, the—uh—more *selective* groups on campus. We have word on good authority that this year's final . . . *character-building* exercises within these specific chapters have much to do with . . . *fraternizing* and *affiliating* with a certain type of woman.

"Women that *we* are proud not to have anything—*anything*—to do with."

At Chapter, nothing ever captures the communal attention. But this did—this did completely. Worried voices, curious ones, probing ones, started to bounce across the room.

Finally, Millie's attention was diverted. We were both fixed on Kathy Van Tassel.

The noise had risen to a pitch, each girl talked to those beside her, their eyebrows were in knots, and their shoulders were in shrugs. *I* have no idea, everybody said, *I* haven't affiliated with them.

Have I?

A senior shouted from their coveted and separate spot on the back stairwell, "Just tell us what the fuck the frats are doing, Kathy!"

Kathy Van Tassel looked grimly across the room.

"If you *must* know—the final contest, for the new fraternal initiated members, the 'pledges,' as they are known colloquially, is this year abhorrently titled: The Pig Roast."

She looked at us with raised eyebrows, asked us if we understood.

We did.

PENNY

For a very brief moment, everything is sublime.
However, I seem to have made a critical error.
There isn't very much in that little bottle that Stella left for me. Not very much at all.
My supply has dwindled.
I don't mean to euphemize. My supply is gone.
The elephant is back.
It's staying.

STELLA

CHAPTER LET OUT BUT EVERYBODY LINGERED. Shimmery curls and lacquered nails taptaptapped, small bodies crowded around one another, howareyou, youlookgreat, canyoubelievethisshit?

I felt Millie watching me even as I got up and wandered toward the front door. My movements needed to appear mindless. I wanted to run so fast that my knees cracked open. Still—once I got out, I forced myself to walk.

Once I was out of the radius of Kappa Alpha's shine, I ran.

My heels hindered my progress, one almost snapped, I ripped them both off, tossed them onto the nearest lawn, a fraternity lawn, some no-name house. Then I really picked up speed, and here the road ended. I chose to go straight ahead, down the dark trails and into the Huron Valley, where I'd once told Penny all of my saddest secrets.

I frequently went out jogging here. I secretly tried to keep pace behind the varsity girls. It wasn't even a close match. Booze and drugs had had their way with me. High school track star I was not. I would run after consuming sugar. Or bread. Anything with volume. If the university gym had closed for the night, and there was nothing else to do but work it off, out here in the dark.

What else was I meant to do? Let the sugar rot and expand? What would be left of me, then?

I had only one thought, but it was loud.

I thought, over and over, about Kathy Van Tassel's warning. *Be careful this week, everyone. It is secret—do not breathe a word.*

Silence had followed the announcement. I'd watched as some of our own pledges blushed with unfortunate recollection: the realization that you might've been the pig in somebody's scheme.

The night was heavy. And it didn't float with any drugs. It was just pure dark night, heavy and suffocating. And I was alone within it. I could hear downtown Ann Arbor starting to light up with the night, everybody drunk and starting to dance, wondering who it would be tonight, who it would be naked with tonight, and then tomorrow, and over again. And I thought about just how dim they'd fallen, how they'd become all equally uninteresting, and equally harmless, through lack of imagination, and through plenty of money.

* * *

THERE ARE NIGHTMARES AND WORRIES THAT are kept on the edges. I keep nightmares out of my bright days with parties, and music—with *him*—and other distractions, drugs, calories, tomorrow's joke. None of it means anything at all to me except for keeping the nightmares away.

Now *I am a pig*.

How long had I been a part of the game? Was there a list of targets? Was I at the top? How many points had I gotten him? *How many was I worth?*

That was why Nico had introduced us, all the way back in August. *We want him, so talk him up.*

It had not been divine work. Nobody was up there. I'd thought that maybe someone larger than me might have been watching, doing their thing, trying to make amends for the bullshit that had come of last Spring.

Trying to return to me—in some sick broken gesture—what I'd lost.

Jack must have already known that night, the night that he went in for his slaughter. That night at Slounge—our first time together.

And that was why he'd stopped the elevator with his foot, dragged me back up.

It's all right—he'd said.

You ask why I am not bothered about romantics. I am so young, you think. So much left to do and see. So many humans still out and about, breeding, and selling, and giggling, and with so much pretty nonsense still left to say.

To that, I just laugh and laugh, and then back again.

I let the fury take me, and I started back toward home.

I thought about the future. How sad it was, how mad it was. How much was mine to ruin.

PENNY

THE PARTIES CONTINUE TO BURN ON.

I understand now that the ketamine has come, and done its thing, and vanished. Soon I will be profoundly unmedicated. I cannot remember a time when this was a remote possibility, the possibility of sitting completely alone with myself. It must've been long before all of this, and I might've even been happy, then.

Who can really remember so long ago?

The night is not stopping, although I'm short-circuiting, and I'm falling. I may just stick around and see what's at rock bottom.

And anyway, I've been invited to a party. A party at The Church—the famous religious establishment that moonlights as a fraternity house. And, as Leah pointed out, it's going to be a *crazy fucking night*.

So, I'll go.

There's just so little difference anymore.

STELLA

I RETIRED BACK TO KAPPA ALPHA late enough that everybody had gone off to the frats already. For all we'd heard that night about their final task, the party that night was at The Church, and everybody went. Before I went to my bedroom, I crept into the dark living room. Dark and still.

Nobody.

It was the godlessness throughout the house, the emptiness so dead and still that I might've been inside my old amphibian aquarium, that one with the artificial light and liminal oxygen.

She's wrecked, Millie had said. What she had meant by it, I could not gather. *She's wrecked*—but how could she be, so fast?

Yet a different thought returned again, the same old nagging one. If she was not here, she must be somewhere, *must be.* It only logically followed that she'd gone to The Church—she'd gone to The Church, to see him.

Up in my bedroom now, it had to be drugs. I'd been putting off this last resort, had tried to forget all about it. I hadn't even checked on the little bottle, because—I think—I'd known all along where it was.

I ripped open my desk drawer, ripped it out so hard that the drawer itself came out flying, hit and rebounded off the wall behind me, then all went quiet as I approached the pathetic scene, looked at the disemboweled furniture, looked long and hard, even kicked the drawer around, turned it upside down—

And, sure enough, the ketamine was gone.

*　*　*

Had to find her, had to find her, had to find her. Something was going to go terribly wrong.

I had to eradicate the unknowns, to feel like God over something, anything at all—and my body would suffice. It always did. Habit has its way with you, seizes you by the tongue and leads you back.

I went about it the old-fashioned way, which is significantly less enjoyable than, say, through a blackout or a bad trip, but it was still effective. It had been a little while—in fact, lately, I'd not thought about it much. But it's still a rote process. Hair goes up. I'd normally prefer the toilet, but somebody might be around, still, sniffing. I used the garbage bin in my bedroom, forced all my insides out.

I sat still afterward.

And I reveled in it.

I tried again, but I had nothing left except bile, and tears, apparently. Those came freely. I tried to shut myself up by gripping my hair tight. I was worried that I might be heard, and then I'd be asked, and then the truth of my involvement in the pig scheme would become public fodder.

I shouldn't have worried.

Everyone was gone.

PENNY

As we walk toward The Church, I hear nervous whispering amongst the girls. They are so hushed and suspicious. I'm in a little herd with Leah and two other Kappa Alphas, and they ask one another series of incomplete questions.

Leah says, "You don't think they. . . "

And they respond, "No, no."

And Leah says, "And you don't believe that Jimmy Crawford actually did the roast . . ."

And they say that they don't know, they can't be sure.

And then somebody adds, "Are we sure we should really go to . . ."

And everybody says, fuck yeah. Of course we should.

When there is a lull, I turn toward Leah. "I think I know why you're worried about . . . your ex. Jimmy. Listen: he was with Millie. Millie upstairs? He slept with her."

She looks back at me in a way that makes me wonder if I had spoken only in my head.

"A lot," I add.

Still, she only looks.

It isn't a look of somebody in turmoil. It is a look of somebody concerned—for *me*.

She says, "I knew that, Penny. I knew that the whole time. What the fuck are you talking about?" I only shake my head. I cannot fathom their propensities of emotion. And I can no longer try. Leah says, "Listen. Are you all right? You barely seem *here*. Are you *even here?*"

"I don't know, Leah. I really don't know."

"*What* don't you know?"

I slow my walk down, and hope that she might match me. She does not. She walks a couple of paces ahead, half skips, and slides back in between her two sisters. She converses with me by peeking her head around and saying platitudes. I feel a sudden need to express myself, because I'm worried that something might go really wrong.

I say, "Leah, I don't know how it's gotten so bad."

And Leah takes that to be an insult, an insult to her hospitality. She says, "*Jesus*, Penny. Sorry about that."

I tell her what I know to be true, which is that it isn't her fault. It isn't her fault at all.

"It's mine," I say. "My fault, in the end."

"Who knows," Leah says. "Everyone thinks that. Just forget it, Penny. Enjoy the party—for fuckin' once."

I tell her that I'll try to, to enjoy the party.

Just like everybody else.

* * *

I HAVE BEEN TO THE CHURCH'S outdoor lot for Football Saturday, but never to their basement, and never at night. I don't know whether this is normal behavior, or if something is going on—something that makes Leah tense beside me, that makes her look around the inside of The Church skittishly, like she's being stalked.

As soon as we enter the basement, Leah abandons me to find more Kappa Alphas. She says there is something extremely important going on, and they all have to talk about it together. The two others go after her, and I am alone in the party.

So it seems perfect fortune when he emerges from the density, right when the music does its awful thing and drops.

The boy from Slounge, the one who had bought me two, three? drinks, and then vanished into himself. Now he recognizes me like an old friend, an arm around my shoulder. He looks at me like I'm letting all of the sun shine in, like he's witnessed hope again on this dance floor.

Now I understand it—what was so flush in silly novels, and what Kappa Alpha girls experienced in real life, real-time, all the time: the simple feeling of being wanted.

I'm dancing.

First with him as two, then with him as one. I've seen this in the movies, read about it in books about being young. The truth, I realize, is that it's really all right, this type of dancing, the type that means you're with somebody, and you're *with* somebody—which makes you feel like Somebody.

Since this type of music has no end, and no beginning, there is no legible place to stop. So we dance on. This is what they felt every night, and I feel just like them, at last, and nobody looks around for the lumpy one, the unbeautiful one, the *visitor:* I could be a Kappa Alpha.

I am.

The boy had brought a drink, and he hands it to me in an interim of sound. When I thank him, he says something which at last makes him fully human to me.

"I remember you, of course."

His hand pets my head now, and runs through my hair, and over my ear, and the crackling feeling that it leaves behind worries me a little, as if my hair might be stood up perpendicularly now. Then he says, "New York? Visiting?"

Which confirms that he does—he remembers.

Now, he invites me elsewhere. To smoke, drink—or both, he says. His speech is nebulous, and slurred, and obstructed by the smile. The lingering ketamine calls to me faintly, and tells me how pretty it all could be, if only I go along with it.

I follow as he walks out toward the bright light of a hallway, and we pass a pack of what I take to be his fraternity brothers. I think that I see Jimmy Crawford there; but they are all hidden by smoke from their cigarettes. When we pass, their watching becomes staring, and the whispers become laughs. Trip says nothing; nods at them, and they go quiet, and nod back.

As Trip turns into a bedroom, and shuts the door, they break again into laughter.

And in the room, I laugh too, just to be among them.

* * *

WE STILL HEAR THE PARTY MUSIC from his bedroom. He offers me a drink, and then, so quickly, a drink is in my hand. He fills a huge pipe, which he's retrieved from nowhere.

He pushes my shoulders down gently, so that I sit on his bed. He sits beside me, and our shoulders touch. He lights the pipe, and sucks in deeply, almost violently, and there's the loud noise of electric bubbles. With his hands, he instructs me to do the same. I put it to my lips and then remove it.

"Uh—I never have," I say.

His sigh is expansive, and depressed.

"Just suck," he says.

I do. He pretends not to notice my reaction, which is sudden, and physical. The smoke from the thing has gone directly into my brain, and it has sublimed into a cloud there. He looks away as I respond with a succession of guttural coughs.

I think that this is kindness—the way he looks off and pretends not to see.

I settle, and he turns back. He looks fully and completely at me—so that his face is all there is, and then we kiss.

There isn't much to say about it. No revelations. Nothing burned; nothing of desire.

It continues on.

And on, and on.

* * *

IT CEASES SO HE CAN REFILL my cup. I ask what we are drinking.

"Jungle juice," he says.

I look into my cup, pitch red, no bubbles, but I could see dust particles in that uncomfortable way made possible by fluorescent light upon a liquid surface at the right angle.

"Delicacy," he adds.

And then the fluorescent light is no matter—he flicks the switch.

Kisses onward again.

* * *

I GUESS THE TONGUE IS UNSURPRISING.

More surprising is the blackout.

And most surprising is the black back in.

This is what Stella had meant when she went on about the significance of being *cross faded,* and hitting the *wall,* and waiting for the blackout to begin, and how the only end to it all is to *pull the trigger.*

I say, "Uh—I think I need the bathroom?"

It comes out like a non-language, and he either does not understand me, or he does not want to.

I'm blacked out again before I can repeat myself.

When I come around his hand is working arduously over the zipper of my jeans, which are borrowed, and the movements make me reflexively suck in the teetering fat that flops over Leah's twenty-five waist.

I try to say, *hang on a second.*

The utterance is unclear again.

Or so it seems to be to him.

He appears awake only to a voice inside his own head, which instructs him onward—onward, then, he goes.

* * *

I MANAGE WORDS, EVENTUALLY. I SAY, "Hang on, what the hell?"

He starts the process of sliding the jeans off entirely.

He sighs—the same depressed sigh, so bitter, and exhausted. Perhaps he finally realizes that I have no capacity for this type of thing, not in my last remaining sobriety, and that I'm deadened, and dull.

He says something determined, then:

"This will be a lot easier if you'd just *be quiet.*"

I believe him, because it's sometimes true, you know. It sometimes makes sense, to shut up, and let everyone else get on with it—and so I do, then, because I think that maybe if I don't say anything, I won't feel anything, either.

*　*　*

I DON'T KNOW IF HE KNOWS that I am a virgin. He does not seem the type to consort with virgins much. Because he goes about his business with vast experience.

I offer pathetic protests.

We know that they are wasted, and that I'm humoring us both, together.

Most of the bits of my brain that still remain have jumped ship now, upon fully understanding at last what the prerogative here is. But sometime in here, I choose to expand the last of my cognizance back out into The Church basement, where I had felt briefly wonderful on this very same night.

At the party, the music still goes, but it has turned in on itself. It is tinny, and it has no rhythm. You cannot sing along to it. You wouldn't want to.

Up till now, music has helped in times of trouble. Yet somewhere between the basement and the bedroom, things change. Nothing, not even music anymore, is making the bad better. All that I love is laughing at me.

I no longer care for my body as it is. Not with him moving above me like he does now.

We haven't spoken a real word since—well, since he told me not to.

And then it ends.

It has to. Everything does.

He stands, then. Covers himself. I lay. I have no urge to cover myself. I am not worth viewing, not worth covering, not worth laying, not worth noticing.

He changes his boxers.

And then, there is a flash. It lights everything bright white. It's pointed at me, so that it doesn't illuminate his face, but I can imagine it—empty, and still handsome. And then there is the soft buzz buzz buzz of a polaroid in mid-development.

This shocks me for just a moment, until I understand:

Proof.

He steps away, and then tosses me a towel.

Leaves me to my privacy.

I move a hand toward the towel. It seems like a strange closing sentiment, the towel.

And then it makes perfect sense, when I feel warmth. It feels like heat, and it feels like comfort.

Blood.

STELLA

I journaled.

I wrote a poem, and it was demented.

I was feeling rather uninspired. Whatever you think of muses, and where they originate, I personally believe they come from aesthetic beauty. Whether that's the kind of mental beauty you encounter when you've had two doubles, are at the apex of giddy drunkenness; or whether it's beauty of the outdoors, you know, the kind that the God Damn Independents are on their bullshit about trees, and other leafy matter; but really, it's beauty true and simple; beauty symmetrical; beauty complete.

None of which I had; none of which I have.

Which was why I could not write a poem—something that Julie had told me to try. She'd told me to try anything creative, anything that required mental dexterity. A haiku, she'd said, might suffice.

Yeah, all right here's one.

Never mind talk therapy

It's bullshit, nonsense.

* * *

My therapeutic expenditures failed. Could I really sit there in my hot bedroom, getting only hotter as my reeking puke diffused throughout the air, and wonder, and wonder, and wonder? That would kill me; it'd kill me clean. No, I wouldn't wait. I wouldn't wait for the results, for the highlight reel, for the big heartbreak. I'd just go to him in the night.

He always knew when I was on my way.

By the time I'd righted myself enough to leave, it was early morning. The kind of early morning that is the end of the night, or the beginning of it. I went out, and this time I did not check into the living room.

I knew that she'd be back. And when she returned, I'd find her in her solitude, and I'd help her sort out the drugs, and I'd pat her head during the horrible ketamine comedown, and I'd tell her calmly *I'm sorry*, and I'd help her from the wreckage.

* * *

THEY'D BEEN RIGHT AT CHAPTER: HELL Week was on its last leg. Because nobody, not even Nico, stood by at the Sigma Rho door. I knocked, and there were the regular shuffles, and somebody that I recognized only by face opened up, and he recognized me too, and said to go on up, Stella.

As I went, I vacillated, and my logic argued with the other parts of me. Every movement toward his bedroom felt like a step toward an ending. He could be in there; he could be in there with *one of them*.

Worse: He could be in there alone—because *I'd been the one*. His only pig.

I wound up before his bedroom door, and I knew that there was no other available direction. I knocked, and he called, Stella?

I tapped the door open, and the bedroom light was on, along with the desk light, which was shined close to *Principles of Economics*, which he had opened at the middle, one finger still placed where he'd been following it on the page.

And as I looked at him, perfectly quotidian, I was incredulous with the far-off places to which my own delusions had urged me. It was Jack, and Jack only, as he'd been since August. And it was me the same, as I'd been since then.

I said, "I can explain why I'm here. I heard—yeah, listen. All right. *I know*. I know about the Roast. I've heard. Right? So, tell me honestly, tell me strai—"

He closed *Principles,* swiveled the desk chair around to look at me direct, his face unmoved apart from the eyes (widened), and the smile (creeping in).

"I didn't play," he said. "Of course I didn't."

"With me, or in general?"

He formed a church steeple with his fingers and gazed at the top of it. This was the first time I'd seen him show emotions on the edge of unpleasant. And I saw that this was something other than sadness; something else—disappointment.

I should've known.

I came closer, kicked off my sneakers, passed by him, and went to bed.

"In general," he said. "I didn't play in general," and then he came to the bed too, and took off his socks, and my delusions felt like nightmares, and I felt like I was awake again.

* * *

I CAME HOME IN EARLY MORNING or very late night, depending on who you asked. And still there were nighttime creatures, aching their way up or down South University, their hair done, and their faces concaved, and loose, and their makeup drudged about as if a car had raced along their cheeks and browbones. They teetered around, cold, and hard in the Michigan night—cold, cold, cold—and still they threw off their shoes, left them behind. One girl had quit before she'd even reached the sidewalk; she slept or was comatose on the front lawn of some disreputable fraternity, one heel still on, and the other in the bushes that groped around her ankles.

The sun was not up yet, which meant there was still sufficient time for me to be comfortably alive. Tomorrow would be for work; I'd ask Jack to come to the library, as we'd done a few times now, and we'd collect our objects, and ourselves, and try to study, and look at each other often.

I shuffled errantly down the road, bundled in two of Jack's sweaters, and felt an ephemeral relief—the kind of breathless understanding that you have been wonderfully wrong, and I jolted slowly along, and allowed the feeling to take me, and give me an occasional shove.

When I got back, I did not peek into the living room.

My contentment was rare, and it was delicate; I wished to take it to my bed and enjoy the night with it. And I'd find Penny in the morning—I'd ask her for friendship back again, and I'd tell her the news, the unusually happy news, that Jack had not played in the game, and that I was not an animal to him in any sense of the word.

This, incidentally, turned out to be one of those unwise choices that feels so good, even right as they happen.

PENNY

I HAVE TO GET HOME. I don't know how much time has passed since Trip's exit from the bedroom, but at some point, it comes to me that to be found here by a stranger, naked in this horror show, would be somehow worse than what had actually happened.

I gather my things, which are only the borrowed clothes that I'd worn to the party. And I steal an article of his, because even indoors I can feel the strength of the coming winter. I leave in one of his fraternity letter sweatshirts, and pull the hood up.

I observe nothing much on my walk home, down South University.

The nothing is obtrusive, and it is full of admonishments. The nothingness, along with the nighttime, announce to me their intentions. Their intentions are no good; their intentions are hellish, and discordant, and they speak to me in electronic droning where music might've been once.

The night, and its intentions together instruct me that there is an obvious course of action; and that it would offer safety from the night, its deep dark sadness, which, I have come to understand, has nothing to do with drugs. No. It's just *me*—it's me, and me only. The darkness is within me, and it probably always has been. It's found a suitable habitat, and I can't expel it. I've tried so hard. I've been trying so hard for so long.

I am nearly back to Kappa Alpha, and I consider my utter paucity. My life is characterized, now, by an extreme dearth of anything at all.

Friendship, for instance:

Stella is gone.

Stella has been gone the whole week. And Stella does nothing undeliberated. She is gone, and she has meant to go. Stella has left me behind.

And what of Michigan now?

Drugs, the drugs are gone too. They might've never been there at all. They might've been here on a brief visit, found a comfortable host in me, played some silly games, and then gone elsewhere, for more favorable conditions.

Back home now, I sit in my new nothing. I sit stark, deeply uncushioned by medicine. I am back on the living room floor.

And I finally understand it, you see. *I finally know.*

All this while I've been someplace else, and it has been briefly wonderful. And I've been with different people, and with them I've seen different things.

I have made a fundamental mistake. Because everything has been new, bright, and beautiful, I have believed that everything is, indeed, bright, and beautiful.

But it was just that everything was new.

Now, I sit. The living room has not changed much, since end August.

I am my only real acquaintance. The difference now is that she is looking at me clearly.

She is telling me to do terrible things.

THE GILDED BUTTERFLY EFFECT

Everything has gone from me but the certainty of this night: how dark it is, how lonely—and here I sit now, calm, and sober. The sun is only just beginning to rise outside, and it's as beautiful as ever.

STELLA

I'D RATHER NOT MINCE.

After tragedy, it's a habit. Adults mince it into soundbites, and heightened prose, and the newspapers deal with it apocalyptically.

I'd like to just finish the story straight, if you don't mind, I'd like to be done with it, this prescribed catharsis, my last struggle through Cognitive Behavioral Bullshit: *recording the trauma*.

Penny had had enough.

Or at least she thought so. It's all in the mind. And hers gave out.

Nowadays, I don't blame her mind, not at all.

She flew off the Kappa Alpha balcony. She crashed. My own small euphemism is that Penny flew. She'd never got the chance to, you know. Never did the flyaway youth thing, was not interested in *reckless abandon*. She flew, but she crashed. This is not a children's book.

The sidewalk in front of Kappa Alpha is concrete. As they tend to be. And as you might expect from such a landing, it had its way with her neck.

They said that, due to the angles, and so on, it was an easy snap.

I'm happy that they chose to say that, whether or not it's true.

THE GILDED BUTTERFLY EFFECT

There was general shock that morning. Kappa Alpha was hit with a wave of performative grief, which soon gave way to a communal awareness of the mortality of the individual, and an absolute draining of all remaining therapeutic appointments that were still somehow unfilled within the Ann Arbor city limits.

Her parents hadn't known where she was for months.

I have heard, from Leah, that Penny's parents will move away from their town in New York. They are trying to escape the new reality of their long, progeny-less lives with a bit of mountain air, and sunshine.

What they didn't do was press charges. They wanted to, but their lawyers advised against it. Because there wasn't anyone to *sue,* they'd said. You can't sue a child, not for owning the prescription drugs that had somehow fallen into—and then out of—Penny's bloodstream. *The Michigan Weekly* had received some anonymous tips, which suggested that hazing might've been involved, and there was a halfhearted call for investigations into certain fraternities. The lawyers, and some raggedy focus group of middle-tier psychiatrics assembled by Michigan Medicine, did a bit of light scoping.

Absolutely no evidence of hazing this season, they'd reported. It appears that the local fraternities are at last in line with our standards of behavior, and etiquette.

The Michigan Weekly, however, had its own bonanza. They reported that Kappa Alpha's current President had been called to Ohio, to face the Kappa Alpha National Board there. Kathy Van Tassel was followed by reporters who wrote that the CEO of Kappa Alpha—an elderly woman, white-haired, and pearled—questioned Van Tassel on the abhorrent practices in her very own chapter.

They interrogated Kathy Van Tassel, and our President cooperated until the very end, when she was invited to speak for herself.

At which point she pulled her travel bible from a briefcase, flicked to a bookmarked page, and said: "Let us pursue the notions of forgiveness. Shall we start on Corinthians?"

And after a while, Nationals forgave.

It made the *Detroit City News*, and then was picked up by NPR. I hear that young sociologists have seized it as a case study for their next shot at federal funding. We look, and we look, and we look, they say, for the crux of the problem with the American youth. And this is it, this is it right here.

It made all the headlines for about two weeks.

And then it didn't anymore. Shortly thereafter, there was an armed robbery in one of the luxury student apartment buildings. And as that took ascendency over the front page, most everyone forgot about the mutilated body found in front of Kappa Alpha.

Maybe they didn't really forget, but memory is tricky. We forget the things that we would like to, and we all continue to go merrily around—as if it's not all still under there somewhere, beneath all the smoke, and the distractions.

* * *

I AM CERTAINLY DETERIORATING. OH, ABSOLUTELY. I fear my brain might be hurdled determinedly in a questionable direction. But I am refusing drugs. I have remained quit from them, and my comedown no longer feels like a comedown.

It feels like normal life, in an underfunded aquarium.

In the weeks that followed, before school broke off for Christmas, I kept two things near. One was Jack. Jack never knew her, nor about the extent of our relations. But when I want to lie still, and be by myself in the company of another, he's there for that.

The other thing that I kept was a souvenir.

I know this might've been an important key to it all. The lawyers, who I heard about but never met or saw, might've wanted it. Or her parents might've been curious. No, not her diary—that was swiped early, for the sociologists, and, eventually, for the poets in need of material.

No, I searched through the remaining living room mess that nobody wanted to touch in the following days. I found, under the pillow that she'd used for sleep, a black sweatshirt with The Church fraternity letters plastered across the front.

A black sweatshirt that I knew, that I recognized. The inside smelled of him. It also smelled, a tiny bit, like me.

One Spring afternoon the previous year, I'd worn that sweatshirt while sleeping in his bed at The Church. I decided then to destroy the object before anybody else could find it.

It is in a landfill now.

Σ

THEY PERFORMED A VERY QUIET CATHARSIS. Only the top two houses went, and they went in communal spirit of the sanctity of Hell Week, and with the understanding that the pledges' accomplishments could not be negated by some sorority tragedy, some sadness amongst the girls that they did not care about.

One dead night, in the solemn hours between the very last bar's closing, and the first God Damn Independent's rising to get a library seat, Sigma Rho and The Church gathered in the Huron Wilderness.

The Pledge Masters had arrived hours earlier, and started the fire, so that by the time the pledges arrived, all in black sports hoodies, it was raging high.

They were careful that it did not climb out of control. Nobody on campus could find them out there, come investigate to see what they were burning, and why.

Trip had handed off his photograph of Penny to a pledge; he had not really been meant to participate at all, but tradition called for the Masters to lead by example—particularly during the final task, when the distinction between brother and pledge was tired, and faded. And this had been an incredible moment of creative brilliance, when he and Nico had created the Pig Roast, so he had wanted a stab at it.

He was glad that the photograph would be burned tonight. Because it was no longer just proof.

It had lately become evidence.

Although who could know about the connection? Who could really fathom? Loads of out-of-towners came out to Michigan on the weekends and got blasted drunk at The Church.

He had not even got a good look at her face, a picture of which had gone viral online, and been featured in *The Michigan Weekly*. So he could not be sure, not at all, whether that girl had been his pig to begin with, and he preferred not to worry about it.

Whether it was proof or evidence, it was burned tonight. And then he could get on with it—everything gets forgotten in the Michigan winter.

Trip Swindle stood back as his pledges walked up, each alone, and tossed their photos into the fire. Some had captured only one; others had gone on a frenzy, tossed in handfuls of photos of naked girls. There was no applause, no acknowledgement. Except: each pledge walked by Trip and Nico after his burning, to shake the Masters' hands.

* * *

JACK ELLIS STOOD ON THE Sigma Rho side.

After they'd learned the nature of their final task, he had gone to his closest friend in his pledge class, and the one who most understood his feelings for Stella. Bleis would sympathize; he had his own reservations about participating, Jack knew, what with some girl in his hometown waiting for him to come back for Thanksgiving, and then Christmas, and then over, and over again, and then forever. Jack had asked Bleis— and then begged Bleis—to snap a photograph for him, *anything*, any proof would do, anything that Jack could burn before the others. And one day Jack would owe him hugely.

Bleis considered, and Jack waited. Jack waited nearly all the way through the final Hell Week task, for Bleis to consider.

Now, Bleis walked toward the fire himself, and emptied one polaroid picture from his pocket, tossed it in.

As Trip watched, he was reminded of the point of it all—because life can be awfully sad, awfully long, without a family to stand with. He wasn't sure what that meant, exactly; but this felt close enough.

Bleis thought he might feel it too, as he walked back to his spot on the circle beside Jack.

Jack walked forward now, stood before the fire. Watched it, and almost started to think—but chose not to. Now wouldn't be the right time for that.

Because in the end Bleis had said no. "I'm sorry, buddy," he'd said. "I can barely stand to do it once. I can't do it twice. I'm sorry, Jack." And, "Jack, are you even her boyfriend, anyway? Does it really matter?"

Jack supposed not. He had continued to suppose not, as he brought the outwardly giddy but inwardly bleak God Damn Independent upstairs, offered her a drink. Do you have beer, she'd said, and he didn't—uh, I have rum and vodka, he'd said. Diet coke?

No coercion necessary; plenty of painful pre-conversation, which included her reflections on how a fraternity house really looked from the inside, *wow*, she'd said. So when can I come back?

Now, Jack emptied his own pocket of his polaroid. She had been mainly covered by blankets, and had not awoken to the flash.

He tossed it in; hadn't looked at it since he'd snapped it.

Jack thought that he might tell Stella in time. When the weather was warmer on them, and the sun more merciful. When spring came around, and put them in quantifiably better moods—he'd tell her then, in spring.

He was the last one to burn.

They stood now in a full circle, and the pledges looked at one another in an expectant way, and then they looked back at their Pledge Masters, imploring: now, they were brothers. Now, they should be recognized as such. Now, as equals, the pledges demanded respect.

Trip looked to Nico, and Nico looked to Trip.

And they realized that nobody had remembered to keep tally.

STELLA

Somewhere in there, springtime started, but no one noticed, or no one cared. When all the madness of the fall was faded, I stared at Julie, whose washed-up fashion sense had persisted.

The room was very white, and there was a buzzing that grated on my mental. It might have been imagined. Some things, lately, had not been sitting quite right up there. I suspect that it may have something to do with contrition, which was what I hoped to sort out that day.

I announced, "Listen: I am a murderer, of a degree. I don't know which. Second? Maybe. But *either way*. That's the truth, and I'm here to admit it."

But the psychiatrist was unmoved, and she only looked at me with her predetermined sadness. She looked at me as one might look at a case of pure delusion. Julie no longer supported my decision to go off drugs. She believed that, unmedicated, I had fallen to incurable patterns of *distorting*, and *catastrophizing*, and *overemotional reasoning*.

Julie: Now, Stella. I do wonder whether you have considered the *nature* of these destructive thoughts. Are you internalizing certain events, or *magnetizing* underlying anxieties? Could it be a projection? Have you been doing your cognitive behavioral exercises?

I said, "It's all real, Julie. These aren't just *thoughts*. Or anxieties. They're real history. Haven't you been listening at all?"

And I told her that our realities were the same; that maybe she hated it, maybe it disgusted her. But my reality was her reality, so *why the fuck wasn't she listening?*

I went on, "It's this deep dark sadness. Madness? Julie, can't you see it? I destroyed her chances—and she'd been close, Julie. To feeling like she was alive, and all of that. But I killed it, and by proxy, *her*, in a way. Jesus *Christ*, it all comes down to me."

Then I watched Julie's face do something different. I watched Julie's face give up.

"Julie, can't you hear me? Listen: it's all germane to the case, so write this down."

Julie nodded. She clicked her pen, and started to write. I watched her work. It wasn't anything to do with Penny, with all that I'd just told her. She was writing out something very distinct, very medical—lots of numbers, and decimals. It was a new regimen, on a familiar pharmacy order form: Vyvaid, a high dose of a new generic Smitherin, Coxydon, and two others, indiscernible. She ripped it from the pad, and her face was absolutely empty of a face, soulless as any soulless place, not a wince of regard in a single eyebrow hair. She looked at me as if she had an easy fix to the heaviness on my chest, which had been there lately, and which might have been there always. Now it was a dense heaviness, foreboding; like something was coming, a loneliness or two.

"Christ, Julie, can't you see? I *smashed* her brain in, therefore she *smashed*—Julie, listen."

She only pressed the medication form across the glass table. She said nothing until I took it up.

Then she said, "Yes. Sometimes, life can really seem that way. Can't it?"

ABOUT THE AUTHOR

HEATHER COLLEY IS AN AWARD-WINNING WRITER and academic. Her short fiction has won widespread recognition, including *The Oxford Review of Books* Short Fiction Prize, the Hopwood Award, and the Desperate Literature short fiction anthology. Her academic work has received various awards such as the prestigious DC Watt Prize from the Transatlantic Studies Association. Heather's academic writing has appeared in peer-reviewed and critical publications including *The Routledge Companion to Gender and Childhood*, *The Oxford Comparative Criticism and Translation Review*, *American Book Review*, and *Gale Review Online*.

Heather is a doctoral student in English Literature at the University of Oxford where she is also a postgraduate member of the Rothermere American Institute and a British Library Research Fellow. She is a graduate of the University of Michigan Ann Arbor and St. Andrews University. She lectures in English Literature at Hertford College, Oxford. Heather was born and raised in New York, and currently lives in Oxford and New York.

RECENT AND FORTHCOMING BOOKS FROM THREE ROOMS PRESS

FICTION
Lucy Jane Bledsoe
No Stopping Us Now
Rishab Borah
The Door to Inferna
Meagan Brothers
Weird Girl and What's His Name
Christopher Chambers
Scavenger
Standalone
StreetWhys
Ebele Chizea
Aquarian Dawn
Heather Colley
The Gilded Butterfly Effect
Ron Dakron
Hello Devilfish!
Ron Dakron
Hello Devilfish!
Robert Duncan
Loudmouth
Amanda Eisenberg
People Are Talking
Michael T. Fournier
Hidden Wheel
Swing State
Kate Gale
Under a Neon Sun
Aaron Hamburger
Nirvana Is Here
William Least Heat-Moon
Celestial Mechanics
Aimee Herman
Everything Grows
Kelly Ann Jacobson
Tink and Wendy
Robin and Her Misfits
Lies of the Toymaker
Jethro K. Lieberman
Everything Is Jake
Eamon Loingsigh
Light of the Diddicoy
Exile on Bridge Street
John Marshall
The Greenfather
Alvin Orloff
Vulgarian Rhapsody
Micki Janae
Of Blood and Lightning
Aram Saroyan
Still Night in L.A.
Robert Silverberg
The Face of the Waters
Stephen Spotte
Animal Wrongs
Max Talley
Peace, Love and Haight
Richard Vetere
The Writers Afterlife
Champagne and Cocaine
Jessamyn Violet
Secret Rules to Being a Rockstar
Julia Watts
Quiver
Needlework
Lovesick Blossoms
Gina Yates
Narcissus Nobody

MEMOIR & BIOGRAPHY
Nassrine Azimi and Michel Wasserman
Last Boat to Yokohama: The Life and Legacy of Beate Sirota Gordon
William S. Burroughs & Allen Ginsberg
Don't Hide the Madness
edited by Steven Taylor

James Carr
BAD: The Autobiography of James Carr
Judy Gumbo
Yippie Girl: Exploits in Protest and Defeating the FBI
Nancy Kurshan
Levitating the Penttagon and Other Uplifting Stories
Hédi A. Jaouad
The Immortal Journeys of Isabelle Eberhardt
Judith Malina
Full Moon Stages: Personal Notes from 50 Years of The Living Theatre
Phil Marcade
Punk Avenue: Inside the New York City Underground, 1972–1982
Jillian Marshall
Japanthem: Counter-Cultural Experiences; Cross-Cultural Remixes
Alvin Orloff
Disasterama! Adventures in the Queer Underground 1977–1997
Nicca Ray
Ray by Ray: A Daughter's Take on the Legend of Nicholas Ray
Aram Saroyan
Before I Forget: A Memoir
Stephen Spotte
My Watery Self: Memoirs of a Marine Scientist
Christina Vo & Nghia M. Vo
My Vietnam, Your Vietnam
Vietnamese translation: *Việt Nam Của Con, Việt Nam Của Cha*

PHOTOGRAPHY-MEMOIR
Mike Watt
On & Off Bass

DADA
Maintenant: A Journal of Contemporary Dada Writing & Art (annual, since 2008)

MIXED MEDIA
John S. Paul
Sign Language: A Painter's Notebook (photography, poetry and prose)

HUMOR
Peter Carlaftes
A Year on Facebook

FILM & PLAYS
Israel Horovitz
My Old Lady: Complete Stage Play and Screenplay with an Essay on Adaptation
Peter Carlaftes
Triumph For Rent (3 Plays)
Teatrophy (3 More Plays)
Kat Georges
Three Somebodies: Plays

TRANSLATIONS
Thomas Bernhard
On Earth and in Hell (poems; German and English)
Patrizia Gattaceca
Isula d'Anima (Corsican & English)
César Vallejo | Gerard Malanga
Malanga Chasing Vallejo
George Wallace
EOS: Abductor of Men (Greek & English)

ESSAYS
Richard Katrovas
Raising Girls in Bohemia
Vanessa Baden Kelly
Far Away From Close to Home
Erin Wildermuth
Womentality

SHORT STORY ANTHOLOGIES
SINGLE AUTHOR
Alien Archives: Stories
by Robert Silverberg
First-Person Singularities: Stories
by Robert Silverberg
Tales from the Eternal Café: Stories
by Janet Hamill, intro by Patti Smith
Time and Time Again: Sixteen Trips in Time
by Robert Silverberg
The Unvarnished Gary Phillips: A Mondo Pulp Collection
by Gary Phillips
Voyagers: Twelve Journeys in Space and Time
by Robert Silverberg

MULTI-AUTHOR
The Colors of April
edited by Quan Manh Ha & Cab Tran
Crime + Music: Nineteen Stories of Music-Themed Noir
edited by Jim Fusilli
Dark City Lights: New York Stories
edited by Lawrence Block
The Faking of the President: Twenty Stories of White House Noir
edited by Peter Carlaftes
Florida Happens:
edited by Greg Herren
Have a NYC I, II & III: New York Stories;
edited by Peter Carlaftes & Kat Georges
Songs of My Selfie
edited by Constance Renfrow
The Obama Inheritance: 15 Stories of Conspiracy Noir
edited by Gary Phillips
This Way to the End Times: Classic & New Stories of the Apocalypse
edited by Robert Silverberg

POETRY COLLECTIONS
Hala Alyan
Atrium
Peter Carlaftes
DrunkYard Dog
I Fold with the Hand I Was Dealt
Life in the Past Lane
Thomas Fucaloro
It Starts from the Belly and Blooms
Kat Georges
Our Lady of the Hunger
Awe and Other Words Like Wow
Robert Gibbons
Close to the Tree
Israel Horovitz
Heaven and Other Poems
David Lawton
Sharp Blue Stream
Jane LeCroy
Signature Play
Philip Meersman
This Is Belgian Chocolate
Jane Ormerod
Recreational Vehicles on Fire
Welcome to the Museum of Cattle
Lisa Panepinto
On This Borrowed Bike
George Wallace
Poppin' Johnny

Three Rooms Press | New York, NY | Current Catalog: www.threeroomspress.com
Three Rooms Press books are distributed by Publishers Group West: www.pgw.com